Rela

Danger without, passion within . . .

"I hope Lord Alington went home, or elsewhere. You do not think he lurks out there, waiting for us?"

"You poor girl," Justin said, his compassion overcoming his good sense. With great strides he was at Anne's side, taking her into his arms, nestling her head against his shoulder. It felt incredibly right and good.

"Forgive me for being a watering pot. I feel very foolish." Anne sniffed again.

He touched her chin lightly so she would have to look up at him. Their gazes met. After that it was difficult to say who moved first.

To say that the kiss was an improvement upon the first was to say daylight is better than the light of the moon. There was little comparison. Justin found her sweet, yet there was an essential passion within her that he could detect. He explored her lips, finding much to his liking. Only a sound in the hall outside the anteroom broke them apart.

Anne no longer looked frightened or lost. . . .

Miss Haycroft's Suitors

Emily Hendrickson

A SIGNET BOOK

SIGNET
Published by New American Library, a division of
Penguin Putnam Inc., 375 Hudson Street,
New York, New York 10014, U.S.A.
Penguin Books Ltd, 27 Wrights Lane,
London W8 5TZ, England
Penguin Books Australia Ltd, Ringwood,
Victoria, Australia
Penguin Books Canada Ltd, 10 Alcorn Avenue,
Toronto, Ontario, Canada M4V 3B2
Penguin Books (N.Z.) Ltd, 182–190 Wairau Road,
Auckland 10, New Zealand

Penguin Books Ltd, Registered Offices:
Harmondsworth, Middlesex, England

First published by Signet, an imprint of New American Library,
a division of Penguin Putnam Inc.

First Printing, September 1999
10 9 8 7 6 5 4 3 2 1

*This book is dedicated to
my daughter, Kirsten Valleskey.
Her splendid help and suggestions,
not to mention her encouragement,
are greatly treasured.*

Chapter One

Anne pushed the heavy oak church door open just enough to allow her to enter. Its well-oiled hinges made no sound in the vast interior of the structure. A lovely mixture of muted color splashed across the interior of the church, cast from the tall windows of stained glass. Dust motes danced in rainbow-hued air. The scent of flowers mingled with the damp mustiness found in churches, unheated and unused so much of the week. Anne found the church as welcome a refuge as people had in ages past.

Before the magnificent altar with its tall ivory candles and array of gold plate, a bishop faced the assembled guests and the couple standing before him. His words echoed in the vastness of the interior.

She frowned at the sight of the wedding taking place at the distant altar. She was late. The ceremony had already begun, and the music she enjoyed listening to had been played. She had hoped to sneak away from her maid long enough to see the wedding of the year—a love match, everyone said. Romantic.

She hesitated, not wishing to join the others toward the front of the church, not wanting to call attention to herself in the least. Glancing about her, she saw several chairs against the wall in a shadowed area where she would be easily overlooked. Gathering the skirt of her violet muslin in hand, she tiptoed over to the last chair, sinking quietly to the woven-rush seat. Surely Dolly wouldn't seek her here. The maid was merely one of the more annoying aspects of living with her aunt and uncle. Aunt Winnefred loomed largely as another, while Uncle Cosmo was the worst. How he and Anne's dear Papa could have been related was more than she could imagine.

Voices floated across the expanse of the church interior, low and commanding, high and sweet. Vows. Soon she would have to make the same vows. How could she avoid them? And if not, could she say those promises to obey, serve, love, honor, and keep him in sickness and in health, forsaking all others? Honor, serve, and obey she supposed must be compelled. But love? Her uncle had declared that he intended to arrange a marriage for her and that she would have no say about it at all. That could not please, for she suspected her uncle's choice would not be hers but one that suited his needs.

Anne had always hoped for a love match and had forestalled her uncle's matchmaking schemes the past few years. But it seemed he would not wait any longer. A few tears escaped to trickle down her cheeks, and she didn't bother to wipe them away. There might be more. Weddings always brought tears, didn't they?

From what Aunt Winnefred had hinted, there were particular *reasons* her uncle was in a hurry to see Anne wed. What those reasons might be had been kept from her, presumably not considered important for her to know. There would be a wedding and soon, if her uncle had his way! Considering her dreadful uncle and his taste, Anne very much feared his choice. Could she bear to live with such a man?

True, there were good husbands to be found. Anne suspected that Uncle Cosmo did not know any of that type. He was a gambler, a crude man, and not one given to kindly consideration of others.

She closed her eyes to think and, ignoring the crunch of her neat little straw hat, leaned her head against the cold stone wall to reflect on the past days of hectic activity. She didn't agree with her aunt regarding the selection of wedding clothes. In fact, she did not agree with her aunt on much of anything, as Aunt Winnefred insisted a love match was foolishness.

Was Anne foolish to desire love in marriage? She was quite convinced her dearest father would have allowed her some say in her future husband. But he was no longer alive to protect his daughter, and her uncle had other notions regarding Anne's future spouse. The very thought frightened her.

Uncle had ordered her to select a wedding gown. Of course

he'd not informed her *who* her husband would be. Never mind it was an accepted way of managing this business of marriage. She was a silly girl to desire more. Yet she did. How she longed to flee her uncle, escape his manipulations. Indeed, she feared his selection, for she had learned to know her uncle well, and she didn't trust him one bit. Sly, cruel, covetous—that was her uncle.

She peeked at the couple before the altar again—what joyous voices, such firm responses. Indeed, it must be as had been rumored, the marriage was the culmination of true love. How wonderful—true love! They had not suffered an arranged marriage as so many young women faced—as Anne faced.

The lack of sleep—result of her worries over her future—caught up with her. In the dim light and faint scent of flowers Anne slipped into much-needed slumber, her cares forgotten for the moment. She didn't hear the procession that paraded from the church, nor the conversation of those guests who followed. Lost in the deep shadows off to the side, she was not noticed.

Certainly, the gentleman who ushered out a tall older woman with a commanding air about her didn't see the girl huddled in the shadows far off to one side. He was intent upon the lady at his side.

With the happy couple seen off on their way to a wedding breakfast, Justin Fairfax, Earl of Rochford, was settling his aunt in his carriage when he exclaimed, "I seem to have forgotten my cane in the church. I cannot think how I managed to set it down, then forget it," he concluded, appearing vexed with his absentmindedness, yet with a twinkle lurking in his eyes. "It's a favorite of mine, the one with the clouded-amber handle. I must return; I'd not have it lost. Why not go ahead without me, Aunt Mary? Besides," he admitted, "I'd as soon not go to the breakfast. I have some business that needs tending."

"I know you find Katherine's mother a dreadfully encroaching woman," Lady Mary replied with a shrewd smile. "I'll offer your excuses. It is quite sufficient she saw you here at the ceremony. What a good thing it is that the newly wed couple are so well liked that most will attend in spite of that woman."

Bestowing a grateful look on his favorite aunt, Justin saw her into the town coach, then returned to the dim coolness of the church. He marched to the area where he had been seated and retrieved his cane from where he had nudged it beneath a chair.

He was sauntering down the aisle, looking about him while speculating on his afternoon when he saw her. She seemed a delectable creature from what he could see; ash blond curls peeked from beneath her little hat—could they really be that lovely color?—and a charming figure, from what he could see of it. Poor girl probably slipped into the church to view the wedding, then dozed off, a victim of a late night ball. He knew well how these young girls plunged into the exhausting whirl of a Season.

Curious, he approached where she sat, noting she appeared sound asleep. What an exquisite mouth she had, now slightly and temptingly relaxed. She stirred, and her clever little hat slipped a bit to reveal more of those charming curls.

Normally the most circumspect of gentlemen, indeed, a man noted for his decorum, he nevertheless felt compelled to quietly sit down beside her. There was something extremely appealing about her, and he certainly wanted to learn the identity of this delightful creature. Her clothes were of the highest quality, evidence of her position. He ignored the odd sensation in his heart, unable to place it. She ought not be alone, and he thought he might offer her proper escort, for he was a *most* proper gentleman. Usually.

When he looked more closely, he was dismayed to see the remnants of tears on her delicate cheeks. Tears for the wedding? Or had she other woes? Poor girl.

An oddly protective and compassionate feeling came over him, quite sweeping away his common sense. Justin did something that was far from his customary behavior, certainly something he could never explain to himself later when he reflected on it. He leaned forward to place a gentle kiss on a tearstained cheek.

His reward was fluttering eyes, the dawning of awareness, and—a look of shock! Sensing she was about to scream or call out, he hurriedly sought her lips, taking his time to sip from lips too tempting to ignore. As a means of silencing a woman, it proved most effective.

Upon her release, she again opened her mouth, and Justin placed a finger over the velvet softness he'd found so satisfying. "Hush, now, I shan't harm you." That he had never done anything of this sort in his life he didn't reveal. He was in a bit of shock himself.

The glare fixed on him by lovely blue eyes should have frozen him on the spot. He carefully removed his finger, quite willing to apply his means of silence again should it prove necessary. When she spoke, her voice was husky with anger.

"I merely sought to view the wedding without my maid. I thought I would be safe inside a church," she declared in elegant accents that bespoke the very best of education and gentry status. "Were I less sensible, I am sure I would have swooned. How dare you, sirrah!" Heavenly blue eyes flashed with indignant anger.

Justin closed his eyes a moment, then met her gaze with a rueful look. How could he explain something he didn't understand himself? "I do beg your pardon, miss. I intended to offer comfort, nothing more."

She sniffed and said nothing.

"What is so bad that it brings tears, or do you merely cry at weddings like so many women?" He hazarded a smile he hoped she would not take amiss. A smile, were it gentle enough, might reassure her he harbored no evil intentions.

"Indeed." Anne glanced at the prettily gloved hands in her lap, clenching and reclenching them as she toyed with the idea of slapping his face . . . or worse. Another tear slipped down her cheek, and this time she searched for and found a handkerchief. Dabbing at the wayward tear, she considered the man at her side. He spoke well, likely a guest at the wedding. Why had he bothered with her, not to mention offered comfort at her tears?

A proper young lady ought to be highly offended by such outrageous behavior as a kiss. It merely served to prove that she was a trifle improper, as Aunt Winnefred often declared. Yet he said he wanted to comfort her, and she'd known little enough of that. She looked at the man again. He was handsome, assured, and from his garb and speech of the highest *ton*. And—while she was no expert judge of the matter—he also knew how to kiss! She waited to see what he might say next.

The elegant gentleman leaned back slightly, one hand on his knee, the other grasping his cane. His dark eyes studied Anne—she felt he searched her very depths. "Why have we not met before?"

"I have been in London for some weeks, sir," she said in frigidly polite tones. "I have but lately entered the whirl that constitutes Society. As to my tears, they have nothing to do with *this* wedding." She fixed her gaze on him, then most improperly inquired, "Who might you be?"

"Rochford," he replied promptly.

"I am Miss Haycroft." Anne relaxed a trifle, although she was well aware that they ought to be introduced by a mutual acquaintance. Even she had heard of the earl, for he was deemed of the highest *ton* in London Society. He also had a reputation of great respectability. Surely he would be trustworthy?

"I have met your uncle," he said, a grim note entering his voice.

"Please, do not mention that dreadful man to me," she whispered, unable to prevent herself from glancing around as though he might pop up from behind a screen.

"I understand he is arranging a most advantageous marriage for you?" Justin asked, his manner gentle.

"Indeed, I suppose he is, although to whom I cannot say." With most uncharacteristic candor, probably because this was the first sympathetic person she'd found in London, Anne continued, "I have been instructed to order a wedding dress, but do not know my groom. I suppose Uncle has not discovered which man will give him the most money. It is the customary thing in arranged marriages, is it not?" She could not keep the bitterness from her voice.

Anne turned away from this stranger in whom she felt she might confide and stared off into the dimly lit church. What could she do? Where could she flee if necessary? How? Instinct urged her to escape, run away while she could. She then gave the gentleman at her side a defiant look and said, "Well, have you no reprimand for me?"

"Do you not have the slightest notion of the identity of the possible groom?" Lord Rochford asked softly.

"A number of gentlemen have paid me particular attentions

as of late, so I cannot be certain. If only I *could* know." She gave his lordship a look of inquiry.

"I am acquainted with most of Society." There was little he could say to ease her fears. He knew of several men who hunted for a wife and whom he had observed in company with Cosmo Haycroft. "Can you tell me the names of some of these gentlemen?" he asked, so as better to understand, not pausing to consider how highly unusual it was for him to become involved in the life of anyone outside his family. That she utterly captivated him didn't cross his mind. He only knew her dilemma called to something good and decent within him.

"Well, there is Lord Bowlton. He was introduced to me at Lady Sefton's rout a fortnight ago by my uncle and proclaimed an admirable *parti.* Lord Gower is another. Uncle insists Lord Alington is *most* desirable. He attended Mrs. Cathcart's musicale last week as I did. I played the pianoforte during the evening, I must say," she said with a shiver, "his gaze was offputting."

Then she tilted her head to study Justin, and seemed reassured at what she saw. "I cannot think why I tell you this."

"Because you sense me as a friend. What brought you here?" He gestured to the church interior.

"I wished to view the wedding."

"Where is your maid?" Justin asked, knowing no heiress would be allowed out of the house without at least a maid, if not a footman also in attendance. If Haycroft might brag about snabbling a husband for his niece, she must be well to grass.

"Actually, she is my aunt's maid. She snoops on me, so I sent her on an errand. I expect she is hunting for me even now." A look of panic settled on her face.

He recalled some of the disastrous arranged marriages he'd seen and inwardly shuddered. As well, he knew something of Alington, who was considered one of the better catches of the Season, and he felt abhorrence at the idea of this innocent girl with such a man.

Justin—who had never before even experienced a desire to interfere in the affairs of a young woman—found himself saying, "I shall help you." As he realized what he had just said, he further amazed himself by finding that he felt drawn to her and fully intended to do what he could for her.

"What can you do?" Miss Haycroft replied, skepticism showing in her voice.

"Allow me to consider your dilemma a moment." It might not be as bad as she suspected. What if the chap her uncle intended as her husband was not the villain he thought? It *was* highly improper for Justin to interfere, but he felt sorry for her. That he also felt something deeper, he ignored.

"I ought not trouble you," she murmured, smoothing the delicate kidskin of her gloves over her hands, unconsciously revealing her distress. "I have no claim on your or your time." She thought of his kisses, how they had stirred her, had made her tremble with their intensity, the leashed desire she sensed in spite of her inexperience. And, she realized with great shock, the kisses had made her desire another! She gave herself a faint shake. This would never do. She was beyond propriety as it was, and to even *think* such a thought was wicked.

He ignored her softly uttered protest, saying, "I believe for the moment you had best return to your uncle's. As soon as you know what fate he intends for you, your plan of action can be decided."

"What plan?" she inquired with a trace of suspicion.

"Your uncle's choice may be none of the gentlemen you imagine. It could be someone you deem most acceptable." From his expression he thought it unlikely.

"I am supposed to attend a musicale at Lady Chalfont's this evening," Anne volunteered. "Lord Alington may be there, for it appears he likes music."

"Do you perform this evening?" When she nodded, he frowned, then said, "I believe I shall also attend. I would enjoy an evening of good music."

She rose from the chair to be joined by Lord Rochford. He seemed concerned, and she was much affected by that. She said, "I cannot thank you enough for any assistance you may be able to offer." She prudently overlooked the infamous kisses. Best not to bring that into the conversation at this point. Offering her hand in a proper farewell, she was disconcerted when he took it in his, bending to lightly kiss it while holding her gaze. No doubt the look from his dark eyes was just as intent as Lord Alington's, but it held an allure missing in that other man's gaze.

Justin was grateful she ignored the matter of the improper kisses. Probably they hadn't stirred her as they affected him . . . nor made her desire another, as he did. His gaze fastened on those tender, delectable lips, and he was compelled to wrench his attention elsewhere. It was not like him in the least to behave in this manner!

Looking down to the cane he held, he thought a moment, then said, "I shall escort you from the church and go with you until you can locate your maid or possibly find a decent vehicle in which to ride to your uncle's house. You should not be alone."

"I am appreciative of your concern. But should someone see us leave the church together, might there not conceivably be gossip? The wedding party left some time ago." She walked at his side until they reached the great oaken door.

Justin placed his hand on the latch. "I doubt there will be anyone of importance about at this hour. All the *ton* are either at the wedding breakfast I had promised to attend or attending to other equally diverting matters."

He opened the door, glanced about, then offered her his arm. They left the scented confines of the church for the chill of a spring day. Few people chanced to be nearby. Fewer yet were those who might be interested in the pair exiting the church.

"There is my maid," Anne whispered. "She looks a bit frantic. She'd never comprehend my wish to be alone."

"I quite understand," Justin replied, thinking that he did discern her wish for privacy and some time to herself. From what little he knew of her aunt Haycroft, the elderly woman was a confounded harpy. He couldn't begin to imagine living with such a woman around.

"Until this evening," she murmured as she drifted down the shallow steps away from the church.

He said with quiet urgency, "I shall see you later."

She turned then, glancing back at him with a flash of those remarkable eyes. Her smile was her only answer, but it was sufficient.

Anne hurried to where her maid stood, anticipating a scold from the older woman, who thought of herself as a chaperon as well as a maid.

"Here I am. I said I would wait for you by the church and I did. I saw a wedding; the bride was so lovely and the groom quite the most handsome of men. Do tell my aunt that I chanced to see the wedding of the Season. I feel certain she will be pleased." Anne knew all that transpired while absent from the house would be reported to her aunt by her faithful spy.

The wedding proved to be a splendid diversion for Dolly; her aunt's maid listened avidly to the invented description. That an account might appear in the newspaper made little difference; Dolly could not read.

When they entered the house, Anne found her aunt in the drawing room and in a dither, not an unusual condition.

"There you are, you unnatural girl. Why you shy away from the wedding planned for you I cannot think. Most any girl would be in alt to find herself betrothed to either of the gentlemen Mr. Haycroft has found for you."

Anne didn't betray her feelings by so much as a flicker of her eyes. "Oh? And who are these gentlemen?"

A crafty look settled on Mrs. Haycroft's face, one Anne instantly mistrusted.

"Why, none other than Lord Bowlton *and* Lord Alington. Fancy that! You have a baron and an earl both a-wanting you."

"How, how . . . interesting," Anne stammered, aware she might have given her revulsion away. So much for Lord Rochford's suggestion her groom might be someone more agreeable.

Her aunt paid her no heed, however. She nattered on about a wedding dress of orange-blossom watered silk with lace, bows, and flounces. She followed with all sorts of other nonsensical plans as they drifted through her mind. Coming to an end at last, she turned to face her niece—actually her husband's niece and hers only by marriage, something of which she was supremely aware. "You best go to your room to ready yourself for this evening. Have you practiced your music?"

Knowing her aunt had little actual interest in her music, Anne merely nodded. She left her aunt as quickly as possible, hurrying to her room with Dolly trailing behind her.

Ignoring the maid's chattering, Anne wondered what the evening might bring. Lord Alington would probably attend, so she had best control her nerves and plan to play her finest. That Lord Rochford might actually be there did not seem possible. And yet she trusted him. If anyone could find her a way out of this dreadful dilemma, she thought it might be Lord Rochford. He possessed an air of resolve, although why he should care about her she didn't know.

"What's the matter with you?" Dolly demanded. "You don't look like a gel who has had two respectable offers of marriage, you surely don't."

"I am merely feeling a bit downish. Perhaps if I take a nap, I shall feel more the thing?" Not waiting for her maid to reply, Anne turned around so she might be assisted from her day gown, then crawled into her bed as though she intended to sleep. There was little the nosy Dolly might do but leave the room.

Privacy! How little of it she could attain. The only time was such as this, by subterfuge, or when she practiced the pianoforte. Dolly didn't like the music Anne played; Bach, Clementi, and Mozart did not please. Dolly by far preferred a jig.

Staring at the gathered folds of the top of the canopy over her narrow bed, Anne considered what best to do. She would run away if she could only get her hands on some money. That was the rub of it all. She was an heiress of some substance, and she scarce had a pound in hand. Unless she walked off with her green traveling bag in hand, she was trapped. And, afraid as she was, she determined she would do precisely that if necessary. Somehow she would find a way out of this unwelcome marriage!

Hours later, Justin strolled into the elegant town house belonging to Lord and Lady Chalfont, where the musicale was to be held, without a hint of his unease. The trick of it was to find Alington and Gower and learn what it was that drew them to the girl. Justin had little doubt as to Bowlton's motivation. All one had to do was to look at Miss Haycroft and know what *that* was; the greasy old wigsby would likely lick his lips when he eyed her.

At first he couldn't see his quarry. The room thronged with the fashionable *ton,* and it wasn't easy to spot a man who was but average in height and as thin as a banister.

Justin was standing to the rear of the concert room when he caught sight of his man. Garbed in black, his white linen cleverly draped about his neck in a neat Osbaldeston arrangement, Alington looked the very image of the elegant peer. Justin wondered what went on behind that bland façade.

When the harpist had completed her charming bit of music, Justin made his way around the back of the room to where Alington stood in anticipation of the next performer.

"Evening," Justin said in his most laconic manner.

"What on earth brings you here, Rochford? I cannot recall seeing you at a musicale before," Alington replied with a faint sneer in his voice.

"I was told that I was missing a talented performer and decided to rectify my error," Justin shot back smoothly, settling into a position at Alington's side.

"The harpist?" Alington inquired lazily, but with the watchfulness of an asp ready to strike.

"No, a young woman quite gifted at the pianoforte."

"Miss Anne Haycroft. She will play next. Your much vaunted charm will do you no good there. Her uncle has plans for her. You may as well leave," Alington said in a harsh whisper, a sly smile on his thin lips.

"Leave? I barely arrived. Besides, I like pianoforte music. You apparently do as well."

"She is perfect," Alington said softly. "A true gem I *must* have. She has looks, breeding, and ability, and will grace my home quite nicely."

Shivering inwardly, Justin thought Alington looked upon Anne Haycroft as an item to add to his exquisite collection of beautiful things. What might happen as Anne grew older? When he tired of her or she lost her looks, would he discard her in favor of a younger, more beautiful woman? He'd likely divorce Anne on some trumped-up excuse, then select another young beauty.

Justin decided at that moment that he would do all in his power to help Miss Haycroft flee her scheming uncle and the men she feared to marry. It was unconscionable to permit a lovely young woman to be forced into a marriage so utterly wrong and distasteful to her.

That he also recalled her response to his kisses was for the moment ignored. He shouldn't allow his personal reaction to affect his judgment in this case.

At that moment Miss Haycroft walked to the pianoforte, seated herself with a minimum of fuss, and when all was quiet, began to play. He had never disliked music, nor had he contempt for the pianoforte. However, this was not merely music, it was magic from the heavens. He listened for a time to the re-markably gifted girl when he chanced to look at the man at his side.

Alington stared at Miss Haycroft with that alarming intensity of which she had spoken. It seemed to Justin that there was a hint of madness in that stare. Obsession gleamed in Alington's eyes; his entire body seemed tensed with his fixation.

At last the ethereal music drew to a conclusion. The people around him stirred, talking in subdued voices as though it were a desecration to speak in normal tones.

"You now see why I must have her," Alington said softly for Justin's ears alone.

"She is not yours as yet, my friend," Justin replied a trifle grimly, not able to keep his contempt out of his tone.

"You want her for yourself? 'Tis not possible. You see, I tendered an agreement to her uncle this afternoon." Alington's smile was not nice to observe. "He won't reject me."

"Indeed?" Justin said in his own quietly menacing way.

Alington's nasty smile broadened. "Indeed."

Justin excused himself and went to the back of the room, wondering how he could get in contact with Anne—Miss Hay-croft, that is. He was about to search for writing paper when he heard a whispered "Psst."

He strolled from the drawing room, then looked about to find Miss Haycroft behind a potted palm in the hall. "You were superb." He wished he had words to tell her how her music had stirred him.

"Thank you," she said with the modesty he might have expected from her. "You sat next to Lord Alington." There was a question in her voice.

Recovering his usual aplomb, Justin swiftly revealed what he had discovered, then added, "What may I do to help? I do not trust Alington any more than you do."

"I must escape, get away from my uncle at once, else I shall be married before I can sneeze—with such choices!" Her eloquent eyes were full of fear. "If I can but hide away until my birthday on June the seventh, I shall be free of Uncle's guardianship—with only my trustee to order my life."

Justin instantly decided to go with his earlier impulse to aid this young woman in any way he could. "Gather what you wish to bring, and I shall pick you up first light tomorrow. You may stay with my aunt. I fear there is no time to waste."

"I agree," she whispered after a small hesitation, a hint of her alarm in her eyes. "Thank you. I hope you will not regret this action."

Justin gazed down at the lovely face and suspected he would. But a man had to live dangerously at least once in his life. "I shall be there."

Chapter Two

A nne peered nervously from her window, silently blessing the fog that had crept into the city during the night. She had scarcely slept, worried about the coming hours, the coming days. Could she succeed? The law would not take lightly her defiance of her guardian's decree. Would Lord Rochford, in whom she had placed such enormous trust, be able to help her attain what she wished? It was risky to abet a girl in leaving her legal guardian. Yet he was a man to inspire confidence.

Now the hour was at hand for her to slip from the house. She had thought long and hard, deeming it necessary that silence reign and she not be discovered by anyone. As unlikely as it might seem, her best way out of the house was the front door. Surely one of the servants would be in the kitchen by this time of the morning. The front door had well-oiled hinges and was close to the bottom of the stairs.

Preparing for her escape had been easier than she would have believed. Once Dolly had thought Anne abed, ready for sleep, there had been privacy and opportunity to pack the most needed of clothing. She was thankful for Dolly's laziness, for one of Anne's cases had been left beneath her bed rather than being stored in the box room. If she could presume upon Lord Rochford to see her lawyer regarding some funds, it might be possible to survive until the relative freedom she would gain on her birthday.

In the faint gray light she noted it was time to depart. She wrapped a warm scarf more firmly about her neck, picked up her single case and left her room. Her simple plan to skim down the stairs on her Moroccan slippers, unlock the front door, and slip outside seemed far too easy.

Every creak of the step, the slightest sound, and she froze, listening. Had her cat still been alive, she might have thought it prowling about, but her uncle had tossed the animal out, declaring it a menace to their health. This, from a man who ate to excess, drank likewise, and gambled stupidly. What a pity he did not occasionally win, she thought, as she continued her cautious way down the stairs. The last flight looked ominous as she stared at the bottommost tread. One thump of her case, one wrong creak of the wood, and she would be found out.

When she at last achieved the entryway, she discovered the key was not where she usually saw it. Heart pounding, she almost groaned. To be so close, only to be thwarted by a missing key! *Impossible!* She tried to think logically. Where might her uncle—coming home late—stow it for the night?

Slowly pirouetting about, she took a closer look at the hideous vase on the entry table. Not logical, she told herself. But she checked nevertheless. *Success.* Inside the vase her aunt took such great pride in was the missing key. After that it was but a small matter to insert the large brass key into the lock, then ease open the door. How glad she was to find herself on the outside of that door! Now for her appointment with her rescuer!

Around the corner she found a carriage waiting. It was closed—an improper arrangement but a necessary precaution. As she neared, the door opened and Lord Rochford stepped down.

"You cannot know how relieved I am to see you," she whispered, still worried that Dolly might rise early and take a notion to check on her mistress. Should she raise the alarm, all might be lost.

"No more than am I to see you. After we parted, I thought of all the obstacles that might present themselves to prevent your leaving." As they spoke, he placed her case in the carriage, then helped her in, looking about him as he did. Although misty fog swirled about the street, the dim morning light revealed no sign of others.

"Let us hope the headache potion I offered Dolly helps her to sleep longer than normal." Anne nudged her case to one side with her foot, then settled against the squabs. There would be time enough, she suspected, to ask Lord Rochford about the money she would need.

"How did you manage something so clever?" he inquired with admiration in his voice.

"She complained about her headache, and I suggested she try a potion I had obtained from the apothecary just yesterday morning. Actually, it was nothing more than a tincture of laudanum. I do not usually take such, but Dolly forgot that in her eagerness to ease her discomfort."

Justin rubbed his jaw while studying the young woman opposite him. He had discovered she was rising twenty-one, yet she looked as fresh as a girl in the schoolroom. He liked the softness of her voice. Even when annoyed—indeed, angry— she had spoken quietly, and she'd had good reason to complain quite loudly. He sensed a gentleness about her, something neither Bowlton nor Alington would appreciate. He did not credit Alington's assertion that the deal was a closed matter.

How feminine she appeared, even in this dawning light when she must have risen early. Her pelisse of a delicate blue and very sensible kerseymere flattered her, as did the pretty dove gray shawl wrapped snugly about her neck. She must be nervous, yet she sat quietly, hands in her lap, looking as relaxed as though she were off to a picnic.

He wondered if she had even slept, yet she looked fresh and neat. Although how she had managed to dress without her maid to help her was beyond him. In his experience no woman could cope with dressing herself considering all the hooks and buttons and tapes required to hold those garments together.

Giving voice to his thoughts, he asked, "You managed to pack and dress without any difficulty?"

She flashed him a look of reproof. A gentleman was not supposed to inquire of such things. Yet she answered him politely, thinking he could know little of the problems she'd encountered. "It was not as difficult as it might have been. How fortunate a gown recently delivered from Madame Clotilde buttoned down the front. It was but minutes to fasten and I was ready." She did not mention the other matters; it wouldn't be proper.

He cleared his throat, looking nervous, perhaps rueful for an indiscretion.

"It is awkward, is it not?" she said with a sympathetic manner. "We are neither fish nor fowl. We are not quite strangers, required to be chillingly polite, nor are we close friends who may resort to familiarity." She was not certain where those kisses fit in, but that episode was best forgotten—if she could.

"Indeed," he said with feeling. Then, changing the subject, he said reassuringly, "My aunt expects you this morning. I explained as much as I deemed necessary. It is up to you to reveal all you think she should know."

"The whole of it, I suspect. I cannot think how she may house me—a runaway—without knowing the entire story, the truth of the matter, before my uncle or others fill her ears with lies. Earwigs abound, gossips eager to tattle a tale whether it be truthful or not."

"One thing about telling the truth, you have no lies to sort out and remember," he pointed out.

"Indeed," she murmured as the carriage drew to a halt before a neat house.

"Lower Brook Street is a desirable address, and my aunt keeps excellent company. You will not want for entertainment." He assisted her from the carriage with what Anne thought a very nice regard.

She stood silently for a few minutes while he gave orders concerning the carriage, her case, and when the driver ought to return. The house was indeed neat. It was also surprisingly large for a town house. Her uncle's home had but a two- and one-window arrangement to either side of the front door. This house contained two on either side, with indications of high ceilings and four stories, rather than her uncle's three.

"Come. Aunt Mary will not be up and about, but we can settle you in your room while I order us a meal."

Thinking this most practical, Anne went before him into the charming entry hall, where black and white tiles gleamed in the pale morning light and a cherrywood chest stood against the wall with a pretty silver tray on it awaiting calling cards.

She pulled off her gloves and untied her best bonnet with unsteady hands. She had done it. She had taken a potentially fatal step. Determined to make the best of her situation, she turned to face her rescuer.

"Your case should be in your room shortly. Potter will bring it there directly the coachman delivers it to the rear of the house. Come, let us repair to the breakfast room. There are bound to be muffins and eggs, not to mention some excellent ham, shortly. My aunt keeps a very good table." He clasped Anne's elbow to guide her along the hall to the rear of the ground floor.

"I would expect nothing less from a relative of yours," Anne replied, her eyes twinkling with amusement and relief that he could be so nonchalant.

He paused at the doorway to a charming breakfast room, his hand lingering on her arm. "How so?"

"It would seem to me that your family must do nothing by halves!" She smiled at his reaction, for he had grinned in return.

"We have never been accused of being slow-tops."

They were seated at the table when Potter entered with a tray bearing all that was required for a most excellent breakfast. Discovering she was amazingly hungry, Anne loaded her plate and commenced to eat with a hearty appetite. About to bite into her marmalade-laden toast, she glanced up to find Lord Rochford's eyes upon her. Thinking she must have preserves on her lips, she delicately licked them, while raising her brows in query.

"I am all astonishment, my dear lady. I had no idea there were actually women who consumed food with an appetite. Whenever I am invited to dine, all I see are women who nibble, protest they cannot eat a bite, and still manage to appear reasonably healthy. How do they do it?" He seemed quite serious, yet Anne detected a hint of mirth in his dark eyes.

"They lie. Usually a lady will eat at home first so as to give the impression she will be economical to keep as a wife. It is all a hum, you see?" Anne placed her fork on her plate and turned serious. "There is something I must ask of you yet again, sir."

"I gather it is not to keep the secret of dainty eating?" He forked a bite of succulent ham into his mouth, then chewed while awaiting her request.

"Indeed, no. How are we to go on? How am *I* to go on? I shall need money. My uncle never gave me but a bit of pocket money for little things. I have nothing."

"That often is the way of it. I would wager he suffers from not the slightest want?" He raised his brows, an expression of contempt touching his eyes.

"Is it possible for you to call on my solicitor, perhaps convince him that I wish some money?" Anne inquired hesitantly, not wanting to put him out still more, yet desperate for funds.

"How are your bills handled at this point?"

"I believe there is a man at the bank who pays my bills and sorts out the accounts. I did all this for my father while he yet lived. I am not permitted to do so for myself," she concluded with irony.

"I have long felt that we men do not sufficiently appreciate the mental capabilities of women—at least some women. I'd not give your Aunt Haycroft high marks." He grimaced and shot her a questioning look.

"Indeed," Anne murmured in reply, her thoughts on the problem of money. "If the solicitor will not cooperate in this, I confess I am at a loss. My uncle will do all in his power to see to it that I am thwarted in my desire *not* to marry his choice."

"You cannot be faulted in that, for certain. Neither Alington nor Bowlton are men to win a lady's regard easily. If I cannot convince your solicitor, I shall think of something. You will not be left without a cent to call your own."

Anne flashed him a rueful smile. "I fear I am naught but trouble for you."

He returned her gaze with a look of warmth and something else she could not identify.

They settled down to discuss possibilities, reaching an accord Anne would not have believed achievable with a gentleman she scarcely knew. Yet she had exchanged far more words with him than either man her uncle wished her to marry. Most agreeable words they were, too.

"What excuse can I offer for leaving my aunt and uncle? Surely the world will wonder?"

Thinking Society would make what it could of the matter, regardless, Justin was about to offer an opinion when his aunt entered the room, her morning gown flowing gracefully around her ample figure. He immediately rose to greet his aunt with all respect.

"Ah, my mysterious guest. Good morning to you both," she said, an eyebrow raised at her nephew with compelling inquiry. She sailed around the table, accepting Justin's kiss on her cheek with aplomb, then seated herself at the end, where she could easily watch the other two. He resumed his place, prepared to talk.

It did not take long for Justin to explain what had happened the evening before. That he had previously alerted his aunt to the probability of her entertaining a guest simplified things considerably.

"I welcome you, my dear," Lady Mary said with a candid look at Anne. "I cannot think of anything so tedious as relatives who insist they must ruin your life. Do not mistake it—it would be utter ruination were you to wed either gentleman. Lord Bowlton is a disgusting creature, and not merely because he is odiously fat. He has buried two wives and one must ask why. As to Lord Alington, he is to be rejected on other grounds."

Justin interrupted his aunt to say, "I believe he fancies Miss Haycroft as an addition to his collection. Whether he desires her for her beauty or her ability to play the pianoforte like an angel is difficult to say. I suspect it is for her skill as a musician."

"You joke. It is bad taste this early in the morning, Justin," his aunt declared.

"I fear it is no joke, dear aunt. He is obsessed with beautiful things, and I could be wrong, but I believe he borders on madness."

"I see." Lady Mary remained silent for a time while sipping hot tea. "So, what are we to do now that you have spirited Miss Haycroft away from the evil guardian?"

"Please call me Anne," Anne begged. "If I am to remain with you for any time, Miss Haycroft becomes a bit tedious."

"So, Anne, have you any ideas?"

Pleased that Lady Mary thought enough of her to believe she might have an opinion worth the listening, Anne explained about the money.

Her ladyship pursed her lips, seemingly deep in thought, before she spoke at last. "I think it might be best if we frank you for the time being. I cannot think it good to allow them the least bit of control, and the money could become that."

"But I'll need a few gowns, shoes, you know what is involved. To be truthful"—Anne glanced at Lord Rochford—"I did not care for the clothes my aunt selected for me. She insisted upon white for most gowns and for others, lime green, coral, and a shade of orange that make me look ill! I managed to purchase a blue pelisse and this violet dress, but I have had little to say about what I wear."

"And Madame Clotilde agreed to this! I am astonished."

"It is obvious you have not met my aunt," Anne said.

"Like that, is she? Well, all the better if you are totally free from their say-so. Do not worry about a thing. I shall keep an account of all that is spent."

"Well, I shall leave you ladies to get on with planning your day. While I am out and about, I will keep my ears open for any tidbits regarding the disappearance of the heiress," Justin said while rising from the table. He bowed politely to his aunt, then to Anne.

She also rose, saying, "I'll walk with you to the door. I have a request to make of you."

"Again?" he said with mock severity.

They reached the front door, and Potter held it open for his lordship, then retreated.

Anne compressed her lips before asking, "Please let me know *all* that is being said. I cannot know how to counter their gossip unless I am aware of what they are spreading."

He nodded. "Very well, I will. It may not be very pleasant, you know."

"I scarce expected otherwise." She held out her hand in farewell and he took it in his, raising it to his mouth. The touch of his lips on her hand was warm and intimate without a glove to shield her. They stood facing each other for long moments, looking into each other's eyes with a searching intensity.

As he turned to leave, breaking that communion, he muttered softly at the sight of one of the *ton*'s gleeful gossips peering at the house with curious eyes.

"What is it?"

"Hortense Finch."

"Oh, no! She's a nasty tattle-basket of the worst sort! But what is that to us?" Anne still felt the pressure of his mouth on her hand and wondered that she had not swooned as those ladies in Mrs. Radcliffe's books were wont to do. Indeed, she must be a wanton sort of girl to like improper things so much!

"I feel certain she saw you. You are not unknown, nor am I. She will doubtless embroider a tale, embellishing upon my departure from my aunt's home at such an early hour after bidding you good-bye."

"Rubbish," Anne said feelingly. She would have cheerfully sent Hortense Finch to the ends of the earth so that she might recall those precious moments when she had searched his rather appealing dark eyes.

"I hope your optimism is well founded."

Anne watched as Justin entered the carriage that had drawn up before the house. What a pity it had not come before, to block that wretched woman's view.

When Anne returned to the breakfast room, Lady Mary said at once, "Something occurred. I must know."

"Hortense Finch," Anne replied with a grimace.

"That could be a problem—she is so clever at embroidering out of whole cloth. Since there is not a thing we can do about her, let us put our minds to what we must accomplish today. We need to strike immediately, the sooner the better. Your uncle will be furious his victim has fled. You must be seen out and about with me. My name and consequence will protect you from him for the time being. However, I believe it wise for you to always be with one of us when you leave here. I doubt we can trust your uncle, my dear."

Well acquainted with her uncle and his ways, Anne promptly agreed.

"Very well," Lady Mary said in a more amiable manner. "I shall dress, and we will make our list for today. Gowns, shoes and slippers, a few bonnets—that ought to take care of you for the present. I believe if we drop a word or two of your story into Madame Clotilde's ear, she will aid our cause. She has a softness in the heart for a young woman who flees a bad marriage."

Anne stood by the door, considering the day ahead of her, then said, "Pray we do not cross Lord Alington's path."

"We likely will, dear girl. We shall give him the cut direct. I trust that a gentle soul like you can manage that?" Lady Mary gave Anne a shrewd look.

"Yes, ma'am," Anne replied dutifully, while wondering how one gave the cut direct to a man as powerful as Lord Alington.

It was hours before they left the house to visit the shops Lady Mary favored. When they reached Madame Clotilde's discreet shop with its curtained windows and soft gray interior with the dainty gilt chairs, Anne felt reasonably secure. Lord Alington would scarcely enter these environs to chase her down. Obsessed though he might be, he also appeared to have a great deal of pride. Pride would forbid pursuing her like a fox after a hare.

"Your aunt is not with you today?" the slender woman with the improbably red hair inquired while leading Lady Mary and Anne to a dressing room in the rear of the shop.

"She is a runaway, Madame," Lady Mary declared. "I am sheltering a young woman who balks at the thought of wedding Lord Bowlton or Lord Alington! My dear nephew thought to offer my home as a haven. I think she shows uncommonly good sense not to tie herself to either of those men. Heaven only knows how she would survive! I feel certain you have heard the same rumors I have, so I shan't repeat them. Shocking!"

Madame nodded her head while selecting various bolts of fabric from stacks on a small table. "Now I shall be able to dress you as I please. Lime green and coral, pah!"

Eyeing the lengths of violets, blues, pale rose prints, and sprigged muslins, Anne sighed with delight. "You will remember to keep a careful account, Lady Mary?"

"Indeed." Her ladyship turned to Madame and added, "Can you imagine that uncle of hers not allowing her a farthing to spend? And she an heiress?"

"Shocking!" Madame agreed while pulling a creamy and most expensive lace from the pile of fabrics.

Once they'd concluded the business of selecting a new

wardrobe, they continued on to other shops to find the necessary slippers and half boots, pretty parasols, and lastly, bonnets.

It was when they were exiting this last shop that they came face-to-face with Lord Alington.

Lady Mary touched Anne on her arm, an unnecessary warning. Anne couldn't have said a word to him had her life depended upon it. She looked past his lordship as though he didn't exist, then turned to Lady Mary and quietly said, "I believe I see the carriage approaching, my lady."

"So it is. I vow I shall welcome a rest. Come, my dear." Lady Mary swept past the ill-fated gentleman to enter the carriage that had fortuitously drawn up before the shop.

Lord Alington was helpless in the encounter. If a woman chose not to acknowledge him, he in all proper manner must remain silent and allow her to pass as though he wasn't there—which is precisely what he did. Anne thought she could hear him grinding his teeth as she passed by him.

"Abominable, to behave so to her future husband," Lord Alington muttered, scowling after the departing women.

Anne reflected it must be galling for his lofty lordship to be given the cut direct. She had no doubt her uncle would hear of the snub. She had to confess that although she had never done such a reprehensible thing before, she had felt very good about it.

"You do realize that he cannot *force* you to marry him. Canon law prohibits a marriage without the consent of the persons who marry. Neither Alington nor your uncle can compel you to wed against your will. But you cannot trust them to be decent and law-abiding. I have heard tales of women being tricked, or drugged, with all manner of underhanded, sly, and tortuous devices employed. *That* is why you must take care. As long as you are with me, there is nothing they can do to you."

Anne shivered in spite of the carriage's warmth. The prospect was both comforting and alarming. They truly could not force her, and with Lady Mary at her side there wasn't much her uncle could do without looking like a fool. Yet she knew her uncle was tenacious, and given the obsession Lord

Rochford thought gripped Lord Alington, she dare not relax a moment.

"Since you are not ultimately dependent upon your uncle for money, he does not have total power over you," Lady Mary mused aloud.

"What a pity I have a modest fortune," Anne returned thoughtfully. "I think the common people have the happiest marriages, for they may wed for love."

"Indeed, once in a while an arranged marriage does well, but where one party has not seen the other until they meet before the altar, it is difficult to imagine a happy union. More often than not, the marriage ends in separation, or worse yet, adultery."

Blushing at the thought of what that involved, Anne looked out of the window at the passing scene until they reached Lower Brook Street and Lady Mary's home.

Potter suggested a soothing cup of tea and perhaps a biscuit or two to replenish her ladyship's energy.

Both ladies thought that splendid and continued up to the drawing room, where each selected a chair upon which to collapse.

It was over tea and ratafia biscuits that Justin found them when he called in the late afternoon. "You have been busy by the look of things," he commented. "I just saw Potter accepting a stack of parcels from a lad. A good day?"

"Indeed." Lady Mary paused, then continued, "We encountered Alington outside Miss Grey's bonnet shop on Oxford Street." With a glance at Anne, she added, "We gave him the cut direct."

"The fat's in the fire now," Justin replied with a grimace.

"Well, he spoiled a perfectly marvelous day of shopping by appearing there. You have the right of it when you say he is queer in the attic. I suspect that doesn't cover the half of it." Lady Mary sniffed, then sipped her cooling tea.

"And you, sir, did you have a good day? I suspect not, for you look suspiciously careworn," Anne said in her soft, velvety voice.

"Indeed, I had a perfectly wretched day. Too bad of you to notice, for I wanted to keep it from you."

"From me? You promised you'd not conceal the gossip, and I suspect that is what you do now," Anne countered swiftly.

"Hortense Finch has been quite busy embroidering her view of this morning. I was astonished to learn I was in the act of bidding you farewell following a night of passion. And in my aunt's home!"

Chapter Three

"Oh, bother Miss Finch. What a pity she does not have a family of her own to plague with her attention!" Lady Mary cried with a vexed expression. She turned to Anne, putting out her hand as though to stay her. "My dear, what are we to do? We will need something to counter this evil woman's gossip."

"Evil, dear aunt?" Justin inserted, thinking his aunt was a trifle dramatic.

"You cannot believe the harm that woman has done with her tattle-bearing. Once words are spoken, they cannot be recalled, you know." Lady Mary spun about to pace back and forth in the drawing room, pausing every so often as though a thought had struck her. Then she would shake her head and continue her pacing. At last she halted, letting her hand rest on the top of a high-backed wing chair, the deep red of the chair blending in nicely with the red print of her gown. "Well? Have *you* any ideas, nephew?"

"The thing to do," Justin said thoughtfully, "is something terribly clever. I believe Miss Haycroft requires a number of beaus, perhaps a serious one as well?"

He captured the attention of his aunt as well as Anne Haycroft at his surprising words.

"Indeed, why did I not think of that?" Lady Mary demanded wryly. "And do you offer yourself as one of them? I thought that was the problem—Hortense believes you to be carrying on a flirtation with Miss Haycroft? Or do you have others in mind?"

"Oh, others, assuredly," Justin said easily. "If there are a number of gentlemen paying court to Miss Haycroft, old tattle-basket Finch can scarcely pinpoint me as the only one. We must do something to save Miss Haycroft's reputation or it will be in shreds before she has a chance to find herself this love match she wants. Perhaps Sidney would oblige us? He owes me a favor."

"So you did bail him out of the River Tick after all?" Lady Mary said with a grimace. "He will not learn responsibility that way, Justin."

"I could not have my cousin deeply in debt to the cent-per-centers. Oxford is expensive, as you well know." Justin crossed to lean against the mantelpiece, one arm resting negligently along the pale marble.

Anne sat down on a conveniently placed chair, wondering if she had come to a madhouse after all. "I do not think it would work," she offered into a momentary silence.

"Why ever not?" Justin demanded, a frown settling on his brow.

She shrugged delicately. "I know few gentlemen, other than those two my uncle selected for me. And they did not do at all, as you well know. My aunt saw to it that every man who came near me had a title and funds. She wanted no gazetted fortune hunter sniffing about." Anne looked to where Lady Mary stood, then to where Lord Rochford lounged so seemingly at ease. Only, she suspected, he was not quite so at ease as he would have them think. He had been angry at Miss Finch's gossip. Anne cringed inwardly at the thought of what might happen were her uncle to hear the tattle.

"Well, you can scarcely blame her for that," Lady Mary said in surprising defense of Mrs. Haycroft. "I do not know of one mother who has a marriageable daughter who does not read through the column of bankrupts published in the *Gazette*. I should do so as well in the same circumstances."

"Sidney is not bankrupt, and he's my heir presumptive . . . for the moment. And I daresay that once Miss Haycroft stands up with me, then Sidney, at Almack's, there will be a score of gentlemen hovering about her. She is a remarkably pretty young woman, Aunt, in case you have not noticed."

"I have," she admitted, "but I thought perhaps it had escaped you." She paused for a few moments, then continued, "I must call on Lady Sefton this afternoon, before the hour is past for calls." A glance at the clock revealed the day was well along.

"You think Lady Sefton would come to the aid of someone she does not know?" Anne queried softly.

"She always desires Justin to attend her parties—he is quite a catch, or so I have heard," her ladyship said, her voice dry, almost acerbic. She turned, walking hurriedly to the door, where she paused. "I shall go at once to see about a voucher. Pray Lady Sefton is in a happy mood."

"Shall I go with you?" Lord Rochford asked, a twinkle entering his eyes.

"I believe you have done quite enough," Lady Mary replied, her words curt, her manner abstracted. She left to fetch her bonnet and shawl.

Anne looked at the lean and most handsome gentleman now following his aunt to the door. "I trust I have not come between you and your aunt. You appear to hold her in high esteem."

"We are ever thus, sparring with words. She has a notion I must wed soon and set up a household complete with nursery. Whereas I am in no hurry at all." He stopped to give Anne a quizzical look. "And you? In spite of your uncle, you would wish to marry?"

She took a deep breath before answering. "I must. What other course is there for a young woman?"

"Surely there is something besides becoming a governess?" He stood, silently studying her with dark eyes no longer twinkling, rather, sober and full of curiosity.

"I have means enough, although not a fortune by your standards I suppose. What a pity I cannot simply disappear!" Anne smiled wanly, wishing she might be elsewhere, away from this disturbing man. His look disquieted, his touch thrilled. She suspected he was extremely dangerous to her peace of mind.

He leaned back against the frame of the door, lounging, yet with that impeccable carriage inbred in him. "You have no other relative?"

"A cousin off in southern Yorkshire near Kingston-on-Hull. We have not written often. I am reluctant to impose on her, for she lives in a cottage alone but for two cats." Anne rose from her chair, crossing to stand before her rescuer. "I again must thank you for saving me from my uncle. I only hope that by doing so you do not find yourself in a bumblebroth."

"You gave Alington the cut direct today," Justin mused, seeming almost embarrassed by her plain speaking. "Let us trust that does not cause more trouble than Aunt anticipates."

"Oh, dear," Anne replied, giving him a worried look. "Let us pray some other creature or thing he simply must have comes into his sight and soon! I hope it is a rare flower and not another young lady."

Justin nodded his agreement, then bid her farewell, leaving the house with near unseemly haste. She seemed far too vulnerable and indeed, kissable, in her simple violet gown, a worried frown creasing her pretty forehead. He had no doubt in the least that with his aunt's patronage and an entrée to Almack's Miss Haycroft would be the evening's star. With her ash blond curls rioting about her dainty head, and those amazing blue eyes soberly staring up in admiration—ah, indeed, she would take. Why the thought did not please him, he didn't pause to examine. Rather, he hailed a hackney and set off for his club.

Anne went to the window to watch Lord Rochford enter the carriage, then disappear from view. Slowly she turned to face the room, her thoughts in a whirl. How humbling that people she scarcely knew would go to such trouble to help her when her own aunt and uncle would not listen to a word Anne uttered. She vowed to make it up to Lady Mary and Lord Rochford. And she would try to see that no hint of scandal would touch his most handsome lordship.

An hour later, Lady Mary entered the house with an amused smile on her face. "Anne, where are you, my dear?"

Anne fluttered to the top of the stairs, leaning over the railing to see what the fuss was about. At her ladyship's wave, Anne sped down the steps to where the older lady awaited her.

"I have the vouchers," the lady declared with satisfaction. "Fortunately, the committee had been meeting when I arrived. They were instantly persuaded to your point of view. I was surprised that Mrs. Drummond-Burrell claimed to know you. Naughty puss, you did not tell me you are somewhat related."

"Distantly, it is true," Anne said slowly. "I had near forgotten, for it is my mother's side of the family."

"Well, it made obtaining the vouchers a simple matter. A relative of a patroness has not the slightest difficulty in obtaining one, no matter how distant that relationship might be. We shall be there come Wednesday, my dear. Just wait until Hortense Finch discovers she has been maligning a relative of one of the patronesses. How I would love to see that sight!"

Anne followed the chuckling Lady Mary up the stairs to the landing, then halted as her ladyship placed a hand to her mouth. "I shall send a note to Mr. Witherspoon to accompany us. The dear man has such presence."

Seeing Anne's expression, Lady Mary explained, "I once thought he wished to marry me, but I flirted with another, and he said nothing more. My parents refused me the gentleman I wished to wed and sought a marriage to a viscount with bad teeth and a terrible lisp. I understand your dilemma all too well."

"Goodness me, I *can* see why you have sympathy for my plight. You endured much the same thing," Anne cried in dismay.

"It was my parents, not my uncle and aunt who were the ones who sought an 'advantageous' marriage for me. Indeed, there were several young men who caught my eye so long ago. One went off to Canada, never to be seen again. I have no idea if he is even yet alive."

Anne watched as her ladyship sailed along to her room, no doubt to pen a missive to Mr. Witherspoon. How comforting for her ladyship to have a gentleman she could call upon for escort.

That Wednesday evening Anne was more nervous than she had even been while performing at a musicale. At least at the pianoforte she had her music to offer an escape of sorts. At Almack's there was nothing other than the company of Lady Mary and the quaintly attentive Mr. Witherspoon. He was what one might call a determined bachelor with beautiful manners and a polished line of address that he intended no lady to take seriously.

Anne greeted Clementina Drummond-Burrell with a mixture

of proper politeness and that vague familiarity one reserves for distant relatives one scarcely knows. Anne suspected Clementina was rising thirty, yet she looked remarkably well preserved, if a trifle stern. Perhaps she took her position in Society too much to heart? The other patronesses in attendance that evening promised to introduced Anne to eligible gentlemen. It was unthinkable that Clementina's cousin should not find a respectable *parti*!

With Clementina to one side and a decent fortune to the other, Anne stood a fair chance to do quite well. Now if only her greedy uncle did not put his hand in to ruin everything.

As promised, Lord Rochford appeared in time to lead Anne out for the opening dance, a stately minuet. She fixed a shy gaze on him, recalling his shocking kisses every time they were required to take each other's hands. Through the fine kidskin of her gloves, she could sense the warmth of his gloved hands. And if it seemed to her that he held her hand a second or two longer than he ought, he gave no sign of his impropriety. His eyes teased her, their darkness seeming to hold amber sparkle in the candlelight. He twirled her expertly, and she could almost feel sorry that the minuet was falling out of favor. The dance offered such fine moments for sharing looks, capturing a partner's gaze in warm regard.

Lady Cowper began the next dance, a cotillion, on the arm of Lord Palmerston. Anne accepted the hand of a young fellow introduced as Mr. Metcalf, recommended by Mr. Witherspoon as most eligible. He was tall and lean with sandy hair that tended to droop over his brow in a poetic way. He danced well, however, and she found much to like in the quiet young gentleman.

Following the cotillion she found Lord Rochford standing at Lady Mary's side with a young man who much resembled him. No doubt this was the wayward Sidney, down from Oxford.

"You may have guessed this chap is my cousin, Sidney Fairfax," his lordship said most kindly, considering his cousin had turned as red as a beetroot.

Anne judged Sidney to be the same age as she, although he had not the poise that had been drummed into her at an early age. One thing she had to hand to Aunt Winnefred was that she had seen to a proper training of her niece. But then perhaps that was in aid of gaining an excellent marriage with sufficient funds for Uncle Haycroft.

A country dance formed, with Sidney standing opposite her in the line. It was easy to be graceful with an accomplished partner, and Sidney did well. In time, he would acquire the same polish as his older cousin.

As the evening wore on, she found to her vexation that she instinctively compared each partner—and there were quite a number of them—to Lord Rochford.

"You are quite the belle of the evening," Justin said when capturing her hand for a dance. She looked ravishing in the suitably demure gown of palest pink Gros de Naples. Her pearls gleamed at her throat above a neckline that was lower than he could approve for a young woman making her come-out. On the other hand, it was vastly becoming and enhanced her assets admirably. Almost too much so, for Metcalf had gazed down at her with too much admiration.

She danced well, as though she could read his mind with each step. And she never made a misstep, nor did she spend time eyeing other gentlemen, not that Justin was accustomed to such behavior. But Anne Haycroft needed to fix the attentions of several men to ward off her uncle's demands she marry his choice. She remained properly attentive to her partner, and Justin admired her for that.

At the end of the dance he caught sight of the flush on her cheeks and said, "The lemonade is tepid and weak, but it is better than nothing. May I offer you some?"

"Only if you do not leave me to languish here," she replied with a laugh. "I hope there is a trifle more air where the refreshments are set out."

"Indeed," Justin said with a grimace. "Few care for them, so there is usually ample room."

They found it to be so. Anne sipped the lemonade with thanks, hoping she might make it last the rest of this dance. Not that she wasn't appreciative for the many partners she had. She reluctantly admitted that she enjoyed Lord Rochford's company far too much!

"Ha! So there you are, ungrateful girl," a familiar voice declared, most thankfully not too loud.

"Uncle," Anne said quietly. She was grateful when Justin moved closer to her, seeming to loom over her in a rather protective manner.

"Fine thing, after all the years we fed and clothed you, to treat us so!"

"I believe my own money was expended on my keep. I have not been that great a burden to you, but thinking perhaps I might be, I accepted Lady Mary Crosscombe's invitation to reside with her for a time. And my cousin, dear Mrs. Drummond-Burrell, was so kind as to take me under her wing. I have met any number of eligible young gentlemen this evening." Anne paused, then added in a very soft voice for her uncle's ears only, "And none of them are old and fat or possessing strange habits, either."

Her uncle reached out to grab her arm, only to find his hand clasped firmly by a stern-visaged Lord Rochford.

"I trust you will not object to your niece taking up residence with my aunt?" Justin glared at the other man, making certain that he knew just what he faced were he to continue with the unseemly behavior.

"Gracious! There you are, Anne, dear," Mrs. Haycroft exclaimed. "However did you come to be here?"

"Aunt," Anne said politely, dipping the briefest of curtsies.

"She now resides with my aunt, Lady Mary Crosscombe, at Lower Brook Street," Justin said, knowing full well that the name and address would impress Anne's aunt more than anything else—save for the Drummond-Burrell connection. "Had you forgotten that Miss Haycroft is related to Mrs. Drummond-Burrell on her mother's side? It is she who saw to it Miss Haycroft is here this evening."

That she had was immediately clear, for Mrs. Haycroft paled and took a step back. She placed a tentative hand on her husband's arm and murmured something to him.

"We shall see you later," Uncle Cosmo declared with a vexed look, then marched off with his wife trailing behind him.

"That was a threat, if I make no mistake," Justin said with

satisfaction. The first encounter was safely behind them, and they had definitely bested the uncle.

When they returned to Lady Mary, it was to find her deep in conversation with an older stranger. The gentleman was tall and well built, his muscled form clad in the best of Weston's coats and the finest of linen. He handled himself with ease, as though quite familiar with life in the *haut ton*. Justin was certain he had never seen him before and felt an instinctive protective surge for his dearest aunt.

Lady Mary seemed flustered, fanning herself like a young girl, her eyes dancing with delight at seeing this man.

"Justin, dear, and Miss Haycroft, may I present an old friend. I would introduce Mr. Edmund Parker, lately of Canada. He came over to see his family and renew old friendships, he says."

"I am amazed to find Lady Mary yet single. Are all the men in this benighted isle blind? To leave so bright a star unwed? I am all astonishment, indeed I am!"

"Fie, Mr. Parker," Lady Mary said with shy delight, blushing like a girl of eighteen.

Justin watched the two parry little remarks with great puzzlement while keeping Anne close to his side. At last, he signaled Sidney, who promptly came to Anne's side to beg a dance. Justin hastily requested another young lady to be his partner and joined the other couple in a country dance.

"How nice for my aunt, to meet an old friend," he said when he met Anne in the figure of the dance.

"I rather believe him to be her old beau. She assuredly did not become so flustered when Mr. Witherspoon came to fetch us this evening. She treated him with all the familiarity of an old friend. I do believe Lady Mary is flirting with Mr. Parker."

"Egad! I believe you have the right of it," Justin softly exclaimed when he next met her in the center of the line. They took their positions, with Justin turning his gaze on his aunt for a few moments before the dance commanded his attention once again.

The dance over, the four were strolling around the perimeter of the room when Justin stiffened. Anne looked up at him, then to where he fixed his eyes.

"It wanted only this," she said sotto voce. "Lord Alington, as I live and breathe."

"I wonder if he knew you would be in attendance tonight." Justin frowned at the unexpected sight of one he now considered an enemy. "You must reject him should he seek your hand," Justin commanded quietly.

Anne was only too happy to oblige this direction. She had no desire to have Lord Alington touch her in any way. "He'd not be able to abduct me from here, surely," she did point out in all honesty.

"I will not have him bothering you," Justin said with soft determination. They reached the chair where Lady Mary held court with Mr. Parker and joined the conversation, albeit somewhat distractedly.

"Miss Haycroft, may I have this next dance?" Lord Alington inquired, quite as though Anne were not with Lady Mary or Lord Rochford.

"She cannot, Alington," Lord Rochford growled at his foe.

Anne had read the expression that someone "growled" at another, but had thought it an exaggeration. She thought it no more. There was leonine menace to the purr of his lordship's voice that sent shivers down her back.

"Who are you to say as to her partners?" Lord Alington said calmly, with a slight sneer.

Anne thought his hearing must be defective if he couldn't detect the intimidation present; she was certain it could be felt.

"The evening is late. I should like to go home now, if you do not mind," Lady Mary declared as though Alington weren't there.

"May I pay a call on you tomorrow, Lady Mary?" Mr. Parker inquired, glancing from Justin to the icy countenance of the challenging Lord Alington.

"I should like that very much. You may tell me what you have been doing these many years you have been away."

"And you shall tell me precisely why you are still unmarried," he replied in a very soft and seductive voice.

Anne thought it delightful, that Lady Mary should have a beau other than Mr. Witherspoon. However, it seemed that while Mr. Witherspoon did not wish Lady Mary for himself, he was not kindly taken with another gentleman eyeing her lady-ship as though she were a comfit!

Mr. Witherspoon glared at the newcomer, tucked Lady Mary's hand close to his side, and said, "Come, dear lady. I shall see you safely home."

Their departure was accomplished with all proper speed. Sidney bid them good evening and set off to the Albany with a friend, probably to beg space for the night with him.

"You have made a dangerous enemy, my dear young lady. Refusing to dance with Lord Alington was not the best thing to do," Mr. Witherspoon lectured gently once they were all in the carriage.

"The man haunts her, Witherspoon. He positively stares holes in her," Lord Rochford insisted from the other side of the carriage. "Given the particulars, I could not permit him to so much as touch Miss Haycroft."

"I see," Mr. Witherspoon said doubtfully, which indicated he didn't see at all.

Lady Mary quietly summarized for her old friend the partic-ulars of Anne's situation and her uncle's unsuitable choices of suitors. Anne sat lost in thought until the four reached the house on Lower Brook Street. They partook of a light supper, then the two men left, each saying they would return on the morrow.

Lord Rochford added quietly to Anne, "We shall talk tomor-row."

"Well, fancy that!" Lady Mary declared once the men had gone. "Imagine—seeing Mr. Parker after all these years. What a strange evening we have had, to be sure." She led Anne off to her bedroom, then paused by the doorway. "I'd not thought to see Edmund Parker ever again."

"Tell me about him," invited Anne, gesturing to the little chair near her window.

Accepting the unspoken suggestion, Lady Mary seated her-self, then commenced her recollection. "He asked me to marry him before he approached my father. I suppose he wanted to as-sure himself that I cared as much for him as he did for me. At any rate, he was a third son and as such no match for an earl's daughter with an excellent dowry. Of course my father refused his suit. I do not know precisely what was said, but Edmund

Parker left England shortly after that. I did not see or hear of him until tonight. And tomorrow he will call." She sighed with apparent delight at the thought of conversing with her old beau.

"He looked very fit and certainly was dressed in the height of fashion. I think he must have a fortune!" Anne said with a smile at her benefactress.

"I do believe he has. Mr. Witherspoon hinted that Mr. Parker has acquired immense wealth."

"If he is a third son, how came he to have a fortune?" Anne settled herself on her bed, enjoying this conversation with the older lady far more than she'd have expected. How good it would be if the dear, generous-hearted lady could find happiness after all this time.

"In Canada, my dear girl. He went to Canada and made a fortune in trees and land," Lady Mary said with a wave of her hand to indicate the vastness of those forests. "Forests with fir in great abundance, not to mention beaver to provide fur for gentlemen's hats. Oh, my parents would have hated him, for he has been in trade!"

"But I do not think that you do," Anne said wisely. "You loved him once, enough to defy your parents?"

"He never sought me to find out whether I would or not," Lady Mary said sadly. "I am not sure if I would have been brave enough to challenge my parents."

"Now you need not worry. There is no one to say nay to anything you might wish to do," Anne suggested.

"On the other hand, it is entirely possible Edmund Parker already has a wife in Canada."

"Somehow I rather doubt it," Anne replied. "He appeared far too interested in you."

Lady Mary rose from the chair and walked to the door. "It almost seems too good to be true, to see him again. I'll confess I look forward to the morrow, to see him, talk to him again."

"Indeed, ma'am, I am sure you do. Let us sleep, for tomorrow should be a busy day." Anne did not reveal what Lord Rochford had said to her before he departed. He had given Anne a look that boded ill and declared he would talk to her tomorrow. It had not sounded promising at all, unlike Lady Mary's anticipated meeting with Mr. Parker.

It would be a wonder if she could sleep a wink, Anne thought before closing her eyes.

Her sleep was disturbed by a dream inhabited by a stern, lecturing figure who strongly resembled Lord Rochford. When she awoke, she wondered what could it be that troubled him so that he had to frighten her to bits?

Chapter Four

Sometime after indulging in a bit of nuncheon, Anne was summoned to the drawing room. Here she found Lord Rochford seated in a comfortable chair and reading a morning paper. At her entry he rose, bowed politely, then gestured to the companion of the chair he had occupied. "We ought to talk."

Since Anne could scarcely disagree with this sentiment, she settled on the chair, smoothing her skirts and looking anywhere but at him. He had occupied her dreams far too vividly last night to make her at ease this afternoon. She was aware he had settled back into the chair, putting the paper aside. She also knew he studied her, quite in what light, she didn't know.

"Lord Alington is a problem," he began.

For once Anne interrupted a speaker to insert a comment, "But he is not of my making. Or rather his attentions are not what I desire." She raised her gaze from a contemplation of the Turkish carpet to fix it on her rescuer. She could see the impatience in his expression and was sorry for it, but all too often she was accused of something that was not of her own making.

"Did I say that you are responsible? I merely indicated that we have a problem, and it might be best if we decide how to deal with it." He gave her the same sort of reproachful look he had bestowed last evening.

"Oh," Anne replied, sinking back in her chair, quite deflated.

"I suspect the best thing to do would be to find you a husband." He rose from the chair to pace restlessly back and forth before her, a watchful eye on her at all times.

Anne was thankful she was not drinking tea at the moment— she'd have choked. Unwilling to give Lord Rochford the satisfaction of her anger, she gazed directly at him and said meekly, "How interesting. Do you have anybody in mind?"

"Curious. Your words are tame, but your eyes are flashing fire at me." He paused, his hands loosely clasped behind him and his head tilted to one side.

"Are they indeed? Perhaps it is because I fled one situation where my life was being arranged not to suit me, and now you threaten to do the same. Why should my eyes not flash, pray tell?" she said with commendable restraint.

He patted the air with his hand as though to soothe her feelings. "I am not here to condemn you for what you cannot help. Nor did I intend to appear censorious to you now *or* last evening." Thrusting his hand through carefully arranged hair, he paused to stare at Anne. "I had no notion you could be so . . . so difficult."

"Why, sirrah, *difficult*? I was under the impression that you would help me. I am most sorry to have troubled you." She began to rise from the chair, only to be thrust back by a definitely impatient hand.

"Woman, you try me too far. Sit still and listen!"

Anne retreated into her more customary gentle manner, but kept hold on her determination not to allow this man to pressure her into an agreement that must be distasteful to any woman of delicacy. "Proceed."

"Thank you," he said with what she deemed exaggerated politeness. "As I said, I think we had best find you a husband . . . but I do not think it is necessary for him to be present."

"What do you mean, not be present?" Anne demanded, forgetting for the moment her determination to be gentle and understanding.

"What I must spell out for you is that I believe we could give it out that you are betrothed to a vague someone who is detained in the country, who has urged you to amuse yourself in London for a time before your wedding."

"What about my aunt and uncle? They certainly would deny such a fabrication. My uncle has made no secret of his intent to marry me off to the highest-ranking peer he can snabble with my dowry." Anne folded her hands in her lap, her down-bent head concealing her distress at the very thought of wedding either of the men her uncle chose for her.

"And you wish a love match, as I recall."

"True," she murmured. "I perceive it is next to impossible."

"Not impossible," he denied. "Just not the easiest thing to accomplish. You see," he said in a near patronizing tone, "the problem is to find a man you can love who will love you in return."

"You sound as though that were beyond being an impossibility." Anne jumped up from the chair and went to the window, staring out with unseeing eyes. "Am I so unlovable, then?" she softly asked.

He strode across the room to her side at once, turning her about to study her face. Anne feared he would immediately take note of her tear-filled eyes and blinked hard to clear them.

"Poor girl," he said quietly. "I am a beast to treat you so. Of course there is a man for you. As I said, it is merely a matter of finding him. It truly ought not be so difficult."

Anne gulped, tears threatening even more at this bit of tenderness, something rarely bestowed on her. "No. It is merely that there are some things difficult to accept."

"Being unlovable is not one of them, for I imagine you must appear most engaging to the right man." He grinned at her, seeming rather appealing—at that moment. She could forgive him much when he looked at her so.

"And how do I find this man who will think me engaging? Shall I place an advertisement in the newspaper? Wanted: one gentleman who will tolerate an engaging young lady who wishes someone to love?" Anne dared to tease, keeping a perfectly somber face as she did.

Lord Rochford touched Anne's chin gently and gave a soft bark of laughter. "What a minx you are."

"Never so!" Anne denied. "I am always proper and demure, practicing the pianoforte with diligence and all the skill at my command. I never seek to aggravate—only you. Why is that?"

He ignored her query, rather turning his attention to her imaginary fiancé. "Shall we call him Alphonse?"

Anne laughed as she suspected he meant her to. "Nay. Nor

Peregrine or Tobias either. Something easy to remember like Cecil."

"Cecil it shall be. And for his surname?"

"It must be one my aunt and uncle do not know."

"Romer? One who hasn't been about much but whom you met and instantly formed an attachment to and with, not to mention a secret engagement? One of those sudden passions?"

Anne ignored the odd expression that momentarily settled on his face to consider his suggestion.

"Cecil Romer. 'Tis a strange sort of name, but . . . I agree." Anne offered her hand, and he took it in his own warm clasp. Neither of them wore gloves, and Anne found the touch of his hand brought her oddly peculiar sensations. She pulled her hand away and trusted he didn't think her capricious.

"So, this is where you are!" Lady Mary declared from the doorway. "What is afoot?"

"I believe we may have solved part of Miss Haycroft's difficulty. We have found her a fiancé!"

"Since last evening? My, that was amazingly quick. Do I know him?" Lady Mary advanced into the room, her gaze straying from Anne to her nephew.

Anne darted a glance at Lord Rochford, then said, "He is Cecil Romer, a gentleman I have not known long, but instantly formed a passion for and agreed to marry."

Her ladyship surveyed the serious expression on her nephew's face, then Anne's equally solemn demeanor. "It is all a hum."

"Oh, dear" Anne exclaimed. "And I thought we might be able to fool someone with our tale. It is mostly for the benefit of Lords Alington and Bowlton, you see."

"Perhaps it might prove effective. I give neither of them high marks for understanding. Lord Alington does not possess a sense of humor, nor does Lord Bowlton, come to think on it. I imagine they will believe what they wish. It is to be hoped Lord Bowlton will fix his attentions elsewhere, for time is getting on for him. As to Lord Alington, he is a different matter altogether. But tell me this, what if you meet someone for whom you may truly care? What then?"

Anne turned aside, deciding to let Lord Rochford handle this objection. *She* didn't know what to say.

"Miss Haycroft can easily claim that she and Cecil Romer decided they do not suit and called off the wedding," he answered easily. Too easily to suit Anne.

"Can it be that simple?" Anne asked, spinning about to stare at him.

"I believe so. Your uncle may be your guardian, but if he has not seen any paperwork, he can scarcely object to the arrangements."

"What if he demands to know details?" Anne inquired anxiously.

Justin wanted nothing more than to console Anne in his arms. He had exerted all his restraint not to yield to his impulses before when he saw tears sparkling in her eyes. Now she looked so forlorn, so worried. Poor girl, to think she believed her charming person unlovable was beyond credulity. Why, she was a delightful, if tenacious, creature with the most beautiful blue eyes he had ever seen and pretty blond curls like an angelic halo about her head. Although, he would be the first to admit she was not angelic. A trifle stubborn, absorbed with details, yes.

"We can worry about the details if and when it is necessary," he said with a sweep of his hand, giving voice to his thoughts.

"I think you are immensely clever," Lady Mary said, an admiring smile on her face.

At that moment Jenkins came to announce, "Mr. Parker to see you, milady."

Miss Haycroft made a move to leave and was instantly waved to a chair. "Stay. I would rather have company, if you please."

"You wish me to remain as well?" Justin asked.

"Perhaps it is foolish of me, but I should wish not to be on my own."

There was no opportunity for additional conversation as the gentleman in question entered the room at that point, bowing first to Lady Mary, then to the others in turn.

"How nice to see you after all these years," Lady Mary said politely, effectively masking her inner thoughts.

"I cannot believe so long a time has passed since I last saw you. And that you have changed so little!" He had a charming smile Anne thought a bit too polished, then she chastised herself. Mr. Witherspoon's acerbic wit and comfortable presence were more to her liking. But surely this gentleman deserved to be judged on his own merits, not those of some other man.

"My dearest aunt has devoted far too much time to her extended family. And we impose on her most dreadfully, for she is always so good-natured and agreeable in all she does," Lord Rochford said, looking as though he wished to get in his oar before he was totally forgotten.

"Indeed, I fancy she was always so," Mr. Parker exclaimed.

They settled into a comfortable coze, quizzing Mr. Parker on his life in Canada and the entertainments to be found there.

About fifteen minutes had passed when Jenkins appeared again to announce Mr. Witherspoon.

Anne fancied that Lady Mary was not unhappy to see him in spite of her old love's presence. Her ladyship was not one to toss her bonnet over the windmill without due regard.

"I see you did not lose a moment, Parker," Mr. Witherspoon said in his blunt way. "Canada seems to have that effect on people. An old friend of mine is due to return from Yorkshire any day now, and he's like that as well. He's spent a good many years in Canada, but most likely not in your area. I understand it is a vast place—Canada."

Mr. Parker smiled. "Indeed it is so, sir—vast and very green. Trees without number, furs, other assets without count. A man can easily make his fortune there if he is willing to take a few chances and work at it."

"Work is not a thing one associates with the gentry," Mr. Witherspoon said dryly.

"You forget the *ventures*," Lord Rochford reminded him.

"Ah, indeed, those gentry and peers who have money to invest, but do not wish to soil their own hands in commerce," Mr. Parker said.

"And where would we be without those who undertake a commercial or trading venture—even if at a distance? They export and import goods at considerable risk to their own fortunes, considering the state of our high seas," Lady Mary inserted. Then, obviously wishing to change the subject, went on to inquire as to Mr. Parker's plans while in London.

"Oh, the theater, a few parties—if I can presume upon old friends to invite me along." His look to Lady Mary gave a clear indication as to which old friend he meant.

"I feel certain you will be welcome wherever you may choose to go." Lady Mary smiled at him then. It was a forgiving smile and revealed much to the others.

"A gentleman of wealth is always welcome in this Society," Mr. Witherspoon observed.

"Where is he not?" Anne wondered aloud.

"Perhaps we can arrange for a theater party tonight, or perhaps tomorrow?" Mr. Parker invited. "I am not up on the current plays or concerts."

"You once were," Lady Mary reminded.

"Indeed. Rather clever at joining theater parties, as I recall," Mr. Witherspoon added in a quiet aside.

Anne repressed a smile at this. She could not have found a better anecdote for her megrims and fears had she tried. There seemed to be a duel between Mr. Witherspoon and Mr. Parker, and it was over Lady Mary!

"I trust this pretty young lady is close to being betrothed." Mr. Parker said with a hint of a query in his tone.

"Her fiancé prefers to remain in the country and insisted Miss Haycroft have a little time in London. It will give her opportunity for a bit of shopping as well," Lord Rochford hastened to say.

Mr. Witherspoon shot Anne a puzzled look, but said nothing.

"I can believe that," the Canadian gentleman said in reply. "I brought a list with me for a few gowns of the latest designs, a bonnet or two, you know the thing," he added with a smile aimed at the gentlemen. "Is ever a man so imposed on as to go shopping for some female? Perhaps I might presume upon your good nature and have your aid?" he said, turning to Lady Mary with a helpless look.

Softening whatever resistance to his appeal that she might have known, her ladyship nodded, eyes demurely down. "I should like that, I believe."

"Good!" Mr. Parker rose, bowed to one and all, then added,

"I shall see what tickets are available and send word to you immediately. I look forward to some good company."

The room was oddly quiet when he was gone.

"Seems like a good chap," Mr. Witherspoon said in a way that made it clear he doubted it.

"Dare I say that time will tell?" Lord Rochford asked. "It is impossible to judge upon so brief an acquaintance."

"Both of you are dreadful," Lady Mary admonished. "The man is here merely to visit for a time, see to a few business connections, and do a bit of shopping."

"For whom? He did not say," Mr. Witherspoon commented as he also rose to make his departure. "Count me as a part of your theater group. I would see more of our Canadian wonder." He exited in the neat way he had of moving, not a motion wasted.

"I do not see why he has to be so cynical," her ladyship said, looking at Anne, vexation clear on her kindly face.

"Perhaps he is jealous?" Anne replied.

"Pooh! Jealous? He has had ever so many years to show an interest!" Lady Mary scoffed.

"But," Anne replied softly, "has he ever had competition for your attention before?"

Lady Mary considered this remark silently for a time before commencing a conversation along another line entirely. They continued to chat for some time until Lord Rochford interrupted.

"Come," he urged Anne, "take a drive in the park with me. We need to discuss this business involving Mr. Romer some more."

Sensing he wished to give his aunt time alone to think, Anne immediately agreed and left to fetch her bonnet and gloves.

"She has a point regarding the matter of jealousy between your old and new beaux," Justin suggested.

"Perhaps, but I doubt it," his aunt replied without any coyness. "What shall you do about Miss Haycroft and her false fiancé?"

"Why, I shall mention him at every turn to one and all. And I believe I shall make all the beaux jealous of his good fortune." Justin bestowed a kiss on his dear aunt's cheek, then left the room, humming softly as he crossed to the stairs after ordering his carriage be brought around.

Justin met Miss Haycroft at the bottom of the stairs and decided his lightly spoken words to his aunt were not far off the mark. Anne Haycroft looked very lovely in her blue pelisse with a pretty bonnet of fine straw trimmed in small knots of blue riband. She was a vision to turn heads, of both men and women.

He held out his hand, allowing her to place hers atop. It was an accustomed gesture, one performed every day, yet it felt oddly good—comfortable, right.

"My carriage ought to be in front of the house shortly. I really meant what I said about discussing your erstwhile betrothed. Cecil must miss you dreadfully and is certainly a good chap for suggesting you have a sojourn in London without him."

"How silly you are," Anne admonished. "I cannot think what my uncle will say when he learns of this latest ploy. And I imagine he will learn of it, for you know what gossips abound in Town."

"Like Miss Hortense Finch, our gossip *par excellence!*"

"She certainly has caused us a great deal of inconvenience, not to mention the necessity for this deceit. I cannot like it. Deceit is something I abhor," Anne declared firmly.

"I cannot say I approve of it either, but there are times when one must resort to such measures to preserve one's self." He looked at her with approval, for it was unusual to hear a woman so soundly denounce deception. Many of the women he had met thought it a game.

"I suppose you have the right of it."

Additional conversation was prevented when Potter informed them that the carriage was now before the house.

It was but a moment for the two to leave, and for Justin to assist Miss Haycroft into the curricle. They set off at a spanking pace, the tiger on the rear deftly hanging on with good will. Hyde Park was as usual thronged with vehicles, the finest of horse-flesh being ridden by accomplished and not-so-accomplished equestrians. Every manner of carriage vied for space on the road through the park.

"We are catching a bit of notice," Justin observed. "Now, should someone stop us, allow me to present you and do the initial talking."

"I am fully able to speak on my own behalf," Anne protested, then wondered how on earth she came to be so bold. Never had she addressed a gentleman, much less a peer of the land, in such a manner.

"I am aware you can speak, my girl. I thought it best were I to offer the background explanation."

"Oh," Anne replied in a very small voice.

A gorgeous barouche of rich maroon picked out in gold approached and came to a halt when it and its occupants came level with the curricle bearing Lord Rochford and Anne. A very stylish lady leaned forward, tilting her parasol to better see the couple in the curricle.

"Lord Rochford, how lovely to see you this afternoon. I trust you have not been indisposed?" The lady flicked a glance at Anne, but her attention was fastened on Lord Rochford.

"Not at all, merely assisting my aunt entertain a young friend. May I have the pleasure of introducing Miss Haycroft? Lady Ellen Worth."

The two women nodded, taking measure of one another.

"Miss Haycroft has taken residence with Aunt Mary while in London. She desires to see a bit of Town, do necessary shopping, the usual. I believe she is fortunate to have a betrothed who is willing to be apart from her for a length of time."

"Ah, she is engaged then? But I thought you were with your aunt and uncle, Miss Haycroft? Did I not hear something of a betrothal to Lord Alington?"

At her side Anne felt Lord Rochford stiffen slightly. He had forgotten how gossip traveled in this Town.

"Her cousin, Mrs. Drummond-Burrell did not approve the match. Naturally, Mr. Haycroft bowed to her feelings on the matter."

Anne remained silent, more than willing to permit Lord Rochford to dig himself out of the pit he had just created.

Rapidly losing interest in what appeared to be dull stuff, Lady Ellen bade them farewell, but only after admonishing dear Lord Rochford to present himself at her coming ball.

"I should have known that your residence with your uncle would be remembered by a few," his lordship muttered once the curricle was moving forward again. From then on, he took care to avoid the matter of Anne's background. That continued until he was faced with Mrs. Drummond-Burrell.

Anne decided it was time she said her little piece. It was inconceivable that she contradict Lord Rochford, so she acknowledged the other, and most powerful, woman.

"Dear cousin, I am pleased to see you today. I have had a most trying time."

When pressed to explain, Anne continued, "My uncle Haycroft seeks to engage me to Lord Alington when I am already betrothed to a fine young man from home. Mr. Romer may not possess a title yet, but he is a gentleman and does not frighten me." Anne allowed her words to trail away, hoping the implication would be taken—that Lord Alington did frighten her.

It was clear that Mrs. Drummond-Burrell thought little of the mushroom gentleman who would impose his petty plans on her cousin. She nodded, her eyes narrowed in thought. "I shall make it plain that a connection between you and Lord Alington is not acceptable to the family. Our family."

Which, Anne concluded, was the family that counted when all was said and done. "It is most kind of you, ma'am. Thank you." Anne's simple appreciation seemed to please the older woman. She nodded again and was off without another word.

Anne thought she would not be the least surprised were the vouchers to Almack's to be withdrawn from Aunt and Uncle. How her aunt would bemoan that loss!

"She is an original," Lord Rochford said before cutting his remark short, possibly recalling that the two women were related.

The drive continued with no other encounters of interest. On the way back to Lower Brook Street, Anne shifted uneasily, pitying poor Lord Rochford to be put in such a position.

"We return unscathed but the better for the ride. Your address to Mrs. Drummond-Burrell was inspired. Add that to the bit I gave Lady Ellen and I believe we have all we need to begin with."

They drew up before the house, waiting while the tiger hopped down from his perch and ran around to tend the horse.

Lord Rochford assisted Anne from the carriage, then walked with her to the front door. There were but two steps up from the walkway, and the door opened promptly, quite as though Potter had been awaiting them.

Anne turned to face his lordship, loathe to see the moment had come to part, yet relieved she must. "Thank you for your assistance. Your aunt is most fortunate in her relatives. Would that I might have one so helpful."

"But you do," he reminded. "Clementina Drummond-Burrell is far more powerful than the Prince himself. I believe you will come about quite nicely."

Anne smiled weakly in reply, then entered the house, leaving Lord Rochford to drive off in lofty splendor, his curricle gleaming in the waning light of the day.

She crossed the entry to the bottom of the stairs when Potter approached with a modest bouquet of white flowers in hand.

"These came for you while you were driving, miss."

Anne accepted them absently, walking up the stairs while holding the bouquet in one hand, her skirts in the other. As soon as she gained her room, she set the flowers down to read the small note tucked deeply inside.

Remember this, my perfection, I do not give up my quest easily. Alington

Anne stared at the innocent bouquet of white flowers. She gathered them up once more, and with the card in hand, hurried down the stairs to find her ladyship.

"Lady Mary?" she asked Potter when she spotted him.

"The sitting room, miss."

Rushing along the hall, conscious she still wore her bonnet and gloves, she entered the room precipitately. "Only look at what has come, my lady."

"White flowers? They look quite unexceptional, my dear."

"Read the card that came with them!" Anne cried, tossing the flowers on the table and marching about the room in a distracted manner.

"Oh, dear," Lady Mary murmured. "He still poses a threat to you, I fear."

"*He* will not care that I have the protection of Mrs. Drummond-Burrell!"

"Do you, now? How interesting! I gather the drive in the park produced results, then?" Lady Mary set the card down on the table, watching her guest pace about the room.

"You might say so. I believe your nephew thinks so. Of course, he does not know about these flowers and the note with them," Anne cried. "What now?"

"I suggest we are where we were before, more or less. You must not leave the house unless Justin or I am with you. It is too dangerous."

At those forbidding words, Anne sank down on the nearest chair to stare at her hostess with dismayed eyes.

"How I wish I'd not been compelled to come to London."

"But it remains that you are now here and must make the best of it. Allow word of your supposed betrothal to wend its way to Lord Alington. It ought not take long if I know our gossips, and I think I do. Then we shall see. Not that I would ever trust that man—ever! He is devious and not beyond doing as he pleases."

Potter hesitated at the doorway, coughing slightly, then offering a crisp folded missive to his mistress.

She absently thanked him, then broke open the seal to scan the contents. "We are invited to attend the theater tomorrow evening. Mr. Parker invites us all, including my nephew. You shall be well protected."

"I need such at the theater?" Anne cried in dismay.

"Particularly at the theater. It is far easier to abduct a woman in the midst of a crowd, for no one pays the slightest heed to her cries."

Anne reflected on this a bit, then rose from her chair. Stiffening her spine, she said, "I shan't allow him to intimidate me."

"Good girl!"

Chapter Five

L ate the following morning, the upstairs maid scratched on Anne's door, then entered to announce that there was a lady below wishing to see Miss Haycroft.

"Claims she is a relative, miss," the maid concluded before returning to her work.

Anne checked her image in the looking glass to see that she was presentable, then hurried down the stairs, thinking it must be Mrs. Drummond-Burrell, for what other female relative would be remotely interested in her? It was likely that elegant lady would be concerned about the preservation of family ties, no matter that they were distant cousins. Anne approached the drawing room with a suitably demure expression.

"So, you dare show your face to me after all? Cosmo said you would not receive me."

The nasal rasp of Aunt Winnefred's unmistakable voice struck Anne's ears with unwelcome force. Anne curtsied properly, then slowly walked forward to greet her unwelcome caller. "Good morning, Aunt."

"Ungrateful girl! That you reject so eminent a suitor as Lord Alington is beyond belief." Mrs. Haycroft stood in the center of the room, arms crossed before her, and looking as much the harpy as possible.

"I am persuaded that we should not suit, Aunt," Anne replied while searching her mind for words to combat this dreadful woman. Relative only by marriage, she still was a force with which to reckon.

"Would not suit? Would not suit! And what is that to say to anything, missy? You ought to be thankful there is a man of his rank and fortune who is willing to marry you." Her aunt emphasized each of her words with a shake of a lace-mittened finger.

"I will not marry him, nor can you compel me to do so. The law is on my side in this matter." Anne clenched her hands at her side, hiding them in the folds of her blue jaconet gown. She longed to be free of her aunt, this room, to hide beneath the bedcovers!

"Since when do you know anything of the law, pray tell?" Mrs. Haycroft demanded. "And when did you become so intimate an acquaintance of Lady Mary Croscombe? I detect something smoky there. Does she seek to marry you to her dear nephew and thus secure your fortune for him?"

Anne could well understand how her aunt's mind worked, for that would be precisely her own motives in taking in a well-dowered young woman. Surely Uncle Cosmo must have some of the same feeling to negotiate a marriage contract that favored him financially? Anne selected her words with care.

"Lady Mary most kindly offered me a room here, partly to keep her company, and partly because I needed a refuge from an intolerable situation." Anne ignored the outraged gasp from her aunt to bravely continue. "I refuse to marry the gentlemen Uncle has chosen for me, and Lady Mary agrees that either marriage would be disastrous. With such support I can sustain my resistance to Uncle Cosmo's demands."

"Hmpf!" Mrs. Haycroft gave Anne a narrow look that promised dire retribution. "And what about the nephew, missy? Hortense Finch says she saw him leaving here at a very early hour of the day. Says he was holding and kissing your hand and making love to you right at the doorway! What do you have to say about that, eh?"

"You may rest assured that nothing untoward has occurred here. Not only is Lady Mary the highest stickler for propriety, her nephew has been nothing other than polite and well-mannered to me, offering welcome help." Anne sternly suppressed the memory of those kisses in the church. Thanks be Aunt didn't know of those! "While driving me in his curricle, he made a point of advancing my acquaintance with my cousin, the elegant Mrs. Drummond-Burrell." Anne did not mention what power that lady held in Society. She felt certain that Mrs. Haycroft knew it all too well.

"I still say there is something decidedly odd about your residence here," Mrs. Haycroft insisted. Her stance was one of someone determined to have her say and her way. Anne wondered how in the world she was to rid the house of such an unwanted caller.

"Good morning. Mrs. Haycroft, I believe?" Lady Mary said as she sailed into the room.

If ever Anne had doubted the aristocratic background of the lady, those doubts would have been dispelled now. She was every inch the daughter of an earl, reared to the highest standards. Attired in a simple gown of striped lutestring in shades of pale green, her bearing gave that simplicity a touch of elegance beyond anything with which Madame Clotilde endowed it.

Some of Mrs. Haycroft's belligerence faded with the entry of Anne's hostess. A note of protest lingered however when she spoke. Mrs. Haycroft was not one to yield easily to a superior force. "Pleased, I am sure," she said in a rather ill-bred way.

Anne performed the introductions, then ceded the floor to one more experienced than she.

"Please join us for a cup of tea, Mrs. Haycroft. Anne tells me that you are in London for the Season."

There was the hint of a question in those words. Anne promptly surmised that Lady Mary prodded to discover whether the senior Haycrofts intended to leave for the country soon.

"Indeed, Mr. Haycroft intends to be here for some weeks." She glared at Anne, then continued, "If this missy would do her duty by him and return to her proper place, we might be more agreeably situated."

"You intend to change your residence?" Lady Mary said with apparent sympathy. "It is always so difficult to find an agreeable house in the city. I understand that renting can be so tedious." Inherent in her words was the satisfied knowledge that she, in any event, had a charming house that belonged to her and was not leased.

Since that was not at all what Mrs. Haycroft had intended to say, she became flustered, floundering on her own words.

"Well, that is, I mean to say . . ." Mrs. Haycroft stuttered. "We own our house in London."

"Perhaps my aunt intended to say that my Uncle Cosmo planned to include a provision for substantial remuneration for himself in the marriage settlements?" Anne offered dryly, a level look bestowed on her aunt.

"Ring for tea please, Anne, dear," Lady Mary said while ushering Mrs. Haycroft to a chair. "I always think it is most pleasant to have conversation while sipping a cup of fine bohea." Lady Mary settled herself on a chair that was slightly higher, with an imposing back to it and facing the caller.

Anne allowed a smile at this ploy when she turned to address Potter regarding the tea. He glanced at Anne's bewildered relative and nodded.

"Now as to remuneration in marriage settlements," Lady Mary said, oozing sympathy again, "it is quite a necessary thing, I know. Had I been so fortunate as to have a daughter, I would have wished her to be well guarded. *I* am blessed with all I desire of this world's goods and could not think of demanding such a settlement. However, I am aware it is customary for some. How good that Anne has a fortune of her own. Her solicitor ought to be able to fix a fine arrangement to protect her and her future children."

The request for tea must have been anticipated belowstairs, for it arrived with amazing promptness. Anne busied herself with filling cups and offering milk and sugar. The talk became general for a few moments.

Apparently Mrs. Haycroft thought her danger past, for she turned to Anne and in her usual hectoring voice said, "You may as well pack your things and return to your house. Your uncle has given Lord Alington to understand you will marry him."

Anne compressed her lips, looking to her hostess and protector for help.

"But I thought you knew!" Lady Mary said with feigned surprise. "Anne is already betrothed to a nice young man from the country—Cecil Romer, I believe he is called? I thought that was what you meant when you referred to settlements! Surely you refer to Mr. Romer?"

A voice from the doorway added, "A substantial young fellow in line for a barony, I believe. Is that not correct Miss Haycroft?"

Anne turned in her chair to see Lord Rochford paused there, taking in the situation in a glance and advancing upon Mrs. Haycroft with a relentless smile. He said with that consummate grace that was always a part of him, "We have met?" Thereby he implied that if they *had* met, he had forgotten all about it. *Masterful!*

Mixed emotions swirled through Anne at the sight of him. Sheer delight, worry, aggravation, and something else she did not wish to name just yet. While Lady Mary performed the introductions, Anne poured another cup of tea, offering it to him with a trembling hand.

Evidently mistaking that her nervousness stemmed from her aunt's accusations, he gave Anne a reassuring smile, then turned to face Mrs. Haycroft. "You were unaware of Miss Haycroft's betrothal? I imagine they wished to keep it secret so that she might enjoy her Season the more. It is pleasant that Mrs. Drummond-Burrell has welcomed our young lady into Almack's with her blessing, is it not?"

Anne closed her eyes for a moment, waiting to hear her aunt's reaction to the masterly cut dealt by Lord Rochford. In one sentence he had reminded Anne's aunt that Anne had a powerful cousin and that she was now under the protection of a family far more powerful than that of Cosmo Haycroft.

"It is naught but nonsense. I never heard of a Cecil Romer." But it was certain she wavered. She studied the cup in her hands as though it offered help.

"You must go back to your good husband and tell him that our dearest Anne *has* a betrothed," Lady Mary insisted kindly as though she was talking to a child. "We will guard her well while she is with us. You may be certain she will be well protected against fortune hunters and the like."

"Indeed," his lordship added, "your husband can cease his efforts on his niece's behalf. She is settled."

A stir at the doorway brought Mr. Witherspoon into the room, bowing and quite his usual acerbic self.

"What's this? Settled? Not on Alington. Dreadful man! Nor Bowlton, either. Buried two wives already. Gower with his nine children! Not to Miss Haycroft, I trust? Who is the fortunate gentleman?"

"Our Anne is betrothed to a Cecil Romer, heir to a barony," Lady Mary informed her friend.

"Never heard of him, but bound to be better than Haycroft's cronies," retorted the fashionable Mr. Witherspoon.

Her guns well and truly spiked, Mrs. Haycroft set her cup and saucer on the nearby table and rose to make hasty adieus. She did not leave without giving her niece a final bit of advice, however. "You will rue this day, missy."

Once they heard her steps on the stairs, then the front door close with a good finality, the quartet relaxed.

Lady Mary finished her tea, then leaned back to study her nephew. "Well done, Justin. That was as brilliant as ever I have seen. I believe we make a creditable pair. What do you think, Anne?"

"I think you are both wonderful, and I thank you from the bottom of my poor heart for your admirable routing of my aunt."

"Like that, is it?" Mr. Witherspoon inquired. "Can't say I admire your aunt, Miss Haycroft. Got a way about her that puts a man off, if you see what I mean. She makes me think of a body who would travel on Sundays!"

"Indeed, I do know precisely what you mean," Anne replied, suitably demure once again.

When invited to join them for a bit of nuncheon, Mr. Witherspoon accepted with alacrity, and before long the four were most agreeably seated in the dining room, partaking of a delectable selection of fricasseed mushrooms, cold ham, and other suitable delicacies.

They had adjourned to the drawing room once more when Lady Mary spoke.

"You *will* attend the theater with us?" she asked of Mr. Witherspoon a trifle archly.

"Indeed. I received a note from Parker," Witherspoon responded dryly.

"Good, we shall make a delightful party."

"Curious chap, Mr. Parker," Mr. Witherspoon mused. "Must remember to ask my friend who is also from Canada if he knows the man. Not that he will, but I find it is a small world when you least expect it."

Lady Mary declared she would take a rest, shooing her friend to his house with the admonition to be back for an early dinner before attending the theater.

"Don't know as I relish going with that man," Mr. Witherspoon grumbled to Lord Rochford before he strolled from the drawing room. Anne followed him, leaving the aunt and nephew alone.

"I want you to join us as well," Lady Mary urged Justin. "Mr. Parker will not object in the least. I do not trust that woman who was here earlier. She has very cunning eyes."

"I agree. Once she informs her husband of the fiancé we conjured up for Miss Haycroft, he will take some action. The problem is, we do not know what he may do."

"You are not sorry you befriended Anne, are you?"

He was clearly disconcerted at her question and strolled away from her, apparently considering his answer.

"No, I cannot say I am sorry. It is a pity she is so beleaguered and with such relatives!"

He left shortly after that, and the house fell into silence for a few hours.

Late in the afternoon Anne slipped down to where the pianoforte stood in grand elegance. It had been most kind of her hostess to insist Anne practice on it whenever she wished. Anne always found her playing to be a solace when she found life more than she wished.

She had played a pretty piece by Mozart when she sensed a presence in the room. Twisting about, she found Lord Rochford seated in the shadows across the room. She half rose, disconcerted at this proximity. "How long have you been sitting there, sir?" she asked with apprehension.

"I have enjoyed a private concert for some minutes now. I

came early for dinner, and when Potter would announce me, I heard the music and begged him to remain below and allow me to slip in here to listen. It is not often I hear such talent as yours, Miss Haycroft." He rose, walking over to join her by the lovely rosewood grand pianoforte his aunt prized. "I trust I have not upset you?"

Anne wondered how she might explain her reaction to him, but failed. "Well, sir, you do not stare so to put me out of countenance as does Lord Alington. I confess I do not care for attentions such as he bestows."

"He often attends the theater. He may be in attendance this evening."

She replied simply, "I shan't pay any heed to him . . . or my uncle."

"But you must," he contradicted. "You had best be aware of where they are at all times. I shan't be far away from your side this evening, nor will Mr. Witherspoon desert you. I imagine Mr. Parker can be called upon to assist if needs be. You shall have a circle of gentlemen about you as a guard."

"Mercy!" Anne exclaimed, her hands fluttering to heated cheeks. "However shall I watch the drama?"

"With any luck at all, we will have an uneventful evening, and you may enjoy not only the drama but the farce that follows." He leaned against the pianoforte, watching her animated face as she listened carefully to all he said.

"I do hope so. My uncle does not like the theater or the opera, so I have not attended either of them. This should be a special evening, to be sure."

"And you are dressed in utter simplicity that will put to shame the excessive display of some of our set," he rejoined, gallantly offering a nice compliment on the pale blue-violet gown she wore. The taffeta rustled as she rose from the straight-back chair on which she had sat while playing.

"Madame Clotilde selected the fabric and design for me," Anne admitted with girlish innocence. "It pleases me very much, for in the past I have had to wear my aunt's choices. Since I am not just out of the schoolroom, I need not wear white as she would insist."

"Say no more. I can imagine what those creations were like."

He turned slightly at the sound of approaching steps in the hallway.

"Ah, such promptness ought to be rewarded," Lady Mary declared as she entered the drawing room. She swiftly crossed to bestow a light kiss on her nephew's cheek.

He turned to where Anne stood fingering her bracelet while giving him a wary look. "I shan't ask the same of you, for I have already been rewarded with your music."

They laughed, then turned to greet Mr. Parker and Mr. Witherspoon. They were accompanied by another friend of Lady Mary's, a Miss Metcalf, aunt of the young Mr. Metcalf Anne had already met.

It was a jolly party that sat down to dinner, then set off to the theater.

"I hope you will not take the evening's offering amiss. From all I have heard, the drama has been well received so far," Mr. Parker said as they approached the theater entrance.

"I believe it is a Gothic, is it not?" Miss Metcalf inquired. "One of Mrs. Radcliffe's books, I think. *Fountainville Forest*? Or is it *The Sicilian Romance*?"

"*The Apparition of the Cliff's*?" Anne asked in delight, for she had indulged in that bit of Gothic charm and shivered all the way through the book, one end to the other.

"Ah, virtue shall punish vice, and we will all denounce the villain of the piece," Mr. Parker exclaimed.

"Pray that is all that happens," Mr. Witherspoon remarked in an aside to Anne as they exited the carriage.

Pushing through the throng of theater attendees, Anne could well see why Lord Rochford wanted her surrounded by gentlemen. People gathered in clusters and all too often would not move, no matter that someone else wished to pass. Lord Rochford politely forged a path for them all, never being rude, his manner forcing others to give way.

When they finally reached the shelter of their box, Anne was delighted to see they were close to the stage.

The play commenced, and the villain dramatically threatened the innocent heroine, claiming he would abduct her so he might have her all to himself. It gave Anne a most uncomfortable feeling, as it was quite as though the play was an echo of the situation she faced at present. Upon glancing at Lord Rochford, she discovered his gaze on her. He looked concerned.

"Do not worry, it is only a play," she whispered. "They are much the same, you know. Poor Rodrigo and his love are fated to go through a great deal of travail before they can have their happy ending." She thought her smile might be a shade tremulous, what with her inner emotions.

"We ought to have attended a different play," he insisted softly.

"It is of no great consequence," she assured him. "I certainly am not going to swoon, nor will I have nightmares from this nonsense."

His look told Anne all too well that he didn't believe her in the least.

When the first intermission came, Lord Rochford and Mr. Witherspoon left the box to obtain ratafia for the ladies. Then Miss Metcalf insisted Lady Mary and Mr. Parker visit a nearby box with her. Since Miss Metcalf had no idea of the threat posed to Anne, it was awkward to say the least. There was no wish to explain, and Miss Metcalf was very determined.

Lady Mary gave Anne a worried look. "I feel I should remain with you."

"I shall be fine. Nothing can harm me here, and Lord Rochford should be back momentarily." She admitted only to herself that she was uneasy. Perhaps it was the play, setting a mood as it were. She looked about the theater interior, admiring the decor, the gorgeous gowns, not to mention the gentlemen's discreet attire. Not familiar with such supreme entertainment, she felt a rush of pleasure that she might at last enjoy it.

The door to the box opened, and Anne turned about to express her pleasure in the evening.

"Hello, niece," Uncle Cosmo said, his voice icy with his disapproval of her behavior. "You will come home with me now, at once. I'll have no more of this nonsense of yours. Silly chit! This bit about Cecil Romer is naught but a hum. Marriage to Alington is the best you can do. And I have arranged it all!"

"Then unarrange it." Anne declared quietly, not rising from

her chair to greet him, refusing to show the slightest respect to the man who cared only for what money she might bring him.

In reply, he reached to grab her arm, pulling her to her feet. "Come!"

Anne thought wildly that this was more of a drama than what she had viewed on the stage, for this was real. Only there was no hero to rescue her. Lord Rochford had helped her once, but he was not here. He had gone to fetch some ratafia, as though that were important!

A faint sound came at the door, causing Anne to take hope.

"What is going on here, may I ask?" Lord Rochford, backed by Mr. Witherspoon, stood in the doorway to the box, effectively blocking any departure Mr. Haycroft might wish to make.

"My niece must come with me now!" Uncle Cosmo declared. "After all, I am her legal guardian. It is my duty to see to her future, and I have arranged a satisfactory marriage for her."

"Satisfactory for you perhaps, but not for Miss Anne," Lord Rochford replied in a deadly quiet voice.

"*Miss* Anne?" Mr. Haycroft cried. "*Miss* Anne, you say? And since when did you become so familiar with my niece?"

"She resides with my aunt. And I, sir, have constituted myself as her defender—with her permission—from your vile intentions. She has stated she has no wish to marry Lord Alington."

"Dashed havy-cavy, that man," Mr. Witherspoon interjected from the doorway, glasses of ratafia in hand.

Mr. Haycroft flicked him a look of dislike, then in the face of superior strength, released his hold on Anne's arm. Lord Rochford gestured to the door, and within moments Mr. Haycroft was gone.

"Here, best drink this ratafia before you go faint," Mr. Witherspoon advised.

"I never faint," Anne declared, stiffening the backbone that had gone decidedly weak.

At that moment Lady Mary and Miss Metcalf returned with Mr. Parker.

"We saw Mr. Haycroft on our way back here. Was there trouble?" Lady Mary queried, her gaze fixed on Anne's pale face.

"You might think so. The man had grabbed Miss Anne and was about to abscond with her," Lord Rochford said indignantly.

Lady Mary started at her nephew's use of the more familiar address to Miss Haycroft and gave him a curious look. She turned to Anne. "I feel dreadful. I should have remained here." She didn't blame Miss Metcalf as well she might have done.

"Please, the play is about to resume. Let us be seated and turn out attention to the stage. I will be just fine. The ratafia is an excellent restorative." To prove her point, Anne gave them a brilliant smile, then sat on the little gilt chair provided for box holders.

The others uneasily did the same, casting looks at Anne as though they quite expected her to faint, burst into tears, or otherwise cause a furor.

The play proceeded with no other disturbance, however. When the next intermission arrived, the ladies insisted they would all remain in their seats, the gentlemen speedily agreed, and the conversation was stilted to a high degree.

"This is all my fault," Anne complained to Lord Rochford. "I feel dreadful. I fear I have quite spoiled the play for the others."

"But you have given them something to talk about that the play does not offer—danger!" He smiled at her with such understanding that Anne felt her fears subside.

"It is good that Uncle Cosmo was of some use," She said dryly.

Justin nodded, then leaned back against his chair while watching the assembled group make their tedious way through conversation that avoided any mention of what was on their minds—the behavior of Cosmo Haycroft.

Was the man so desperate for funds that he would sell his niece to Alington? Apparently. Desperate enough also to have his niece spied upon, for it was surely no coincidence that Miss Haycroft's uncle was at the theater the same night as Miss Anne. Justin didn't know what had possessed him to use the more familiar form of address for Anne Haycroft. Miss Anne! He hadn't meant to be so casual, so intimate. He certainly did not consider he had been particular in his attentions to her. She resided with his aunt. He called upon his aunt frequently. Perhaps he called on her more often than usual, but he confessed he was concerned about Anne Haycroft and feared for her.

The drama ended at long last, to be followed quickly by the lighthearted farce, but Anne felt as though she were a hundred years old. The strain of appearing gay and happy had taken a toll on her spirits.

Mr. Parker was at her side as they left the theater building. Anne sighed with relief upon seeing their carriage waiting.

Suddenly Anne felt someone grab her arm. She gasped in pain as she turned to her accoster—it was her uncle. "I have you now, missy. Your fine friends will do nothing in this crowd!" He began to pull Anne with him, ignoring her protests.

Mr. Haycroft proved to be no match for the muscular Mr. Parker. The Canadian gentleman lunged for Mr. Haycroft, catching him by the arm. At a quick twist of the limb, Mr. Haycroft cried out, releasing Anne to the refuge of her friends.

"The nerve of the creature!" Lady Mary exclaimed as they hurried Anne to the carriage and away from her grasping uncle. During the drive to Mr. Parker's hotel, they all offered advice to Anne, exclaimed over Mr. Haycroft's behavior, and in general talked a great deal.

Over the elegant meal Mr. Parker had ordered, he was toasted as a hero for saving Miss Anne.

Anne smiled, joining in the toast, but inwardly she wondered how long she could hold out against her determined uncle. Could she escape him once more? Would the third time be lucky for him?

Chapter Six

While Anne slept late the next morning, Lady Mary found herself entertaining an early caller.

"Mr. Parker, what a surprise," she said, wondering what possibly could have brought the gentlemen to her door before the proper time for calls.

"I have been most concerned for Miss Haycroft, and the notion came to me in the night that it would be well if we could give her respite from those who want to abduct her even if for but a few hours."

Lady Mary motioned the gentleman to a chair and sat opposite him, finding his sympathy much to her liking. "And what conclusion did you reach?"

"A boating party!" he exclaimed, looking enormously pleased with himself.

Much struck with the idea, Lady Mary nodded slowly, and said, "That would be good. There would be no possible way in which they might touch her while she is on a boat. The Thames, I suppose?"

"Indeed, ma'am. I thought a boat going toward Margate to be the best. We can turn about whenever we please, for I shall hire it for the day, and we shall be the only ones on board save the crew."

"How good you are, to take such trouble for one you do not know." Lady Mary impulsively leaned forward to lightly touch his arm.

"But she means something to *you,* my dear Lady Mary. And I seek to please you if I can." Mr. Parker leaned back against his chair to smile at his former love.

Blushing like a girl, Lady Mary dropped her gaze to the floor for a moment or two, then once again studied Mr. Parker. "Very well. A boating party it is. Shall we make up a merry group?"

"Your nephew and Witherspoon, Miss Metcalf, to begin with. Who else should we include?"

"Young Mr. Henry Metcalf and Sidney Fairfax—another nephew of mine. Perhaps two more young ladies to even numbers? Does that please you?"

"If it pleases you, my dear Lady Mary." His eyes conveyed a warmth that could only delight and charm the heart of the spinster.

"When shall we enjoy this treat?" Lady Mary inquired, turning her head slightly when she heard a sound in the hallway. Unless she was mistaken, Anne was coming down the stairs and would join them in a moment.

"Two days' time? It will take a bit of organization to assemble all the necessary items, not to mention obtain a seaworthy craft. I wish a smooth sail for us. Just pray for good weather." He rose as Anne entered the room looking not the least disappointed at the interruption, to Lady Mary's observant eyes.

"Oh, good morning, ma'am, sir. I did not know there was a caller or I'd have remained upstairs." Anne turned to leave the room and was brought to a halt by the light touch of Mr. Parker's hand on her sleeve. He had crossed the room at amazing speed to reach her side.

"Do not go. We were just talking about you, making plans that include you. I suggested to Lady Mary that we have a boating party on the Thames. Would that please you?"

"How delightful!" Anne exclaimed, clapping her hands together after a quick glance at her hostess to see if the scheme met with her approval.

"Mr. Parker is good enough to arrange it all for us in two days' time," Lady Mary inserted, pleased to see the shadows flee her young friend's face.

"You shan't be plagued by unwanted relatives or suitors while out on the water, I'll wager," Mr. Parker said with a self-satisfied expression.

The front door was heard to shut, and soon Mr. Witherspoon entered the drawing room with more speed than usual. He seemed disconcerted to see Mr. Parker installed at such an early hour of the day.

"Good morning. Another early caller, I see," Mr. Parker said with the sharp joviality they were coming to associate with him.

Mr. Witherspoon straightened his coat and moved with his more familiar grace across the room to stand near Lady Mary, giving Mr. Parker a bland look.

"Had Haycroft on my mind—the old man, not you, Miss Anne. Must keep the girl away from him. Bowlton was bad enough, but Alington is a worse character. She is too nice a gel to be parsoned to the likes of *him*."

"We just now agreed to a plan for such a thing," Lady Mary inserted. "Will you join us for a boating party? Mr. Parker suggested a ride on the Thames two days' hence. We think it a most agreeable notion," she concluded. She noted her old friend was not best pleased that Mr. Parker had outshone him with his planned boating party.

"Boating party. Well, I suppose that is as good an idea as any, providing no one falls into the water. I shall join you with pleasure," he said, casting a look of suspicion at Mr. Parker that Lady Mary thought quite unwarranted.

Mr. Parker left within minutes, and Mr. Witherspoon did not remain much longer. He declared he would have to see about a new umbrella to take with him on the boat in the event it rained and suggested they do the same.

"I do believe you have two beaux, my lady," Anne teased. "Mr. Witherspoon was not pleased to find Mr. Parker here."

"I doubt there is anything to cause him alarm. I suspect Mr. Parker simply likes to enjoy himself and have those around him take pleasure as well. Witness his concern for you, my dear. One might think he was setting his sights on you."

"Oh, never," Anne exclaimed in dismay. "I doubt that sincerely. Now, what shall we wear? Who all is to come?"

"I shall send invitations to Miss Metcalf and her nephew Henry, and Sidney Fairfax ought to be here shortly. You know he is Justin's cousin and heir presumptive—for the moment."

"Does your nephew plan to marry soon?" Anne asked with a deceptively casual air.

"Not so he has told me, but he must, as you well know. Although Sidney is a good lad, he does not have the conduct and grasp of matters regarding the estate that Justin does. After all, he was born and bred to be an earl."

Anne reflected on these words and all they implied for a few moments while her ladyship sat lost in thought.

"I have it, Jemima Green and Susan Price will be most agreeable companions for you on the boating party. You have met them?"

"Indeed, on several occasions. It would be pleasant to further our acquaintance, ma'am," Anne said agreeably.

"And I believe Caroline Bonham as well. She has been casting lures at Justin for ages. Perhaps she will at last have a chance without anyone else to compete?"

Anne missed the mischievous look sent her way by Lady Mary. Instead, she averted her face and crossed to the window to stare out at the street below. "How, er, nice," she said rather lamely.

Lord Rochford and a Miss Bonham? Could it be? She was surprised to see how displeasing the notion appeared to her. While Anne might find him appealing, and definitely having polished manners, and certainly the most handsome of all the gentlemen she knew, he could look for a woman with larger fortune and greater beauty than she possessed. And whatever put *that* idea into her head?

"Could you help with the invitations?" her ladyship requested. "I have observed you have lovely handwriting."

Setting aside the thoughts that plagued her, Anne quickly agreed to take on all the writing necessary. She would enjoy inscribing the names and messages on the elegant cream paper with the rich brown ink Lady Mary preferred to use. It was but a few minutes time, and the list of addresses had been located, paper produced, pen trimmed, and ink set out on the writing table.

Anne went to work with a will, wishing she did not have to inscribe Miss Bonham's name on the outside of the pretty note. And when it came to writing Lord Rochford's name, she found herself very careful to form her letters just so. She was a fool to even think the direction her mind took her. Better dismiss such thoughts as utter nonsense. And *she,* who had heretofore always been so sensible!

A clatter in the entry drew her attention. Since it was followed with much talk, then the sound of footsteps pounding up the stairs, she wiped her pen and set it to one side.

Within moments Sidney Fairfax marched into the room to bow correctly before Lady Mary, then step forward to give her an enthusiastic hug.

"Sidney, how good to see you!"

"Charmed, dear aunt." He turned to bestow a smile at Anne. "Jolly good to see you again, Miss Haycroft. I trust you are well?" He gave her an exaggerated bow, mischief lighting his dark eyes.

"Indeed." Anne curtsied properly, while Sidney walked over to her side, bowing and holding her gaze with eyes remarkably like his cousin's. Wearing a well-fitting blue coat and gray breeches he looked as fine as did Lord Rochford, although Sidney did not have the breadth of shoulder. However, his waistcoat was a shocking puce with a pattern of exotic birds that his lordship would never have owned, much less worn, Anne guessed.

"Sidney," his fond aunt said with a laugh, "you will frighten Anne with your enthusiasm."

"I do not frighten that easily, dear ma'am," Anne returned with a laugh. "I am glad you are come, sir. Now I do not have to write you an invitation."

"Invitation? That sounds interesting. Where do we go, or what do we do?" He turned from Anne to his aunt, looking for an answer.

"A boating party on the Thames. An old friend of mine is organizing a party on the water. It is to keep Anne away from her uncle and anyone else seeking to abduct her for at least the space of one day," Lady Mary said with deliberation.

"Abduct?" Sidney said, seizing upon the one word to capture his imagination.

Nothing would do but his aunt had to acquaint him with the details of all that had transpired. His reaction was all that one could wish.

"Zounds!" he exclaimed when his aunt had completed her tale. "What a story!"

"So you see that we need to take great care regarding Miss Haycroft," Lady Mary concluded.

"I should judge that to be a most agreeable task. But what about Justin? He has always been rather clever at deception and making micefeet of sinister plans."

"And good morning to you, cousin," the gentleman in question said from the doorway as he entered the drawing room.

"Justin!" the younger man said with obvious pride. "Good to see you." Sidney glanced to Anne, then back to his cousin. "I was just saying that you have always been good at making micefeet out of bad intentions."

"And so we shall in this instance." Justin crossed to shake his cousin's hand, taking note of Anne's rosy cheeks and sparkling eyes as he did.

"We plan a boating party two days' hence," Lady Mary inserted.

"Clever idea. Who thought of it?" He looked at his self-conscious aunt, then to Anne, who wore a playful expression, and continued, "Allow me to guess. Mr. Edmund Parker. Am I right?"

"Indeed," Anne said, sparing her hostess the necessity of a reply to this probing. "He has kindly asked us all to join him on a boating trip down the Thames as far as we please."

"I am to ask others to make up the party, so I added a few to his original list."

Lady Mary handed the slip of paper to her nephew to await his thoughts, perhaps to see a reaction as well.

"You are still short a gentleman, Aunt. Maybe Sidney can think of someone young and foolish?"

"Would George Harcourt be acceptable?"

"Sober George? Not foolish, but perhaps a very good idea after all," Justin replied with a grin.

"Fine, I shall add his name to our list if Sidney could give Anne his direction." Lady Mary turned to Sidney, an expectant look on her face.

"Better than that, I shall deliver his in person."

"You will move over with me while in Town, cousin?" Justin

said, noting the manner Sidney had adopted toward Anne Haycroft. It was definitely not that of a brother.

"Thank you, I should like that. Inscribe that invitation while I run down to give my man instructions. I thought to move to Ibbetson's. But I would far rather stay with Justin than share rooms at the Albany."

When the clatter of boots on the stairs retreated, Justin looked to his aunt. "He could afford to stay at Ibbetson's, you know. It is a decent hotel and economical for a student. One can intrude on a friend at the Albany only for so long."

"But he thinks the world of you, Justin. Never deny him the pleasure of your company," Lady Mary said with tolerance befitting an aunt who liked to spoil both her nephews.

"It will be an excellent way to keep a watch on him," Justin agreed. That his cousin might confess any amatory interest he acquired crossed his mind as well. Sidney was too young to think of settling down. True, he was the same age as Anne Haycroft, but she seemed far more mature than his cousin. But then, she had suffered a number of trials of late, and he had observed that difficulties tended to age a person. He glanced over to where Anne addressed the invitation to George Harcourt.

The sound of steps recurred, and soon Sidney entered the room to accept the invitation for his friend from Anne. "Do you have Henry's as well? I shall be seeing him, too."

Anne turned to the stack of invitations she had written, then handed Harcourt's to Sidney as well as his. "Mind you do not misplace them. We do not wish someone to be left out of the party."

"Indeed," Justin added dryly, "it would make the numbers uneven."

"Well," Sidney said in his endearingly boyish manner, "I am off. I'll be at your place later, then?" he added to Justin.

"Early dinner. I go out this evening."

When he said no more, Sidney gave him a puzzled look, then dashed from the room, again clattering down the steps at great pace.

"I trust he does not break his neck, the young fool," Justin said with affection.

"What brought you here this afternoon?" Lady Mary said,

taking note of how Anne carefully avoided looking at Justin and how he couldn't seem to look away from her.

"There is a musicale this evening—a very private affair. I thought it would be safe for Miss Haycroft to attend. I obtained permission to bring you both if you are free?" He was rewarded by a delighted smile from Anne and an exclamation of pleasure from his aunt.

"The very thing. This ought to do very well. It will not do for Anne to sit home and worry."

"I am not the brooding sort, dear ma'am. But I confess that I should like a musicale very much. It is always a pleasure to hear talented musicians. What time should we be ready?"

Justin gave them the particulars and promised to pick them up as soon as he had sent Sidney on an errand for the evening. With a cautionary look at his aunt, Justin said, "Sidney was always good at mousing about for information. I seek to know what Alington is about. Bowlton is no longer of any concern. I heard he is making overtures to that platter-faced niece of the Smythe-Joneses."

"Never say so!" Lady Mary exclaimed. "Well, well."

Anne and her hostess dressed and dined early, then settled to wait for Lord Rochford to fetch them.

"Potter assured me that all the invitations were delivered this afternoon. Miss Green and Miss Price have already sent their acceptances. Jane Metcalf also sent word that both she and her nephew will join us on the boating trip. Let us hope that the weather will hold. We are having an unusually warm May this year."

"That leaves Miss Bonham. Mr. Fairfax seemed certain that his friend Mr. Harcourt would accept," Anne said by way of a reply.

"I make no doubt that Miss Bonham will leap at the opportunity to ever so discreetly chase Justin. Whether or not he will encourage her remains to be seen." Lady Mary glanced to where Anne sat and added, "Not that I would wish that alliance to form. Caroline thinks very highly of herself."

"Indeed?" Anne murmured, sinking into reflection that was cut short by the arrival of their escort for the evening.

"You sent Sidney out on his mission?" Lady Mary murmured quietly so Anne might not hear.

"He has instructions to mouse around, learn what he can. Of course everyone knows Sidney is my cousin, yet he is so disarming that nearly all tell him things they would not tell another. Amazing, but there you are."

He turned to Anne, complimenting her on her demure gown of lilac muslin. She resembled a spring flower and seemed as fresh as any schoolgirl. He could not help but contrast her to the overblown charms of Caroline Bonham. He trusted his aunt was not promoting that connection: it would never answer. Miss Bonham simply did not appeal to him.

The carriage awaited them, and they drove off in splendid fashion until they reached—not so far away—their destination.

"Mrs. Calder is as careful of her guest list as she is of the musicians she has to perform. I believe you will enjoy your evening, Miss Haycroft," Justin said as he assisted her from the carriage. He turned to help his aunt and thus missed the sight of Lord Alington bearing down on them.

Anne clutched at Lord Rochford's arm in spite of being resolved in her determination to repulse that man on her own. She forgot how intimidating he was.

"Ah, I wondered if I might see you here, Rochford. And with Miss Haycroft and Lady Mary as well."

"Alington, I know you are not on the guest list at the Calder musicale. I confess I am surprised to see you. Excuse us, we do not wish to be tardy." Justin made to usher his aunt and Anne Haycroft past the other man, but found his arm in Alington's firm grip.

"You will lose in the end. I *must* have her for my own, and that is it," Alington said defiantly.

"Pity," Justin said with disdain. "Someone has already claimed her hand. You have been deceived, my good man." With those terse words, Justin pushed on into the house, thankful the footman was there to shut the door firmly in Alington's face.

"Has he no pride?" Lady Mary whispered to Justin as the women handed their cloaks to a maid.

"I gather he is without that sort of thing when it comes to

what he wants to collect." He glanced to an exceedingly pale Anne and moved to her side at once. "Do not worry about him. See how we brushed through that scene? He cannot take you."

Anne gave him a worried look, then glanced across the room to see the comforting form of Mr. Witherspoon. "I see we have a friend here."

"Indeed. He enjoys music unlike a good many other men." Tucking Anne's arm close to him, Justin led her and his aunt to join Mr. Witherspoon.

The evening improved immeasurably after that. The performers were of professional caliber, enormously talented. Anne found her fears slipping away as she lost herself in the music of Haydn, Handel, and Mozart.

"Had I known you were able to come, I would have asked you to play as well, Miss Haycroft," Mrs. Calder exclaimed when she met Anne following the first group of performances. "I heard you play at the Chalfont's musicale, and I was quite enchanted."

"Thank you, ma'am." Anne curtsied to the older woman, then turned to Justin. "Lord Rochford?" Anne pleaded. Two guests nudged her as they pushed past.

She had paled, her hands trembled. He knew what she wished without asking. Leading her through the throng of people, he at last found an anteroom where she would be free of the crush.

She left his side at once, walking to the single window across the room. The view was not inspiring, giving on to the street as it did. "I hope Lord Alington went home, or elsewhere. You do not think he lurks out there, waiting for us?"

"You poor girl," Justin said, his compassion overcoming his good sense. With great strides he was at Anne's side, taking her into his arms, nestling her head against his shoulder. It felt incredibly right and good.

She sniffed, fumbling for a handkerchief in her reticule of netted silver thread.

In an instant Justin pulled forth his own square of linen, offering it to the delicate yet sturdy young woman in his arms. Odd, how she could manage to look so fragile, yet cope with matters that would fell stronger-looking women.

"Forgive me for being a watering pot. I feel very foolish."
Anne sniffed again, dabbing her eyes.

He touched her chin lightly so she would have to look up at
him. Their gazes met. After that it was difficult to say who
moved first.

To say that the kiss was an improvement upon the first was
to say daylight is better than the light of the moon. There was
little comparison. Justin found her sweet, yet there was an essential passion within her that he could detect. He explored her
lips, finding much to his liking. Only a sound in the hall outside
the anteroom broke them apart.

Anne no longer looked frightened or lost.

Justin felt as though he had been struck with a pole. He
cleared his throat. "I suppose we had best return to our seats?"

"Indeed," she whispered. "Justin . . . that is Lord Rochford,
I . . ."

"Say not another word. I apologize—I did not mean to insult
you. Do you wish to compose yourself before leaving here?"
Justin berated himself for being all kinds of fool. A gentleman
did not behave in such a manner with a gently bred young lady.

"Yes, please. Go, go. I shall follow in a few minutes."

He reluctantly left the little room, glancing back from the
door to see her standing so resolutely all alone in the light offered by a single candle. Once in the hall he shortly found himself beset by the charming and beautiful Miss Bonham, who
begged a moment of his time.

Back in the anteroom, Anne fanned her heated cheeks until
she felt more the thing. What a little fool he must think her, to
so forget herself and permit—no, encourage—his kiss. She
couldn't believe she had done that. Yet she had to confess in the
deepest part of her heart that she had more than enjoyed his
kiss. It had surpassed those first kisses at the church by far. She
was well and truly lost!

Feeling at last she could return to the musicale guests and
slip into her seat at Lady Mary's side, Anne left the anteroom,
walked along the hall, and saw Justin deep in conversation with
Caroline Bonham. It was like being hit with cold water.

They made a splendid pair—he so tall and dark, and she so
very elegant and equally dark, her hair dressed atop her head in

complicated curls and braids. He stood close to her, gazing down with that amused grin he sometimes wore. Her smile was enticing, alluring, and the sort that Anne decided would lead a man to do almost anything.

She ignored them both, gliding through the clusters of guests until she reached Lady Mary.

"The music is about to begin again. Where is Justin?"

"I last saw him speaking with Caroline Bonham," Anne said with commendable dignity. She wanted to howl, cry, stamp her feet, and perhaps smash a priceless vase on the floor. Instead, she neatly seated herself on the little gilt chair that always seemed to be found at these occasions.

"Oh, good," Lady Mary whispered, for the musician next to play had come forth. "Now he can learn if she will join us on the boat."

"I rather think she will," Anne observed sedately.

And so it proved. When Justin slid onto the chair next to Anne's, he said, "I ran into Miss Bonham, and she said she would be delighted to join us for our boating party."

"I felt certain she would," Anne whispered back with a knowing smile and a lift of one brow.

Justin frowned. What had happened since he left Anne in the anteroom? She had seemed so sweet and innocent, and he had felt such a cad. Now she looked at him as though he were the enemy, as though he had betrayed her somehow.

Well, perhaps he had. He had taken advantage of her, but he admitted he would do so again given the opportunity. He felt a compulsion to hold her, protect her from her enemies. And he certainly felt a strong desire to kiss her again!

Anne glanced at the man sitting beside her, ignoring the exquisite music for the nonce. What made him look so grim? Had he wished to remain with Miss Bonham? Had he been reluctant to return to his charge, the woman he felt obligated to protect? Anne shifted, uncomfortable on the little gilt chair.

It was going to be a long evening.

Chapter Seven

The day of the boating party dawned reasonably fair with the promise of sunshine to come. The weather had continued unusually mild for May.

Anne checked her bonnet for the second and final time, then sighed. There was nothing remotely eye-catching about her ensemble. What was different about a neat straw bonnet tied with blue ribands and an ordinary blue pellisse over a simple blue-sprigged muslin dress decorated with knots of blue ribands? York tan gloves—she checked to see they were spotless. Jean half boots, which were most sensible, if ordinary. Only the pretty gold cross at her neck was special, for it had been the very last gift from her papa. Alas, it was concealed beneath her pelisse.

"Are you ready, my dear?" Lady Mary inquired from the doorway to Anne's room.

"As I will ever be," Anne said, then chastised herself for being a silly ninny. Here was a treat such as she had not known before given her by a near stranger. The thing was to enjoy it and totally ignore Lord Rochford and Miss Bonham.

The very man she had determined to ignore awaited them at the bottom of the stairs.

"Hurry. We wish to catch the outgoing tide if we can. It makes the sailing so much easier."

Anne didn't know much about things like that, but accepted his word as so. Within minutes the four of them—for Mr. Witherspoon was in the carriage as well—were off to the Westminster dock, where they were assured the boat awaited them close by.

"Who is fetching Miss Bonham . . . and the others?" Anne

inquired, firm in her intent to be proper and polite—if it killed her.

Lord Rochford leaned back against the squabs to think a moment, then said, "George Harcourt offered to take Miss Price and Miss Bonham along with Sidney. Henry and Miss Metcalf drive with Miss Green and Mr. Parker. I believe that is all of us."

"Goodness," Anne said in a faint voice, "it does seem like a large number." She peeped across the carriage to where Lord Rochford lounged in comfort. It seemed no matter what, he was always in control of himself and any situation. It must be lovely, she reflected, to be so disciplined. She would be quite pleased if her heart would just behave while near the earl. He had such an effect on her that she wondered she was not in a constant blush, at least while around him.

"It should assure us that we do not become tired of one another," Lord Rochford said with that charming grin Anne had observed on more than one occasion. The last time she saw it had been when he was with Miss Bonham while at the musicale. Whatever blush she had, faded rapidly at the mere thought of him standing close to Miss Bonham minutes after kissing Anne nearly senseless.

"Well, it will give Anne a chance to relax and become acquainted with Jemima Green and Susan Price," Lady Mary remarked.

How astute of Lady Mary to know that Caroline Bonham and Anne would have nothing in common. Since Anne had resolved to be polite, if distant, it would be a simple matter to remain at the opposite end of the boat, surely?

Once at Westminster Bridge, they carefully walked down to the narrow landing from which they climbed up steps to the boat. It was a long packet boat with masts fore and aft. Anne looked for the sails. They remained furled, and there was no sign they were to be undone. In the center of the boat was what she at first had thought a mast. Only it had smoke rising from within the tall shaft. Anne was about to suggest they had a serious problem when their host spoke.

"This is a steam packet boat, Miss Haycroft," Mr. Parker declared with pride. "They have only recently gone into service on the river and do not normally carry passengers. I arranged for us to hire it for the day." He modestly did not reveal the sum involved, which must have been several guineas.

"Goodness! Is it safe?" Anne wondered aloud to Mr. Witherspoon.

"We can only hope that it is," he said with a gloomy look on his kind face. He gestured to the covered semiround shapes amidships and added, "Those are the paddle wheels powered by the steam, much like the mill wheel is powered by a river. All I have to say is that if the steam is so good, why do they still have the sails?"

"Mr. Trevithick has known some success with steam engines, so I have heard," Anne said to encourage her companion to continue his talk. Anything to keep from having to observe Miss Bonham flirting with Lord Rochford. She was daintily stepping aboard and insisted she needed a strong arm upon which to lean. Who else could have an arm precisely the right sort, Anne wryly reflected.

"Aye, he has a steam dredger at work along here somewhere. Helps to keep the passage open to the more shallow docks. That *Catch-me-who-can* steam engine of his didn't last long. Rails kept breaking. Fool thing! People keep wanting to go faster and faster. What good it does is more than I can see."

"Well, if they can save time in travel, perhaps more business can be transacted," Anne said. She could see where shortening travel time might be of use. Goodness knew the long coach drive from the country house to London had been tedious. She'd have welcomed a faster trip.

Once all had boarded and settled in various chairs, the boat was cast off from shore, and they commenced their trip. Anne ignored the peculiar clankings and occasional thumps from belowdecks. After glancing about her, she could see the men who tended the boat seemed not the least alarmed. Very likely all was normal. She hoped.

An unforeseen surprise was the noise from the paddle wheels. It effectively blotted out the voices to the rear of the boat. Mr. Witherspoon soon ambled back to where Lady Mary sat in the shade of a vast umbrella, leaving Anne on her own. The wind was moderately fresh, and Anne found it invigorating. Along the shore various gardens could be seen and then wharves where men were scurrying around with bales and boxes. Farther along reared the construction of the much-needed new bridge designed by John Rennie, and shortly beyond that the unmistakable sight of Somerset House. Most of the quays and yards were not very attractive, and she soon tired of them, moving to the other side of the boat and the wilder far shore of the Thames.

She strolled forward, watching the passing land with great interest. The fresh breeze brought exotic scents to her, the marsh grasses, salty hints of the distant sea, sun-warmed banks with decaying seaweed—all alien to a country-bred girl. On the river she observed the bustle of ships coming and going—hoys and smacks, and other enormous sailing vessels bound for the London docks or departing for foreign shores.

"You like sailing, Miss Haycroft?" Mr. Parker said at her elbow.

"So far it is entrancing. You are certain it is safe?" She could hear more strange sounds from belowdecks, chugging and hissing and others undefined. "It won't blow up?"

"Shouldn't," he said cheerfully. "I predict that someday there will be steamboats crossing the ocean between Canada and England with regularity."

"Goodness," Anne exclaimed, thinking it would be some time off into the future before anything so grand took place.

"Here you are. Hiding from us, Mr. Parker?" Miss Bonham inquired archly while sidling up to him on his far side.

Anne wondered where Lord Rochford might be. The last she had seen Miss Bonham was making a dead set at his lordship, looking as though she intended to claim him as her own property. Surely she had not been defeated so early in the day?

"Well, now, I thought as how I would see what Miss Haycroft thought of the scenery from up here."

"Sandbanks and ships from foreign ports, dirty little boats, and boys to carry sacks of goods," Miss Bonham said, dismissing all with a wave of her hand.

"I find it fascinating," Anne inserted quietly. Surely the bobbing of the small dipper birds captivated one with their ability to search under the water for food.

"Come, Mr. Parker, join us, do." Miss Bonham tugged at his arm, and the genial Canadian strolled off with her to the rear of the steam packet boat, where the others gathered.

Anne remained where she was, taking great pleasure in the fresh wind and thankful her bonnet was securely tied 'neath her chin. She lifted her face to revel in the feel of that breeze, inhaling deeply of all those strange aromas, so mysterious and unfamiliar.

"You will get freckles," a voice cautioned.

"That is a small price to pay for such glorious sights," Anne replied to Lord Rochford. "Look, now we pass the Tower of London in all its splendor. What terror must have struck the heart of those who were brought to the gate there," Anne said, pointing to the traitor's gate, deeply overhung and just visible from the center of the river.

"Certain it was unlikely they would ever leave. Few did," he commented.

"I am thankful our present ruler is not quite so vengeful," Anne said quietly. "It is not comfortable to have the threat of danger hanging over your head."

He briefly placed his hand over hers, removing it when she gave him a look.

"The others wondered what interested you so, and I offered to learn what you saw that we did not," he said, leaning against the bow as Anne did, searching the banks for birds and the river for boats.

"It is like the highway. When passing, the boat must stay to the left just as a carriage does," Anne murmured, unwilling to look at the man at her side, or even speak in a normal tone.

Overhead, black-headed gulls wheeled and dove, searching for food found by shallow plunge diving. Anne smiled when one bird managed to snatch an insect in the air before another could reach it.

"Predatory, are they not?" he said.

"They must live. Unlike people who are often predatory merely to make trouble."

"Hortense Finch, for example?" he queried, turning to look at Anne.

"Not just Miss Finch, but Lord Alington. You must admit he

is predatory. How nice to spend a day free from the worry of him," Anne admitted.

"Will you join us? There is lemonade and biscuits for now with the promise of a feast when we arrive at Gravesend."

"I trust that will be more agreeable than the riverbanks and buildings we see now?" Anne inquired, eyeing the wharves and docks overflowing with human ants going about a day's business, unloading the smacks, hoys, and smaller boats. As they passed Fresh Wharf hard by London Bridge, Anne spotted a large ship and turned a questioning look to her companion.

"That is a schooner unloading its cargo. Next to it you can see a smack—that's a coastal trader."

"How do you know all this?" Anne wondered.

"I am one of those commercial venturers mentioned before, and I speculate in shipping cargo. You do not think me deplorable for engaging in such commerce?"

"Not in the least," Anne shot back with alacrity. "I should think ill of you were you to waste your inheritance without trying to improve on it, or your lot."

"Well, you are not very social, I must say," Miss Bonham said with a gay, if somewhat shrill, laugh as she drew near.

"I am most remiss," Anne said politely. Ignoring Lord Rochford, she held out a hand to Miss Bonham and suggested, "Perhaps we might join the others?"

Miss Bonham eyed his lordship, then declined. "You go ahead. I shall take a turn here to see what is so interesting." There was no mistaking her coy glance or the flirtatious flit of her fan.

Anne deplored her coyness even as she admired her stratagem. The woman had but one goal and certainly did not miss a single opportunity. But then, it might be frightening to be her age and remain unwed. Miss Bonham had known three Seasons.

The walk to the rear of the boat was pleasant if one ignored the sound from the paddles and the clankings from below. Mr. Parker had produced a small band, which now began to play for the assembled guests.

"That's a lively tune, my gel," Mr. Witherspoon said rather loudly so he might be heard.

Anne merely smiled and nodded in return. *A band! Amazing.* What would Mr. Parker think of next? She looked to Lady Mary, who still sat in the shade of the vast umbrella, sipping lemonade while fanning herself. In one respect it was difficult to believe one was onboard a boat traveling down the river!

"It is good to be free of worries for a day, is it not?" Mr. Parker declared, studying Anne as though he feared she might effect a swoon at the thought of her peril from Lord Alington.

"I quite forgot for the nonce," Anne confessed. She wished the others might forget it for a bit as well. With everyone frequently reminding her, it was difficult to disregard her nemesis.

"Lemonade?"

Started from her thoughts, Anne was surprised to find Lord Rochford at her side with a glass in hand.

"But I thought you were with Miss Bonham? How . . ." Anne accepted the glass and immediately took a long sip. How thirsty one became out in the fresh air and sunshine.

"George Harcourt joined us, and Miss Bonham found him more amenable company. I have a lamentable lack of knowledge regarding the latest in fashions. George keeps abreast of all the newest styles." The earl quite ignored his own perfectly styled garments of the highest elegance.

"He seems a serious young man in spite of his tendency toward dandyism." Anne slanted a mischievous look at his lordship and added, "Miss Bonham ought to have an agreeable chat, for it is obvious she is *au courant* with the most recent innovations."

"Miss Haycroft, I say, we are attempting to get up a dance," Sidney said, rushing up to where his cousin and Anne stood in conversation. "Will you try it with us? Leave my stodgy cousin to his ale," he added with a teasing smile and a laugh.

Knowing how Sidney admired his older cousin, Anne did not think he realized how such a remark might cut. It was something that might not occur to a younger man. Anne did not pause to think that Sidney was the same age as she.

Offering an apologetic look to Lord Rochford, Anne went along with Sidney to where Miss Green and Miss Price stood with Henry Metcalf.

"Join us!" Miss Price cried with delight. "But where is Lord Rochford? We must have him as well."

"I figured as much," said that low, pleasing voice Anne liked far too much for her own good. "Sometimes my cousin miscalculates."

"Jemima, you pair with Mr. Metcalf, I shall have Lord Rochford, and Miss Haycroft can partner Sidney," Susan Price decreed, smiling and laughing as everyone found places.

"A proper dance, mind you. Nothing skimble-scamble if you please," Miss Price said to the leader of the band.

"Poor fellow," Lord Rochford said to Anne in passing. "I doubt he has an idea what she means. I don't."

"And," Miss Price insisted, "for the duration of the trip, we shall address one another by our first names. I, for one, am tired of saying Mr. Metcalf when Henry is so much simpler!"

This brought forth a great deal of uneasy laughter and glances.

"Very well. Anne, take my hand and we shall begin this thing," Sidney said with an engaging grin.

The band, at first hesitant, then steadfast, launched into a familiar air that was easy to follow. The steps were simple and all knew them. Anne found herself laughing with the others as Susan Price made a point of calling out the first names of each couple as they reached the top of the line.

They were breathless when the first dance concluded—more with laughter than with the effort of the dance.

"Well done, Anne," Justin said, liking the sound of her name on his lips.

"Your aunt calls you Justin, but it does not seem the least proper for me to say that name as well," Anne rejoined.

"Please?" He smiled at her, and with the sun behind him, he resembled more a sun god than a mere man. Anne paused, intent upon her vision, breaking it only when Sidney demanded her attention. She turned away from Justin, almost glad to look elsewhere.

They performed another dance with more laughter than grace, for from time to time the boat rocked with the waves produced by a passing ship.

"I think they must envy us," Caroline Bonham declared

when she gracefully swept onto a chair offered her by George Harcourt. "This is truly a most delightful day, Mr. Parker. How kind you are to us all."

Mr. Parker nodded, watching Anne stroll along with Sidney while Justin spoke with his aunt.

They at last landed at Gravesend. Mr. Parker saw to the ordering of their picnic while the others managed to go from the boat to the shore by wherries that eagerly put forth to fetch them.

Once onshore, Anne shook out her skirts, now thankful that she had worn a simple muslin under her old blue pelisse with sensible half-boots. How much more practical her garb was than Caroline's elegant pink jaconet worn with a very pretty brown velvet spencer. That young lady was already fussing about the sand on her skirt and exclaiming over the delicacy of her Morocco slippers.

Anne ignored her and walked on with Jemima and Susan. They exclaimed over the abundance of wildflowers to be seen, especially masses of red campion and banks of Germander speedwell. Early ox-eye daisies bloomed here and there as well, not to mention the pervasive bush vetch with its splash of pinkish lavender flowers.

Lady Mary brought forth a parasol for Anne to use. To Anne's chagrin the other girls had remembered to bring theirs. Even with her bonnet she would likely have some wretched freckles from the sun, then considered it might not be a bad thing, for Lord Alington might think it dreadful!

A grassy knoll proved an admirable site for the picnic. The men from the boat set up the chairs and a table for the food, along with the huge umbrella Mr. Parker had found in London.

They enjoyed strawberries and cream, various buns stuffed with ham and cheeses, plus other delicacies that Caroline Bonham declared were simply too delicious to eat. Yet Anne noted that the young lady managed to consume a tidy amount without ever seeming to put a morsel in her mouth.

"She is so clever," Susan said softly. "We all envy her in a way, for she is very lovely. How strange it is that she has known three Seasons and not made a match of it."

"Perhaps she is like me—she wants a love match," Anne quietly replied.

"And perhaps it is because she has set her cap at a particular gentleman"—here Susan glanced at Lord Rochford—"and he has not been forthcoming?"

"One cannot always have what one wishes," Anne observed sagely.

"And what do you want, Miss Anne, that you cannot have?" Sidney Fairfax asked with a wicked little grin, popping up unexpectedly at their sides.

"Peace, silly," Anne flashed back at him.

"I am wounded," he cried dramatically. Placing his hand to his heart, he cried, "Miss Anne Haycroft has wounded my heart. I shall never recover. At least, not until tomorrow!" He staggered about a bit, then collapsed on the grass to beg a bowl of strawberries from Mr. Parker's man.

"That is indeed a bit of silliness." Anne accepted her bowl of strawberries liberally topped with cream and settled to enjoy the treat. "Does having a picnic make one silly?"

"Not to look at George," Jemima said with a chuckle. "He is as serious as ever." She rose from her chair to march to his side, drawing him off from the others with the demand he walk with her to view the river.

Immediately Susan requested Henry Metcalf do the same, declaring that the birds along the river looked ever so cunning.

Miss Metcalf looked on with apparent pleasure while Mr. Witherspoon chatted to her about his friend from Canada who was sure to show up in London one of these days—if the chap ever finished his business in Yorkshire. Just why Mr. Witherspoon felt it so necessary to ask his friend about Mr. Parker was not clear. Anne thought it some manner of jealousy, for it was clear that Mr. Witherspoon scrutinized his rival with a jaundiced eye.

Caroline Bonham was not pleased when Lord Rochford did not hover over her, so she turned her smile to Sidney, instead. Anne watched him assist her along the narrow path to another excellent viewing area that would not soil her fine Morocco slippers.

"What a foolish woman," Justin said quietly to Miss Haycroft. "She has her thinking askew."

"Her thinking?"

"Forget her for the moment," Justin requested suddenly. "How do you go on today? I would wager a goodly sum that you are enjoying your bit of peace and freedom very much."

"Indeed, I am. And it is agreeable to chat with Miss Green and Miss Price as well."

"I notice you omit Miss Bonham."

"I suspect she is difficult to know," Anne replied with what seemed like evasive care.

Justin smiled. "Oh, I doubt that. I believe I know her very well, indeed."

"Indeed?"

"Now, Miss Anne, do not freeze me out! What I meant by that is . . ." Justin compressed his lips when of a sudden his cousin Sidney dashed up to where Justin sat in peace with Anne Haycroft.

"Mr. Parker thinks we ought to return. See, there is a bank of clouds moving in from the west." Sidney pointed in that direction in the event they had not already looked.

Justin immediately rose, offering a hand to Miss Haycroft. She looked a trifle self-conscious, and while she accepted his help, would not permit him to hold her hand nor her arm on the walk down the slope to the path that led to the dock.

Drat the clouds in the west, Justin thought, not to mention his cousin, who even now was paying his own sort of court to Anne Haycroft. Not wishing to make an issue of the matter, Justin watched the two laughing young people board the steamboat and envied not a little Sidney's easy manner with Anne.

"I declare, Lord Rochford—or ought I call you Justin as Susan insisted?" Caroline Bonham gaily sang out. "Shall we follow the others?"

"By all means," Justin responded politely. Trust Caroline Bonham to find a way to cling to his arm, smiling and flirting as she so enjoyed doing.

It was surprising how quickly all could move when motivated by the threat of coming rain. Before they could believe it possible, they had all returned to the boat with the picnic things gathered and stowed onboard as well. Mr. Parker was nothing if not efficient.

The trip back to London was not so delightful as the trip down. For one thing, the ladies, concerned about a wetting, were not much taken with the small shelter available for their use. For another, Justin could see that Anne Haycroft was avoiding him, and he wondered if he was to be allowed to make a complete explanation to her. Just why this was so important he could not say.

The sweet memory of those kisses at the musicale haunted him. He had kissed many a woman over the years, yet none of those had touched him as the innocent ones from Anne Haycroft. Perhaps if he could simply explain to her that Caroline Bonham meant nothing to him and that he intended to remain heart whole and quite free of entanglements, their former agreeable relationship might be restored?

Mr. Witherspoon joined Justin by the rail, looking out over the water and watching the clouds approach.

"I thought the day might end like this," Mr. Witherspoon said with obvious relish.

"I had hoped to be spared rain, I'll admit," Justin said absently, his mind still half on Anne Haycroft.

"He's a flattering rascal," Mr. Witherspoon said with a nod toward Mr. Parker.

"Yet, you joined us today," Justin reminded.

"Of course. One must keep the enemy in sight during an engagement of battle." Mr. Witherspoon half turned to see what Mr. Parker was up to at the moment.

"That is a curious way to phrase it," Justin said, his attention caught.

"I'd not thought of it as a battle, I'll confess. But the more I see of him, the more I am convinced that I do not wish to see your fine aunt taken in by that conniving man. Bah," Mr. Witherspoon grumbled. "There is something dashed havey-cavey about him, mark my words."

Justin agreed merely to humor the older man, not seeing anything sinister in Mr. Parker or his intentions. Of course he would be sorry to see his dear aunt sail off to Canada. But on the other hand, after all these years of yearning for this gentleman, surely she deserved a bit of happiness if it worked that way?

"Blinking idiot," Mr. Witherspoon muttered before taking himself off to be agreeable to Lady Mary.

Justin wondered if Mr. Witherspoon referred to Mr. Parker or himself. Surely after their abrupt departure at Gravesend it would seem that his own much-vaunted polish was sadly lacking.

Anne sat with Jemima and Susan, ostensibly chatting about the various parties they had all attended, but a part of her mind was on Lord Rochford. What had he been about to tell her regarding Miss Bonham. Surely he did not have to reveal anything of his affairs. But he had been about to do just that when Sidney came bounding up with the news of the impending rain.

A glance behind them revealed they would likely outrun the storm. The crew of the steam packet boat assured their passengers they had sufficient power to reach the Westminster Dock in good time and would spare no effort to that aim.

No matter that she had enjoyed the day immensely, Anne knew she would be glad to reach the house on Lower Brook Street once again. Just then, Miss Bonham sauntered over to join Lord Rochford, smiling and looking her alluring best. She tripped on a coil of rope, quite falling into Lord Rochford's strong arms. Anne doubted Caroline was truly hurt, but she certainly made the most of her little injury. The sight of Miss Bonham so close to the earl was painful, and compelled Anne to look elsewhere.

This trip had been a well-meant effort for Anne to get away from the threat of Lord Alington, and to that end it had succeeded. It had also proved the means of making Anne aware of just how great her attraction to Lord Rochford was.

What a muddle! Truly, she was like that character in *Two Gentlemen of Verona* of whom was said, "She hath more hair than wit, and more faults than hairs, and more wealth than faults!"

Chapter Eight

When they reached the house on Lower Brook Street, both Lady Mary and Anne were tired from the day's outing.

"All that fresh air is exhausting," Lady Mary declared upon entering the house. Mr. Parker's carriage had drawn away, so he was spared her mild complaint. She handed her parasol to Potter, then eyed her guest with a judicious look. "Would you not concur, my dear? And as to dancing while on a boat, well, I thought it looked most fatiguing!" Her eyes gleamed with the memory of Anne prancing through a very lively country dance in perfect step, face alive with happiness.

Anne agreed absently, her thoughts on Miss Bonham and her maneuver to require Lord Rochford's assistance. That stumble on the coil of rope was nothing but a ruse for his attention; Anne was certain of it. By the time he had finished helping her from the ship, the others had settled in their carriages and the first two were departing. *Foolish man.* If he couldn't see through Miss Bonham's schemes, he was welcome to her! She had failed to snare him yet, true, but she was not one to give up easily. She was as tenacious as Lord Alington in her own way.

After advising Anne to rest in her room, Lady Mary walked to the rear of the house to consult with her housekeeper regarding the supper to be served later that evening.

Preoccupied with her somewhat dire thoughts regarding the fate of the beauteous Caroline Bonham, Anne climbed to the second floor, feeling thankful for the outing but downcast in spite of it.

Atop the small table on the landing reposed a folded piece of white paper. Upon closer inspection Anne could see her name inscribed across it in bold script. With more than a few misgivings, she broke open the seal and commenced to read.

She might have been away all day, but Lord Alington had not permitted her respite from his attention.

"What is it, my dear?" Lady Mary inquired as she joined Anne on the landing. "Potter said a missive came for you and had a maid place it on this table. I trust it is not bad news?" Lady Mary was not actually probing, but allowing Anne to know that she might confide should she so wish.

"Lord Alington wishes to remind me that he has requested my hand in marriage and has been given permission by my uncle to pay his court to me." Anne offered the paper to Lady Mary so that she might see for herself what had been written. "Will the man not give up his delusion that I will yield to his demand? Never! I will flee to the most remote place I know before giving up. I have a cousin far away from London who ought to take me." Brave words, indeed, when Anne hadn't heard from her in ages.

"Now, my dear, it is not to that point as yet. Take heart from the support you have. Remember, Lord Alington cannot hold a candle to my nephew, who has the ear of the Prince Regent. Should it prove necessary Justin could appeal to his highness for assistance."

"I cannot keep depending on your nephew, ma'am," Anne replied at once, thinking it would be inconceivable for the Prince to be troubled with her affairs. "It is not fair, nor is it proper. Think how it might appear to others. I reside with you, his aunt, and he has shown me particular attentions. Remember Hortense Finch. She is ever on the alert to spread a tale abroad whether there be truth to it or not. No one else, other than you and his lordship, knows the full extent of my fears, my aversion to the marriage proposed by my uncle."

Anne studied the crisp paper that Lady Mary had replaced in her hand with loathing, for it represented the man she was coming to truly detest.

"One cannot help but wonder *why* your uncle is so very insistent upon this marriage. For you must know there are many fine gentlemen from whom a guardian with an heiress may select one for a husband." If Lady Mary also wondered about the particular attentions her nephew paid to this girl he scarcely knew, she did not mention it.

Little was said during their late supper. Desultory conversation continued throughout the meal. Anne's thoughts kept straying to Justin's whereabouts. Had he taken Miss Bonham home, then returned later to escort her to the ball that she had mentioned attending? Although Anne was fatigued, it seemed that Miss Bonham was of sterner stuff, ready to dance through the night, a veritable owl—even after tripping on that coil of rope! The notion brought a grimace to Anne's lips. Noticing her hostess had turned to look her way, Anne hastily smiled.

"Something pleases you? I am glad," Lady Mary said warmly. "You looked a trifle wan, and I worried the boat outing might have been too much."

Anne spooned the last of her trifle, savoring the delicious taste before saying, "Not in the least. If Alington would disappear, I would be as right as a trivet in no time." She exchanged knowing looks with her hostess, who nodded sagely in reply.

They both went to bed early, but not to sleep well on Anne's part. She fell into an exhausted slumber in the wee hours, no closer to finding a solution to her dilemma.

The morning after the steamboat outing, Sidney paced around his cousin's library with determined steps. He paused, looking at Justin with a frown. "Dash it all, Alington isn't buying this false betrothal Miss Haycroft supposedly has with Cecil Romer. That's a half-witted name, you know. Cecil ain't so bad, but Romer?"

"Well, it was the best we could devise on a moment's notice," Justin shot back dryly. "Pity you were not here to give us the benefit of your wisdom."

Sidney ignored the barb and continued his pacing. "It will not do, you know."

"I am aware there is a problem in that corner," Justin replied evenly.

"Heard Alington spout off as to how he intended to wed the fair beauty, the talented Miss Haycroft regardless, for he had her uncle's permission, something Romer doesn't. There are too many rumors going around about Alington to make me feel the least easy in my mind."

"I know. I have heard disturbing things as well." Justin was about to add to this remark when his butler entered with a folded missive in hand.

"From your aunt, milord. The footman said she wished you to receive it immediately."

Justin expressed his thanks, then broke the seal on the brief letter.

"What does she say? Anything about Anne?"

Justin raised his brows in inquiry. "Aren't you being a trifle familiar? None of us are family, nor has she given us permission to use her Christian name."

"You are always so stiff-necked, cuz. I cannot imagine you ever doing a thing that ain't proper. Keep this up and you'll be an old wigsby," Sidney complained.

Justin turned so his face would not reveal his thoughts— amusement that Sidney thought him so very proper when the memory of those improper kisses at the church were still fresh in Justin's mind, not to forget the passionate exchange at the musicale, which he couldn't.

"I doubt I am as dull as all that, my lad."

"Faugh! You don't even keep a mistress," Sidney charged.

"That is quite enough, cousin. I may send you to Ibbetson's after all." Justin bestowed a stern look on his younger cousin that revealed his annoyance. He did not have to answer questions of that sort regarding his private life.

Somewhat abashed at the reminder he was but a guest in this house and as such ought to mend his manners, Sidney mumbled an apology, then turned back to the matter at hand.

"Well, what to do about Anne?"

"Miss Haycroft, Sidney. And I suppose we ought to have found someone more agreeable, better *ton*," Justin mused, tapping his aunt's note against his hand as he leaned back in the leather chair behind his desk.

He looked about him as though he might find inspiration in the room lined with leather-bound volumes standing in neat rows upon solidly built mahogany shelves. They reflected his existence until he had happened upon Anne Haycroft in that church. Since then his life had been turned upside down, and he wondered if things would ever be normal again.

"You still have yet to tell me what our aunt deems so important," Sidney reminded.

"She is worried about Miss Haycroft, just as we are. She says Anne received a note from Alington telling her that Cosmo Haycroft has given permission for Alington to pay his court to her. It seems that even removing her from her uncle's house does not free her from his pressure." Justin looked at the note again, not revealing the final sentence, which demanded that he do something about the matter. His aunt placed too great a faith in his ability to solve problems. She also wished to know precisely why Cosmo Haycroft so desperately wanted this marriage to proceed.

"Well, it is clear that neither Haycroft nor Alington believe in that fake betrothal. Do you have an alternative plan?" Sidney threw himself down on the leather armchair opposite Justin's desk, staring at him with yet another frown.

"We discussed allowing people to think she and Romer have agreed to part ways and that she has become enamored of someone here in London," Justin revealed with reluctance. He was not the least surprised when Sidney jumped to his feet and leaned over the desk to confront Justin with his grand and instant scheme.

"*I* shall become her fiancé. After all, I am your heir presumptive, and you don't show much sign of getting leg-shackled. I ought to be a prime catch for someone like Anne who seeks a good marriage. You may be an earl, as is Alington, but *your* estates are in far better heart. I have heard a rumor he has had to sell one of his minor places—no doubt to buy more for his collection. Same person also said Alington is a poor manager of his property. Too involved with his precious collections. Not a regular out-and-outer like you." Sidney preened a trifle until he caught the derisive look on his cousin's face.

"You are too young," Justin objected. "Besides, you know how Society is. You might find yourself marching down the aisle before you know it."

Sidney paled at this home truth, but valiantly declared, "Makes no difference to me. I would be glad to marry Anne should it prove necessary. She's a beautiful girl, nice as well, and I would welcome her fortune, although I'd not marry her because of it. Likely she would be happy to stay in the country raising a family of little ones. She don't seem the sort to hanker after Town life. You know how expensive that can be. Fellow was telling me the other day that he figures it cost him somewhere around ten thousand to get his daughter fired off." Sidney faced Justin squarely. "Anne ain't a bad sort of girl. Fellow could do far worse."

"Your honesty is refreshing, cousin." Justin said, hoping his feelings were not revealed in his face. *What irony!* Poor Anne to be so dismissed.

"Suppose I talk to Anne about it? I could go to see her now," Sidney declared with the attitude of one who desires to dispose of an unpleasant task as quickly as possible. He reminded Justin of earlier days and the disagreeable duty of taking Sidney to the tooth-drawer.

"By all means. I shall come along with you. Perhaps I can persuade her that merely by pretending an interest in you she does not necessarily commit herself to marriage. It could be that she does not wish to marry you any more than you wish to wed her."

At first Sidney looked affronted, then relieved as he assimilated his cousin's words. "But I meant what I said," he insisted, intrepid to the last.

Justin laughed, then urged the younger man toward the door to join him on his mission. "Come, I imagine my aunt expects us. She has always insisted upon immediate action regarding her suggestions."

The prompt call to the house on Lower Brook Street was more of a success than either Justin or Sidney had expected it to be. It appeared that his aunt had been discussing the matter with Miss Haycroft and their way was well paved.

"I suggested to Anne that if we could find a substitute for Cecil Romer, her uncle and Lord Alington might be more accepting of her refusal. She can hardly accept Alington if she has a fiancé that he knows, rather than some stranger. It ought to be someone she's already met, someone with ready entrée in the *ton*."

Justin had the uncomfortable feeling that his aunt expected him to step forward to offer his services as the temporary betrothed. He was actually on the verge of doing precisely that when Sidney spoke.

"Miss Haycroft, I would deem it an honor if you would accept my offer of marriage—temporarily, of course," he added, quite spoiling the effect of his proposal. His expression was hesitant, as though doubtful of the outcome of his offer— mostly because he probably feared it would be accepted.

Anne bit back a smile, for she surmised that it took great courage for Sidney to make his generous offer. Her difficulty was in that she could not refuse to accept his offer—even a temporary one. Under normal circumstances his proposal would have been one seriously considered by any intelligent girl. Sidney was considered a "good catch," as some young women phrased it—a crude but telling way of saying he was quite eligible.

Lady Mary gave Anne an encouraging nod.

"Perhaps we could go about—balls, parties, and the like, while I manage to avoid Lord Alington," Anne began. "It may not be necessary to actually announce an engagement." She turned a hopeful face to Justin.

"*Will* you be able to avoid him?" Justin inquired seriously. "I do not wish to see either of you pushed into something you do not want. As it is, about the only place you are not likely to see Alington is in church!"

Anne exchanged a guarded look with Sidney. She rubbed her forehead in dismay, lowering her gaze to study the fine Turkey carpet underfoot. Why did everything have to be so difficult? At last she looked at Lord Rochford, wishing he might be the one who had volunteered. Of course, were he interested in Miss Bonham, he would not want to offer anything of the sort. Swallowing with care, Anne faced Sidney again and gave him her acceptance of his reluctant proposal.

"I do accept your kind—if temporary—offer of marriage, Mr. Fairfax." Poor Sidney looked pale but determined. Anne could well feel for him.

"I shall leave you to work out your plans for the coming week," Justin said, suddenly wanting to be gone from the house. The very notion of Miss Haycroft being even temporarily engaged to his young cousin did not please him.

Lady Mary gave him a quizzical look, then walked with him down the stairs to the entry hall, where she placed a detaining hand on his sleeve. "You will investigate that other matter, will you not?"

"Haycroft's motive for pursuing the marriage to Alington?" Justin looked up the stairs to where Anne and Sidney could be heard arguing like brother and sister. "I intend to begin that immediately." He added, "If those two continue in that way, no one will believe they are in love or considering marriage. They sound as though they are already related!"

"I promise to speak to them about it. I am glad you are mousing about to learn what you can of this sorry business. Poor girl—she is so sweet and loving, not to mention a splendid musician. I dearly enjoy having her here with me. It is not *just* that she be so plagued."

"Need I remind you that there is much in this life that is not just?"

"Do what you can for her," urged his aunt before seeing him out the door.

Justin found Henry Metcalf and his aunt approaching the house as he left. After greeting them with the politeness they merited, he commented on the fineness of the day and made a move to leave.

"One moment, Rochford, if you please," Henry said quietly while his aunt walked forward a few paces to the front door.

"How may I serve you?" Justin inquired of the younger man. He knew Metcalf only slightly, but had enjoyed his company on occasion.

"Miss Haycroft . . . she is betrothed? This Mr. Romer, is he a man of substance? Someone to capture her heart as well as her name?" Henry asked earnestly.

"I fear Mr. Romer and Miss Haycroft have reached a parting of the ways—quite mutual, I assure you. It is difficult to sustain regard when apart for a long time, and Miss Haycroft found that the esteem was too slight on her side to continue the betrothal," Justin said reluctantly.

Metcalf's face lightened considerably as he absorbed this

news. "I see. Well, I shan't give up hope as yet." He tipped his hat and marched off to join his aunt.

"Poor chap," Justin muttered to himself. If Henry Metcalf actually sustained an interest in Anne Haycroft, he was doomed to disappointment.

Justin headed for the nearest hackney stand, leaving his aunt to retain control over matters. He directed the jarvey to the first of his clubs. If he was to learn anything about Cosmo Haycroft's motive for insisting upon Anne's marriage to Alington, he must spend some time at the places where he was most likely to find the truth.

Lady Mary welcomed her dear friend Jane into the drawing room, taking note all the while that Henry had immediately set aim for Anne Haycroft, ignoring Sidney completely.

"Oh, dear," she murmured, then had to convert those words hastily into another thought entirely. "My dear Jane, how good to see you."

"I enjoyed yesterday, did you not?" said Jane Metcalf with a smile at her dear nephew chatting with Anne Haycroft. "How kind of Mr. Parker to be so considerate of Miss Haycroft. How is she today?"

"I doubt she slept well, but she is not one to complain about much of anything." Lady Mary looked over to where the three young people were presently discussing an upcoming event, a balloon ascension from what could be heard.

"Henry has spoken of little but Miss Haycroft's charms and talent since yesterday," Jane Metcalf said with an inquiring look at her friend.

"Pity," Mary replied, thinking it was far more of a pity than anyone knew. "She and Sidney have become very close these past days. I'd not be surprised to see them make a match of it now that she and Mr. Romer have parted ways."

"It is a pity about Mr. Romer," Jane said in reflection. "But a determined young man never gives up hope until the banns are called, does he?"

"And not even then at times. Do you remember that scandal involving Henrietta Elton? She had been engaged to the Earl of

Wendover, and it was after the banns had been read the third time that she eloped to Gretna with Lord Snelgar."

"The Snelgars are an old, respected family, but that is scarcely the proper behavior for a young lady."

"I understand she has cause to rue her change of heart. The last I heard she had given birth to her twelfth child and seldom sees her husband. He spends his time in London, gambling and speculating on the 'change."

The two spinster ladies exchanged a speaking look, then turned the conversation to more pleasant matters.

On the other side of the room Anne's spirits lightened notably with the frivolous chatter of her two companions. If it distressed her to have Sidney take a somewhat possessive attitude toward her, she reminded herself that it was but temporary, as temporary as his proposal.

Within minutes Jemima Green and Susan Price were shown up to the drawing room and the merriment increased. Soon Anne was playing the latest dance tune for their appreciation, and nothing would do but Henry and Jemima insisted that Sidney and Susan join them in learning the new steps. Since these were a variation of a dance they already knew, it proved a relatively easy task.

Lady Mary smiled her approval of the frolic, tapping her armchair in time with the beat. Jane Metcalf did not seem to mind the attention Henry paid to Jemima Green in the least. But then, Jemima was the only daughter of a wealthy baron, and as such considered a very good catch.

Justin looked about the interior of White's, thinking it was unlikely he might catch sight of his quarry here at this time of day. Yet he felt compelled to search him out. He'd seen Haycroft gaming here recently. And if memory served him right, it was with Alington.

"Good afternoon, Rochford," Lord Alvanley said in greeting. "Surprised to see you here at this hour of the day. Will you not join me for a chat and a glass of wine?"

Justin settled down with his old friend for a comfortable conversation in the hope that one who saw a great deal and recalled nearly all of it would drop a useful remark.

"Excellent wine," Justin began. "Anything happen of interest? I have been so occupied with a number of things of late that I have surely missed some event of curiosity."

"Ah, do I detect the fine hand of Miss Bonham in your days?" Alvanley inquired with a look that on a woman would be called coy.

"Not so I would notice. Miss Bonham may be all that is agreeable, but she does not interest me." Justin recalled a soft smile and gentle manners in a girl who possessed a melodious voice that ever pleased him. Anne was never far from his mind it seemed. "My aunt has a guest staying with her who has a problem. I have offered to assist her in finding an agreeable solution."

"Ah, the talented Miss Haycroft. Rumor has it that she is to marry Alington. Not true, is it?" Alvanley inquired with a narrow-eyed look.

"You have the right of it. She will never marry him, no matter what *he* thinks. My cousin is extremely fond of her. She and Sidney might make a match of it." Justin thought he would choke on the words he forced himself to say.

"Alington seems dashed certain he will be the one, however. Overheard him declare he had permission to court the girl. Claimed he has her uncle in his pocket. Does she truly have a fortune?"

"Well, as to that, it is no more than a modest fortune, but I wonder why Alington would say he has Haycroft in his pocket."

"Curious, I agree," Alvanley replied, retreating to his contemplation of a glass of fine claret. "I do not have any knowledge to offer there, my friend." He was silent for a time, then said, "Do you attend the Prince's levee this coming week?"

"Indeed, I suspect he would be offended if those he counts his supporters were not there." Justin gave his good friend a frank look, then leaned back against his chair, feeling slightly defeated. Alvanley didn't know much more than Justin did. Learning that Alington had declared he had Haycroft in his pocket was not exactly remarkable.

He remained for a time, conversing on the matters of the day with one who was cleverly knowledgeable. Eventually he took himself off to wander over to Brook's. Here, he had dinner, wishing he could be eating with Anne and his aunt instead of this rather uninspired food. He was at his cheese and biscuits when he spotted another affable fellow, one who enjoyed a good bit of conversation.

"Selwyn, good to see you," Justin said, rising to greet the good-natured gentleman. With a wave of his hand Justin invited the other to join him. Poodle Byng entered the room and without demur by the others, also joined the table.

Some excellent port was brought and savored in silence until Byng eyed Justin a long moment before inquiring, "Are you setting to fix on the estimable Miss Bonham?"

"Egad! Was ever a man so plagued? That is the second time this evening I've been queried about my intentions in that direction. I will say now, and I devoutly pray that you will both pass it along to others you know, that I am not interested in Miss Bonham, nor am I likely to offer for her now or ever."

"So there is someone else," Byng mused.

"I fail to see why there must be someone else simply because I have no interest in a woman who is enjoying her fourth Season," Justin said with a distinct snap in his voice.

"I sense it," Poodle Byng insisted. "I have a reputation for knowing about these affairs of the heart. Can you honestly say there is no woman who holds your interest?"

Justin thought of Anne Haycroft and was silent for a moment too long.

"Aha!" Byng declared triumphantly. "Rochford is too discreet to reveal the lady's name. Perhaps we may guess?" At a look from Justin, he amended his query. "But then, perhaps it is better to remain quiet."

"I hear Haycroft lost again, and badly," Selwyn said suddenly. "He does not come here now, but I saw him across the street before I entered. I did not know he had those kind of resources." There was a hint of question in his tone that Justin decided he could answer.

"I think you are right to question that. It is my understanding his estates are encumbered by considerable debt. Perhaps he has delved into money not his own? It is merely speculation on my part, you understand."

"You think he may be diddling with his niece's inheritance? I should think that would be grounds for dismissal as a guardian," Selwyn said quietly. "I have no knowledge of law, but if I knew Miss Haycroft, I would counsel her to seek out her solicitor. Providing he is not in Haycroft's pocket, she might be free of that particular onus."

"You know her, do you not, Rochford? Does she not stay with your aunt? Seems to me you would be in a fine position to warn her," Poodle Byng advised.

"Where does Alington come into this all?" Justin inquired, steering away from Anne's name.

"He gambles with Haycroft. A lot of fellows don't like to play with Alington, y'know. Seems to have phenomenal luck," Selwyn inserted.

"Perhaps less than honest luck?" Justin asked softly.

"Precisely," Poodle Byng said in reply. "I never play with him myself."

"Well, well," Justin concluded, thinking he might have found his answer after all.

Chapter Nine

It was two days before Justin was again able to visit his aunt. A jaunt with the Four-in-Hand club had demanded his appearance, an event envied by many and neglected by few.

He met her at the top of the landing, where she awaited him.

"I am glad to see you, Justin. How good you are to come. Was it the Windmill or the Castle Hill yesterday for dinner?" she inquired, referring to the inns at Salt Hill, where the coaches were driven by the driving club. The gentlemen drove their coaches to Salt Hill the first and third Thursdays of May and June, taking their meals at alternate inns. Considering it was the third Thursday of May, she had hardly expected him to be elsewhere.

"The Windmill, dear aunt. The food was fine, but not as good as you serve," he said with a grin lighting his handsome face.

"You are too serious," she scolded. "When you smile, you look younger and even more handsome than you are otherwise. My, you must make many a heart sing," she said with a gleam in her eyes.

He ignored her teasing, leading her across the room and away from the doorway. He seated her on the sofa, then joined her. When he spoke, it was in soft tones that could not easily be overheard.

"I have done a bit of mousing around, as you put it, and have learned something of interest. It seems Alington has problems with his estates and has had to sell one of the smaller ones. As well, it also seems as though a good many gentlemen do not like to play cards with him, especially the younger fellows. From what Poodle Byng told me, Alington has phenomenal luck, perhaps *too* phenomenal?"

"Anne will be joining us shortly, so tell me anything else I must know that perhaps might be kept from her," Lady Mary urged.

"Her uncle has been gambling and losing far more than his estates and holdings would easily tolerate. And it seems he plays with Alington more than anyone else. Selwyn told me that Haycroft no longer comes to Brook's, but favors White's for play. It is common knowledge that Alington has been barred from playing at Brook's."

"Blackballed? How interesting," Lady Mary murmured.

"There is speculation that perhaps Haycroft is diddling with Anne's inheritance. I've been told I should advise her to see her solicitor."

"Yes, do. Perhaps he will release her money, or at least a bit of it. It seems dreadful that Cosmo Haycroft should have the use of it when Anne cannot."

"How does Anne do?" Justin said, congratulating himself on his patience. He had wanted to inquire the moment he entered the house and had endured the questions and reports to his aunt with decided forbearance.

"Why, very well, my dear. Sidney and Henry Metcalf came over yesterday along with Jemima Green and Susan Price. I believe they picked up George Harcourt and made a day of it at Richmond Park. I sent along a basket of food to add to their picnic as well as James to help serve."

Justin smiled, for James was the burliest footman he had ever seen and hired by his aunt to intimidate anyone she cared to impress.

"It is well they had a large group, not to mention James."

"Being safety in large numbers, you are thinking? So did I," Lady Mary agreed. "And James could handle almost anything that came along. He reported that the young people had a good time. I believe they stayed pretty close to Anne, protecting her as it were, in the event that Alington or someone in his hire should take a notion to abscond with her."

Light footsteps were heard on the stairs shortly, followed by the appearance of the one discussed.

Justin rose immediately as Anne entered the room.

"Hello," Anne said somewhat awkwardly for her. She had

looked forward to the moment when she would see Justin again, but now she felt as though her tongue was tied in knots. "We had a lovely day yesterday. I suppose Lady Mary has told you several of us went to Richmond Park?"

"Indeed," Justin replied, wishing his aunt was elsewhere. "You have been busy of late."

"I have been neglecting my music; it is difficult to practice when so much is going on." She crossed over to sit in a chair near the sofa, where Justin had been conversing with his aunt. When she sat, he did as well, but not quite so close to his aunt as before, rather at some point in the middle.

"Mr. Parker is joining us shortly," Lady Mary inserted. "He called here yesterday, and I thought this might be a small recompense for that delightful boating trip we had. He was very generous."

"Miss Haycroft," Justin said, ruthlessly interrupting his aunt, but wishing to speak with Anne before Parker joined them, "it has been strongly suggested to me that I advise you to seek the counsel of your solicitor. There is speculation that your uncle is dipping into your inheritance to support his gaming. Someone ought to look into the matter for you."

"I might have known it was something of the sort," Anne said bitterly. "It seems to be like a fever with him. I do not believe he could stop, no matter what."

"He has no right to touch what is yours. It is usual for some monies to be used in support, clothing for you, pin money, that sort of thing. From what little you have said, he has been remiss in that line," Justin concluded.

"Then I must see my solicitor. I know little about him other than he has an office on Threadneedle Street. I believe it is close to the Bank. His name"—she thought a moment—"is Mr. Kestell."

"I have heard of him—he is a partner of my own solicitor. Would you like me to arrange an appointment for you?"

"And go with me? I know it is improper for me to even appear in that area, but I suspect this is a time when it is necessary to break conventions."

"I will let you know as soon as it is arranged," Justin said

softly. He could hear footsteps coming up the stairs and surmised Mr. Parker had come to join them.

Dinner was charming, with excellent food and conversation.
Anne enjoyed the lemon pudding while Mr. Parker and Justin
favored the trifle.

They chatted for a time, with Mr. Parker mentioning the balloon ascension in the park.

"Several of us are going," Anne confided. "Mr. Fairfax as
well as Mr. Metcalf, and of course Miss Green and Miss Price
are attending as well."

"That leaves you a man short," Justin observed, wishing he
hadn't promised to see the solicitor tomorrow morning.

"Mr. Harcourt was invited, but he said he had a previous engagement." Anne wondered if George Harcourt's engagement
was with Caroline Bonham. She had not missed his particular
attentions to Caroline, nor his disappointment when she was
not one of the Richmond Hill party.

"Be sure to take James along," Lady Mary insisted. "He can
handle almost any situation, and we want you safe." She didn't
add anything beyond that, presumably because of Mr. Parker.
Anne appreciated her concern.

"Indeed, fair lady, you ought not go about without protection
in this day and age. 'Tis a fearful business, London. Not the
least like Canada," Mr. Parker inserted.

"True, true," Justin murmured in reply, then excused himself
after complimenting his aunt on the fine dinner.

Anne decided to exit as well, bidding Justin good night at the
top of the stairs. She whisked up to her room rather than rejoin
the others. There was a great deal to consider, and she suspected they enjoyed their conversation without her.

Late the following morning Sidney came for Anne with
Henry Metcalf, Jemima Green, and Susan Price already in the
carriage. There was no opportunity for private conversation
with Sidney to inform him of her coming meeting with the solicitor. In fact, Anne wondered at his rather odd behavior. He
was far too attentive to Susan Price. Come to think of it, he had
paid her a great deal of attention at Richmond Hill as well.

Anne sat back against the seat, watching the pair with puzzled eyes. This might prove to be a problem, one that none of them had anticipated.

"We are early enough, so we ought to be able to find a grand position," Sidney informed them. "No need to draw too close. We mainly want to see the balloon go up."

Carriages were parked along the roadways and off onto the grassy area of the park. Throngs of people strolled about the park, inspecting the balloon, its basket, and asking questions of the patient balloon handlers.

The coachman guided the landau into an excellent position for viewing the ascent, then the elderly man settled down for a doze.

Susan asked a question, and Sidney eagerly explained all to her in great detail. To Anne's other side Jemima and Henry Metcalf fell into a discussion of the possible uses for hot-air balloons.

Deciding that she might as well sit back and enjoy the amusement offered, Anne settled against her comfortable seat to watch people. With many different sorts, she found it interesting to see how they behaved. It was while she was searching the crowd that she thought she spotted Lord Alington. Then she decided she must have made a mistake, for whoever it was disappeared from sight.

"Look, it is going up now!" Susan exclaimed, grabbing hold of Sidney's arm in her excitement.

How fortunate that Anne did not mind in the least.

They all turned as one to see the green-and-gold balloon soar upward in awesome glory. It truly was magnificent.

"How wonderful," Jemima said. "Think what you might see from up so high!"

"Someday I would like to go sailing like that," Susan said with a shy smile at Sidney.

"Then you shall," he replied fondly. Or at least to Anne it seemed quite a fond look.

Jemima turned to the footman and said, "James, would you be so good as to fetch me a lemonade from that stand over there?" She gestured to a small stand set up to one side of the park, where a woman was doing a brisk business.

He immediately set off to her satisfaction.

"It is such a warm day, is it not?" Jemima asked.

"Warm for May," Anne replied. She was about to add more when her arm was clasped tightly by someone. Fearing to see just who it was, yet knowing she must know, Anne turned to face Lord Alington. "You!"

"Indeed, Miss Haycroft. If you would be so kind as to step from the carriage, we shall be on our way. I believe I have been patient long enough. A parson awaits us at your uncle's house. Come, my dear!"

"I shan't put one step from this carriage, sirrah." Anne braced herself, placing a foot on the opposite seat and clasping the side of the carriage with a firm grip in spite of the pain in her arm. "I have repeatedly said I will not marry you. Why do you not understand?"

Sidney lurched forward with the obvious intent of saving Anne from Alington's clutches.

"Stay where you are, Fairfax. You aren't as formidable as your cousin is. I can dispatch you with ease." To emphasize his point, a wicked little knife flashed into Alington's hand, aimed straight at Sidney.

The pressure on Anne's arm became nearly intolerable. None of those in the carriage seemed to think of a thing they might do to help. Indeed, they sat like so many stones! Henry drew Jemima against him while Sidney placed a protective hand toward Susan.

When Anne tried again to wrench her arm away, Alington tightened his hold to near bone-crushing level. She didn't think she could hold out much longer.

The milling crowd ignored what appeared to be a pleasant scene. Anne suspected if she screamed they would pay her no heed, thinking it a game.

Reluctantly, she glanced at her enemy and began her careful descent from the carriage. She reached the ground and prayed for help.

"Now walk straight ahead. My carriage awaits us."

She glimpsed a black traveling carriage with a crest on the door, standing ready to depart.

His finger prodded her in the back, a hard stab she could not ignore. Yet she stayed. She had tried so hard to avoid this marriage with this dreadful man. Why could she not think of something, anything, to prevent it?

He twisted her arm painfully, causing her to cry out.

Sidney moved forward again. "I say, old man, you can't do that! Ain't right. Leave her alone, I say!"

"Yes, indeed, Alington. I suggest you drop Miss Haycroft's arm immediately."

Anne almost fainted with relief at the sound of Lord Rochford's voice. She had thought its rich deepness appealing, but never so welcome as now. She turned to him, her eyes round with fear.

He stared at Alington with a narrow gaze that frightened. In Rochford's hand was his customary cane, only now it was aimed at Alington, and there was a sword point jutting from the end of it. And that point was dangerously close to Lord Alington's back.

Lord Alington slowly turned his head until he became aware of the cane with its deadly shaft so near to him.

"I suggest you walk to your carriage *now*, leaving Miss Haycroft here, safe with us," Rochford said as though discussing an oncoming storm.

In view of the sword pointed at him by a man who would not hesitate to use it with utmost force, Lord Alington had little choice but to walk to his carriage as directed. He fumed and looked as angry as Anne ever cared to see anyone.

But she was free. The full realization hit her, and again she almost fainted. Her arm ached, throbbing like fire in her veins.

"Your arm? He hurt it?" Justin asked with a worried frown, the sight of her white face stabbing into him like a pain.

"Looked to me like he was trying to break it," Sidney said, appearing greatly abashed with the knowledge he had failed in his duty.

"Indeed," Anne whispered, her voice catching. "I do not feel quite the thing."

She would have crumpled then, but Justin scooped her up in his arms just in time.

"I'll see you later," he warned Sidney, who had the grace to turn slightly red in the face.

Anne nestled against Justin's coat while he carried her to

where his tiger waited with the curricle. Alington's carriage was nowhere in sight. Justin placed Anne gently upon the seat, then took up the reins and clambered up beside her. At his nod, the tiger released his hold, then dashed back to jump up behind.

Perhaps the young chap sensed it would be a fast ride through Town. At least it was as fast as Justin dared to go, considering the condition of his passenger.

"We shall be there soon. Just hold on to me—lean against me all you can. I shan't let you fall."

He wrapped one arm about Anne, holding her against him, hoping she would do as he said. Managing the reins with one hand was simple for a man of his experience in driving. Their dash through Mayfair might have caused a bit of havoc; neither of them cared.

Once at Lower Brook Street, the tiger again jumped down to run to the horse's head. He stood proudly, awaiting orders.

"Walk him," Justin said, then hurried up the shallow steps to the front door, carrying Anne.

Potter was there of course, opening the door with alacrity, asking what he could do.

"Notify your good wife that Miss Haycroft has been injured. She will need care at once."

Without waiting for a response, Justin carried Anne up the stairs. He could hear voices in the drawing room. His aunt appeared at once, looking curious, then horrified when she saw his burden.

"What has happened?"

"Alington tried to steal a bride in Hyde Park. I took Anne away from him, but not before he badly hurt her arm. Cursed devil of a man," Justin muttered as Anne at last gave up and fainted from her pain.

"Mrs. Potter," Lady Mary cried.

In the background Justin could hear the voices of Mr. Witherspoon and Mr. Parker as well as Miss Metcalf as they exclaimed over the near disaster.

"Town isn't safe nowadays," Miss Metcalf said.

"Never was," Mr. Witherspoon shot back. "Probably never will be."

Ignoring the guests, Justin hurried up the next flight of stairs to the bedroom he surmised would be Anne's. He nudged open the door with his foot, then crossed the room to place his precious burden on the bed, as carefully as a fragile flower.

"Oh, I do hurt," Anne whispered as she began to come around. "Never say I fainted. I have never done so in my life."

"When pain becomes too great, the body has a way of blotting it out," Justin said quietly. "Where is that woman," he muttered, looking to the door for Mrs. Potter. The housekeeper was not to be seen. "I'll help you. First we must remove your pelisse. May I?"

"Please," Anne begged. "I think it would be much better if you did."

It was not a simple matter, but with a gritting of teeth, Anne slipped her left arm from the pelisse first, then her injured right arm. She knew that her bruise was not pleasant when she heard Justin's sharp breath.

"That is going to be rather painful for several days. I only hope that Mrs. Potter—if she ever gets here—will have a remedy for it."

Then at last aware of the impropriety of his being in her room, Justin awkwardly took her hand in his. "I am sorry that Sidney let you down."

"Well, things have changed a little there," she began. Justin placed a finger on her soft lips to silence her.

"Tomorrow we can talk. I shall call early to see if you feel up to going to see Kestell."

The housekeeper finally entered, carrying a basin of water along with a maid who bore a basket of assorted items. Justin hoped that one of them might ease Anne's pain.

He walked slowly down to the drawing room, pausing in the doorway. "This was not quite the way I intended to spend the day."

"We were about to join in a nuncheon. Do you feel you could eat anything at all? Shock usually takes away my appetite," Lady Mary said, offering Justin an excuse should he wish to leave.

"I could manage a small bite. I'd like to stay until Anne is feeling better. You haven't seen her bruise—I have. It is a nasty thing."

"Oh, dear," Miss Metcalf said, looking quite pale.

"Allow me, dear lady," Mr. Parker said hastily and rushed to her side, leaving Mr. Witherspoon to walk with Lady Mary. Mr. Witherspoon gave his rival a sly smile and said nothing at all.

A very subdued group went down to nuncheon. Justin went last, glancing to the upper floor from time to time, wondering what was being done for Anne. So great was his concern that he failed to realize he had thought as well as spoken of her as Anne to others.

Anne slept for some time following the tender care from Mrs. Potter. The willow bark potion helped her to sleep, and when she woke hours later, it seemed her pain had eased quite a bit.

"Oh, miss," cried out Cherry, the maid, "think you to get up? I best fetch her ladyship. She's been looking in here often to see how you be. Do not move, I beg you."

Anne remained quietly on her bed, reconsidering her desire to rise. It might be better to get up. Otherwise, she could have a difficult time sleeping later. She was about to slip her feet off the bed when Lady Mary breezed around the corner, followed by Lord Rochford.

"What's this about rising?" Lady Mary demanded.

"I need to talk with your nephew, ma'am," Anne countered, hoping this might answer.

"There is a problem?" his lordship asked from the doorway, a worried frown on his brow.

"I should like to go to the drawing room and perhaps recline on the sofa. That would not be the least unseemly. It is but my arm that is bruised, not my entire body, you know." Anne blushed at such plain speaking, but decided it would be best for her to move about.

"I shall carry you if you insist," Justin said. "We should talk and cannot talk here."

With a flurry of activity, Justin brought Anne to the drawing room. Cherry carried assorted shawls, pillows, and anything else Lady Mary could find. Lady Mary entered the drawing room last, crossing to study Anne.

"I cannot think this good. I believe I shall consult with Mrs. Potter." She did as she said and left the room at once.

"What is it you wished to discuss? She will return before long, and we won't have another chance to talk." Justin pulled a chair close to the sofa, where Anne lay in as great a comfort as her bed.

"The reason Sidney was not paying close attention to me is that he was mindful of no one but Susan Price. I noticed a little of this while at Richmond Park. Today his interest was quite marked. I fear we shall not be able to count on Sidney as my counterfeit fiancé any longer."

"After today I do not believe you need one. In any event, I decided it would be best were I to assume that role."

"You?" she whispered.

"You object?" he said, drawing away from her.

"No, no, that is not it at all. I was merely surprised. I thought you to have an interest in another quarter." Anne pleated the delicate throw that Cherry had gently placed over her, avoiding her arm as though it could bite. "I thought you were interested in Caroline Bonham."

There—she had said it. He would undoubtedly look down his aristocratic and most handsome nose to inform Anne that she trod where she ought not. He didn't.

"I have no interest in Miss Bonham. On the contrary, I find that lady to be rather forward. I have tried to be polite, but I find that is to little avail. I keep hoping she will turn her attention to George Harcourt."

Anne was so relieved that she didn't even feel the pain in her arm for a moment.

"So you may tell Sidney he is free from any obligation," Justin said, a sparkle in his eyes.

"What was that about Sidney, my dear?" Lady Mary inquired as she entered the room, followed by Mrs. Potter.

"We have decided on a different plan, and so Sidney need not pretend any longer—if, indeed, he ever did," Anne concluded under her breath.

"He is downstairs and begs to see you."

Anne exchanged a look with Justin. "Let him come up for a few moments."

"It did not take long to convince Sidney that Anne would survive and that his services as a pretend fiancé were no longer needed.

"Dreadful sorry about what happened," he said for the third time before his departure.

"You were, I believe, rather taken with Miss Susan Price's charms at the moment," Justin drawled.

"I fear I was," Sidney admitted. "She is a dashed nice girl, you know."

With that, the young man was shooed from the room and seen out of the house by Potter.

Anne rested against the sofa, wishing she did not feel like a limp rag.

"What about the morning?" Justin asked. "Do you think you will wish to see your solicitor?"

"Come early, as you said, and we shall see then. I cannot promise more."

When Justin appeared in the morning, trying not to look as anxious as he felt, he found Anne much improved.

"Mind you," his aunt declared, "I would never approve Anne's going out otherwise, but considering the circumstances, I deem it not only permissible but advisable."

And so Anne entered the now familiar curricle and they were soon off to Threadneedle Street.

The visit with Mr. Kestell was most revealing. The elderly solicitor had been assured by Uncle Cosmo that she had quite sufficient money to hand. When informed of the true circumstances, the solicitor had been angered, drawing up in a dignified and rather grim stiffness. He immediately wrote out a draft from Anne's funds, then offered it to her, advising her she could have access to what she needed.

Taking the paper that Justin could give her banker, Anne left the building, feeling much more assured. "Now I can pay my bills, and buy what I need without worry of imposing. It is dreadful to bother others, and I feel very keenly that I presume too far upon your aunt's kind generosity."

"I shouldn't worry were I you," Justin said. However, he and Anne failed to observe Cosmo Haycroft watching them from the intersection where Threadneedle merged into Cornhill and Prince's Street. It was exceptionally busy, and Justin had his hands full with guiding his horse through the traffic.

Anne was glad once they returned to Lower Brook Street and she could rest in bed. The morning might have been beneficial, but it had been exhausting.

"I shan't see you tomorrow, most likely. The Prince is having a levee, and I must attend. If necessary, I can mention the problem we have with Alington, but I doubt we shall hear from either your uncle or Alington again. You may sleep tonight; rest assured that your troubles are over."

Anne's smile was a trifle wan, but Justin thought he left her in good heart.

She bid him farewell and went up to her room with the hope of a nap. She was not quite so optimistic as Lord Rochford. But then, he did not know her uncle very well. She did.

Chapter Ten

Trustees could be good and they could be wretched, Anne decided, while listening to the conversation of her new friends. Uncle Haycroft was in the wretched category. Jemima and Susan had come to cheer her, but their chatter did not ease her mind. She felt a certain disquiet about her Uncle Haycroft in spite of all the assurances she had received from everyone.

Following the call to Mr. Kestell, she ought to have felt immeasurably better, yet she didn't. Even after Lord Rochford stopped by this morning to leave a packet of money he obtained upon written draft by the solicitor to the banker, she still worried.

"Anne, you fret too much. Lord Alington has been vanquished. Your uncle has no more power over you," declared Jemima Green.

Mr. Parker, who had just entered the room with his usual jovial air, agreed. "My dear Miss Haycroft, you do not have a thing to fear. In Rochford you have found a formidable ally. I feel certain he will not allow a thing to happen to you . . . that you do not wish." This last was said with a twinkling smile full of meaning that was not totally lost on Anne.

"Perhaps I am being foolish," she admitted at last with a polite smile at Mr. Parker as he took a chair near Lady Mary.

"One can never be too careful in this life," Mr. Witherspoon said as he paused in the doorway. "You never know what is around the corner." He darted a glance of dislike at Mr. Parker, then crossed to where Anne reclined on the plum damask sofa.

"You look more the thing today, young lady. I am pleased to see the bloom in your cheeks once again." He nodded to the several bouquets of flowers on a nearby table, adding, "I see others thought to assist the return of color to your face?"

"Mr. Fairfax and Mr. Metcalf each sent flowers, as did Lord Rochford." She discreetly did not add that with Sidney and Henry's flowers came notes of abject apology for their lack of action the day before.

"Aye," Mr. Witherspoon said softly, "and I'd wager his is the largest."

"Indeed, sir, you are right." Anne suspected she blushed, but it could not be helped. There was unspoken meaning in Mr. Witherspoon's words, and she was not about to question him. She might not wish to hear what it was.

"Come, let us play a game," the lively Jemima cried.

"I doubt Miss Haycroft wishes to join in anything spirited," Mr. Witherspoon admonished.

"Perhaps something quiet?" Susan Price suggested.

Thus it was when Lord Rochford entered the drawing room some time later, it was to find the three girls playing a game of cards. This was readily abandoned when Sidney Fairfax and Henry Metcalf followed upon his heels.

"I stopped by to see how you do. I must dress for the levee, but I could not go without knowing you are feeling better," Lord Rochford said to Anne while Sidney and Henry drew the other girls away to chat.

She noted he had been properly polite to the other girls, but to her he had bestowed a warm smile, and she basked in his regard. "I thank you for the packet you left this morning before I was down. It is much appreciated, sir." Anne thought how comforted she felt just knowing she possessed enough money to pay her bills and even flee London if necessary.

"I think Anne is much better today," Lady Mary said with a kind smile at her guest.

"And you are to attend the levee? How very grand you will look," Anne dared to say.

He grimaced. "I am pleased the overly ornate court dress for men is becoming outdated."

"Never say you intend to wear something that is not embroidered!" Mr. Parker said in very shocked accents.

"My coat has a narrow line of embroidery along the outer

edge and on the pocket flaps, with an equally narrow row of cream embroidery on the cream waistcoat," he explained to the other men.

"The coat color?" Mr. Parker inquired, being much interested in fashion for gentlemen.

"Coat and breeches are dark blue," Justin replied with a glance at the women. They appeared not to be listening to such a warm discussion, but he suspected they did. Normally a gentleman did not mention something like breeches in the presence of ladies.

"Well," Anne said turning to look at him with warmth in her blue eyes, "I believe you will outshine them all. Do promise to tell us about it later."

"I thought that if you felt up to it, we might all go to Vauxhall tomorrow evening."

"Jolly good, sir," Henry Metcalf said, making Justin feel positively ancient.

"I shall look forward to that," Jemima said in happy agreement, clapping her hands in anticipation.

"Think it safe?" Mr. Witherspoon inserted during a moment while Justin was making his parting bow to Anne.

Justin gave the older man a thoughtful look. "I believe Anne will be safe with us to guard her."

"Mind you, I would like James to come along," Lady Mary declared. "and no sending him off on errands," she added with a look at Jemima.

Jemima blushed and looked at the floor.

"She had no way of knowing that Alington would pop up in the park, ma'am," Henry said in defense of his favored young lady.

"True. And we do not think Alington will show up at Vauxhall either." Lady Mary bestowed a disdainful look on the young people so careless of her favored guest, quite ignoring that she had allowed herself to be drawn away during an earlier incident.

With that terse remark ringing in his ears, Justin left the subdued group behind and ran lightly down the stairs and out to his curricle.

It didn't take long to change into his court dress. He adjusted the short frills on the front of his shirt and at the cuff, then picked up his chapeau bras. "Good luck, sir," his man said as he watched Justin leave the house.

Justin nodded, then set off to St. James's Palace in his more stately carriage with his elderly coachman and a footman in attendance. Traffic was incredibly thick as they neared the palace.

Once in the palace, he handed a card to the page in the Presence Chamber, who directed him into the Audience Chamber. He removed his gloves, tucked his hat firmly under his arm, then gave the remaining card to the Lord in Waiting who subsequently announced him. Justin kneeled on his right knee, kissed the royal hand, rose, bowed correctly, and backed away, giving the Prince a look that communicated much.

He was grateful that the royal Prince favored cleanliness. From what he'd heard, the French royalty had rarely bathed or washed their hands. Small wonder the French drenched themselves in scent.

He left the chamber and was not surprised when a page approached with a message to follow him. Justin shortly entered an antechamber where a small, highly select group of men gathered, awaiting a more personal chat with their future king.

Since he had deliberately arrived as late as he dared, Justin was fortunate that the line behind him was short. He didn't have long to wait before the Prince Regent joined them.

There was a genial intermixing about the room, gentlemen politely conversing about the latest news from the Continent and affairs of the country. Gossip was carefully avoided at a levee. When Justin was permitted to approach the Prince, he made his point quickly. The matter of Alington was common knowledge by this time, at least among the upper ranks of Society.

"I have warned Alington he is not to continue in his pursuit of Miss Haycroft, Your Highness. I trust there will be no repercussions?" It was not easy to deal with another peer. Had Alington not been of the nobility, the matter would never have arisen. He'd not have been considered as a groom for an heiress.

"We are aware of the problem. Everyone has been talking about his odd behavior," the Prince replied, frowning slightly.

"I would not wish Miss Haycroft to be in danger again, Your Highness," Justin said.

"Indeed." They chatted a bit longer. Justin had been able to perform a number of delicate missions for the Prince, and for that reason, if none other, he was quite a favorite.

By the time he left, Justin felt the seed had been planted and that the precarious matter of Anne's fortune and the dreadful trusteeship of her uncle would be dealt with due concern. Even though the Prince did not have the power royalty once had, he still had certain influence.

It was a relief for Justin to return to his town house and change from the court dress into something more his own style. Within a short time he was off to see his aunt—and of course, Anne.

Upon being ushered into the drawing room, Lady Mary warmly greeted him, "So, how was the levee? You have been gone for hours."

"The usual thing. There was a line of fine coaches a mile long, I fancy. And Mr. Parker will be pleased to know that not everyone has gone to the more sober sort of court dress. I vow there were some veritable peacocks in attendance."

"Tell us more!" Anne cried breathlessly, fascinated by this glimpse into court life. Her aunt and uncle had not the *ton* to sponsor her for a presentation, although Anne merited such.

"Did you have an opportunity to speak with his Royal Highness?" Lady Mary inquired.

"Briefly, but long enough to feel we have a sympathetic friend in the Prince." He met his aunt's gaze with a nod, letting her know he felt more secure about matters involving Anne Haycroft.

"I have been telling Anne about my own come-out years ago. Little of the dress has changed over the years."

"It seems odd they would cling to the enormous hoop skirts, the lappets and all," Anne observed quietly.

They fell to a discussion of court clothes, and Justin wondered how Anne would look in an exquisitely draped hoop skirt with the plumes and lappets above her soft blond curls, now styled in a sort of Titus.

"You must be presented someday," he said of a sudden.

"My Aunt Haycroft would like nothing better. However, the sponsor must have a social standing she does not possess to make a request of the Lord Chamberlain for the proper cards."

Justin said no more on the subject, turning instead to the coming outing at Vauxhall.

"Shall you wear a domino?" he asked Anne.

She looked to Lady Mary for the answer.

"I think we will dress simply but without a domino. We have no need for masks, do we?"

"I would hope not."

On his way home once again, Justin considered Anne's uneasiness and decided she was merely being overly concerned. There was nothing Alington could do. With James along and surrounded by men who would be far more on the alert—he hoped—Anne ought to be as safe as though she were at home.

The following evening found Anne feeling far better. Her arm was still very tender. She was careful to avoid coming close to anyone, lest they inadvertently bump against her.

"What a becoming gown Madame Clotilde has made for you. Such pretty pleated mameluke sleeves, too. Just the thing to wear this evening. I have always liked pale amaranthus as a color, and it is most becoming to you," said Lady Mary with delightful enthusiasm. She walked around to inspect the back of the pinkish purple gown of fine muslin.

Lady Mary reached out to puff up the many-tiered sleeve on Anne's right arm. When she winced, Lady Mary frowned. "Are you certain you wish to go this evening? It will not be too much for you?"

"Not at all." Anne's arm was still tender, but she did not wish to deny her friends a lovely evening. Surely she could manage the excursion with care?

Subsequent speech was cut short by the arrival of Jemima Green and Susan Price. Within minutes Sidney and Henry Metcalf were shown into the drawing room, closely followed by

Miss Metcalf, Mr. Parker, and a decidedly testy Mr. Witherspoon.

"This is like setting bait to catch a poacher," he grumbled,
while shaking his head at Anne.

She gave him a demure look.

"That won't cut butter with me, missy," he added with a bark
of laughter. Justin joined them at that point, and Mr. Witherspoon turned to him to add, "Fine minx you have here,
Rochford. Enjoys a bit of teasing, she does."

"I have no doubt of that, but I am pleased to see she feels up
to such sport." He looked about the room to note all had arrived. "Shall we depart for Vauxhall? I have the town coach and
Witherspoon has his. Sidney?"

"Indeed, I requested the family coach, and when Father
heard you were in charge, he gave leave to use it," Sidney
replied, revealing how esteemed his cousin was within the family circle.

Anne joined Lady Mary and Mr. Parker in Justin's coach,
and they set out in the lead of the others, who had not been slow
to enter the remaining coaches. They crossed Westminster
Bridge in a fine little procession.

Once there, Justin produced the prettily engraved silver
medallion to gain entrance to the box he held for the Season.
Once settled, the ladies sat for a time, admiring the costumes of
those parading past and appreciating the protection offered by
their escorts against insults offered by too familiar a gentleman.

As one box allowed for accommodation for six, or at best,
eight people, Justin had arranged for the adjacent box, rented
by one he knew, to be open for their use as well.

"Is this not exciting?" Jemima cried to Anne across the barrier that separated the two boxes.

Anne agreed, but wished she felt more at ease about being in
such a public place.

However, as the evening wore on, it appeared that her fears
were for naught. They had a splendid supper, then left the boxes
to stroll along the various walks. The only ones forbidden to
Anne by Lady Mary were the Hermit's and the Lover's Walks.
Not surprised in the least at that, Anne agreed and set off with
Lord Rochford as her guide to the gardens.

Anne glanced off to the Hermit's Walk and commented, "I can see why your aunt did not wish me to go there. It looks exceedingly dark, and so very narrow."

Their feet crunched loudly on the gravel path as they strolled on for some minutes before Justin said, "Do you not trust me, then?"

Anne thought back to those brief moments in the church. "I am of mixed feelings. You seem quite different from what I first thought you to be. But, yes, I trust you. Perhaps it is myself I do not trust?" she added softly.

In reply, Justin tucked her left arm, the uninjured one, close to his side, chuckling as he did. "You are wise. *I* shouldn't trust me at all, were I you."

"Fie, sir. How you do talk!" She laughed at his expression, a teasing smile on her lips.

A man brushed close to them, almost forcing them off the walk and up against the espaliered enclosure of Chinese design.

Anne cried out in alarm and in mild pain as well, for it was her right arm that had been shoved against the espaliered tree.

"Rude fellow," Justin said in disgust. "I ought to chase after him to give him a sound thrashing for such behavior, but I suspect that might be just what he wants."

"I shan't demand an explanation of that," Anne said quietly.

"You believe it might be someone from Alington?"

"Maybe. Or perhaps my uncle? I doubt he has given up all hope of compelling me to wed his choice, in spite of what you say."

At this point Mr. Witherspoon and Lady Mary joined them, and they strolled along to the first of the pavilions, which they found highly pleasing. Leaving this elegant, if simple little building with the intent of looking over the Cross Walk, they came face-to-face with Cosmo Haycroft and his wife.

"Uncle Cosmo!" Anne cried. She ignored her aunt for the moment; it was her uncle who was her concern.

"Anne, I see you are with your *protector*," Mr. Haycroft said in a snide manner, implying Anne was in Rochford's keeping.

"How dare you, sirrah," Anne said with deadly calm. So intent was she that she scarcely noticed Lord Rochford's arm go around her in a sheltering gesture.

"Miss Haycroft resides with my aunt, Lady Mary," Justin declared coldly, "as you well know." He gave the pair a scathing look, then added, "I do see Miss Haycroft from time to time—she is a charming young lady—but you labor under a great misunderstanding if you believe what you implied."

"See here, Haycroft," Mr. Witherspoon said, taking an intimidating step toward Anne's uncle, "you keep your nasty insinuations to yourself, hear me? How dare you insult a fine young lady and a gentleman who has the ear of the Prince!"

Anne could tell that her uncle did not believe Mr. Witherspoon, in spite of his impressive bearing.

"Take care, Uncle. Beware of who it is you antagonize," Anne cautioned.

"I will see you wed to Lord Alington, dear niece. One way or another!"

Not permitting Anne to utter a word, Justin swept her along with him, leaving his aunt and Mr. Witherspoon to trail behind. He couldn't recall when he had been so angry—other than when he had come upon that snake in the grass Alington, attempting to force Anne to go with him.

"I believe you may let me go now," Anne said with commendable calm, considering what had just transpired.

"I cannot believe that man is a relative of yours," Justine declared.

"My father did not particularly care for him either. It is unfortunate Uncle Cosmo had to be the only one remotely suitable to serve as a trustee—along with the solicitor who is so ancient I expect his demise any day."

"Mr. Kestell might be elderly, but he should be able to thwart your uncle at every turn, especially now that he knows what is being attempted. Your uncle seems unaware of one clause in the trust. You may not marry without your solicitor's approval, and knowing what we have told him, he will never permit a marriage to Alington. The letter reminding your uncle of this odd little clause ought to reach him by tomorrow. Do you suppose your late father suspected such unworthy intentions in his brother?"

"I was but thirteen when Papa died, and it seems such a long time ago. It is not impossible he thought that far ahead. He must have known Uncle to be a gamester even then." Anne paused by Lord Rochford's box to add, "What about an abduction? You foiled his plot the other day, but who is to say he will not try again?"

Her voice wobbled a trifle on the last word, and Anne hoped his lordship did not think her a watering pot. She'd not cry, but she was afraid. Why did some people seem to be able to break the law with impunity? And why was she so desirable? She was not so foolish as to think she was a great beauty. Nor was her playing on the pianoforte beyond anything remarkable.

"I do not understand any of this, you know," she murmured to Lord Rochford as he assisted her to a chair.

"You are a lovely, talented young lady who happens to have an uncle who likes to gamble. That he appears to gamble mostly with Alington is puzzling. I shall get to the bottom of the mystery before long. Your uncle's estates are in need of money, yet he gambles as though he had unlimited funds."

"Yes, so you said before," Anne said with a sigh. "And you think he may be using mine. Cannot Mr. Kestell cut off the money from Uncle?"

Justin smiled rather wickedly. "He has done precisely that as of today. It is bound to make your uncle furious when he receives the letter reminding him of the marriage clause followed by the notification from the bank that he will no longer be permitted to draw on your account for anything."

"That is setting the cat among the pigeons!" Anne cried. "Surely he will be more determined than ever to wed me to Lord Alington—or anyone else he can find who will oblige him."

"I'd not thought of that aspect—that he might turn to someone else."

"Must I remain a prisoner in the house, unable to go about in the least?"

Justin frowned, staring off into the crowd of people. "I would take you to the country house, except I'd not wish to interfere with Aunt Mary's happiness. She was denied her heart's desire years ago, and I'll not have her happiness withheld again."

"You mean Mr. Parker?" Anne inquired, knowing what he meant, yet unsure that it was what Lady Mary truly wanted.

"If she so wishes. That places us in a dilemma. Shall we tell her of the danger hanging over your head? She will insist upon finding you the safest place possible until your birthday." As an afterthought, he asked, "Just how long away is your birthday?"

"I shall be one-and-twenty come the seventh of June," Anne primly replied.

"But that is only weeks away! Do you think you could manage until then? The day of your birthday you will be free."

"So I shall. And all of you will be free of me as well," Anne said with a strained smile. "By that I mean there will be no more need to worry and fuss about me, no anxiety that I will be snatched from a carriage or . . ." She paused at the look on his face. "What is it? What has occurred to you now?"

What it was she was not to learn, at least not at the moment. Sidney and Susan along with Jemima and Henry returned from their stroll in the gardens. Immediately behind them came Mr. Parker and Miss Metcalf with Lady Mary and Mr. Witherspoon.

Anne thought it odd that Mr. Parker had offered to show Miss Metcalf the cascade rather than showing it to Lady Mary. Of course, a nasty little voice prompted, Miss Metcalf had inherited a considerable fortune from a recently deceased grandmother who had lived far longer than anyone had believed possible. But surely a devoted love of many years standing meant something? And pigs might fly!

Lord Rochford insisted they should all enjoy a late supper of the famous shaved ham plus a sampling of the equally famous rack punch.

"I shall have ratafia, dear," his aunt decreed. "And I believe Anne should have some as well. She looks rather pale, which isn't the least surprising, all things considered."

At that Lady Mary and Mr. Witherspoon were begged to explain all to those who had been elsewhere and missed the confrontation with the Haycrofts.

"Oh, Anne, you poor dear, to be so plagued," Jemima cried, wiping her eyes, of what Anne wasn't sure. It was fashionable to be emotional and cry over the least little thing. Anne thought the fashion silly and rejected it. Apparently Jemima thought it clever.

The ham and rack punch, along with the requested ratafia,

were served, and much praised. Following their supper, the group, surrounding Anne in a snug cluster, strolled off to see the fireworks before leaving the gardens.

There were Catherine wheels and sky rockets, a clever outline of a maiden, and sundry other inventive explosives. Anne jumped every time, no matter how the others reassured her. She wished she might cling to the earl, who stood so close to her yet not close enough for comfort.

"It sounds like a gun," she explained to Lord Rochford at last.

"That was what I was about to tell you. I hope your uncle does not take it into his head to assault our carriage on the way home." He had spoken close to her ear so that none of the others would overhear him.

"I truly did not have to hear that," Anne protested, turning to give him a dismayed look.

"I did not mean to upset you, but you should be prepared for any event."

"I believe I am, at that," she muttered, wishing she possessed a stout stick with which she could cudgel any and all males!

Chapter Eleven

In spite of Lord Rochford's fears, their carriage was not attacked by armed men on the ride home. Although Anne had been quite afraid, upon later reflection she decided they had worried for naught. Now, if the confrontation had come *after* Uncle Cosmo had received the notification from the bank and Mr. Kestell's reminder of that clause in the trusteeship, she would have thought it far more likely.

When she went to bed later, she thought that on the whole the evening had gone very well. She at last had seen Vauxhall, the beautiful gardens of which she had heard so much. And the much praised shaved ham as well as the rack punch, of which she had taken just a sip, was a treat not to be missed!

But now, the matter of her uncle returned to haunt her. What could he do? She had felt so safe with Lady Mary. It was a pity that Hortense Finch had seen fit to spread her gossip about Town. Such a magpie should be banished—or severely punished!

The following afternoon Anne welcomed Susan and Jemima to the drawing room, inviting them to join her for a cup of tea. Talk of the latest fashions, novels, and which lady had been observed dancing with which gentleman was a most amiable pastime.

The girls were agreeably occupied with precisely such topics when Mr. Witherspoon charged into the drawing room, waving a newspaper in his hand. "It is in the *Chronicle*!" he cried, huffing slightly from his haste. "What will come of it, I dare not say. Here! Read for yourself. Where is Lady Mary? We must talk with her at once!"

Anne accepted the newspaper from him to note that a particular item had been marked. It was a blessing she was sitting down, for if not, she would have likely sunk to the floor in a swoon. "This is not possible! Tell me it is a mistake!"

"What is it?" Jemima cried, snatching the paper from Anne's suddenly limp hands in her eagerness to see what had caused such alarums. "Heaven forbid!"

Susan peered over her shoulder, read the item, and gasped. "How terrible!"

"Your uncle has gone beyond the pale with this," Mr. Witherspoon declared with a look of pity for Anne.

"A suit claiming the seduction of his niece? But Lord Rochford has not seduced me!" Anne cried in vexation. "Why would Uncle do this to me? To Lord Rochford? The poor man, to be so ill rewarded for his kindness to me."

"I fear this suit of seduction is brought before the court all too often," Mr. Witherspoon replied dryly. "Most frequently people see it as a means of obtaining easy money. And if a girl has been, er, compromised, they use it as a means of buying her a husband."

Potter ushered Mr. Parker and Miss Metcalf in shortly thereafter, and it was apparent that they had also seen the latest issue of the London *Chronicle*.

"I just read the shocking news. Pray Lord Ellenborough does not handle the suit," Miss Metcalf said to no one in particular.

"Why should Lord Ellenborough, our chief justice at King's Bench, not handle the suit and what suit, may I ask?" Lady Mary quizzed upon sweeping into the room. She greeted her friends rather absently while fixing her gaze upon Jane Metcalf in particular.

"Well, he tried a suit of seduction of this sort and obtained a settlement of a considerable amount of money from the jury for the plaintiff. A truly dreadful amount of money! Lord Eldon tried a similar suit in past years with much the same result. The precedent has been established all too well."

"What I want to know is *why* he is doing this?" Anne demanded quietly.

"Why, who is doing what!" Lady Mary demanded, looking quite frustrated, her glance darting from one to another.

"Uncle Cosmo is reported to have instituted a suit of seduction against Lord Rochford. He is claiming the loss of his niece—me—as a potential bride to a peer and a loss of planned income to my uncle and aunt. It says he insists that a reliable witness saw his lordship leaving his aunt's house early in the morning—actually, around ten of the clock—and improper behavior occurred even at the doorway."

"Did it?" Jemima eagerly asked, before she realized how she sounded. She looked abashed and retreated in her chair, hands folded, face meek, but with eyes agleam.

"Only what Hortense Finch imagined she saw when Lord Rochford was leaving the house and I said a proper good-bye to him, thanking him for his assistance in finding me a refuge from my uncle." Anne omitted the kiss on the hand. For some reason she did not wish to bring that bit out at this moment. It had been precious to her, and to discuss it before one and all seemed ill-bred.

"He brought me here early, and we discussed matters over breakfast. Lady Mary was most gracious regarding her early morning guest," Anne said quietly, ignoring that she had been alone with the earl for much of that time.

"Nothing improper has occurred in this house," Lady Mary stated firmly. Then, after a glance at Anne, she turned to the young ladies and added, "Do you girls plan to attend the Eldon ball this evening? I imagine you intend to rest so as to look your very best. You know what a crush their balls are. Everyone who is anyone attends."

Such a delicate hint was caught at once. With understanding looks and softly worded encouragement, Jemima and Susan said good-bye to Anne. They left the house with many backward glances and much whispering.

"I fear that does not help my cause, ma'am," Anne said quietly. "They may assume the worst and then tell their mothers, who will of course tell their best friends who will tell their best friends, ad infinitum."

"If that is the case, you are well rid of the girls," Lady Mary said with a sympathetic look at her guest.

Mr. Witherspoon sat down on the sofa beside Anne, patting her gently on the hand as he gave her a sad look. "I fear the coming days and weeks will not be easy for you, my child. If you go out and about, you will be the recipient of stares and speculation. It will be assumed that Lord Rochford had his way with you and you are now a debauched woman. Never mind that nothing happened between you."

"And," Miss Metcalf continued, "be prepared for men to make improper advances to you, calculating that you will be fair game for dalliance."

"Yet I cannot hide here as though I were guilty of some crime—which I did *not* commit!" Anne wailed.

"Bravo!" came a familiar voice from the doorway. Lord Rochford entered the drawing room, looking grimmer than Anne had ever seen him. "I take it you have seen the morning papers? The suit is reported everywhere." He turned to Anne and added, "Your two friends looked at me as though I had suddenly sprouted horns and a beard."

"Then they are no longer welcome in this house," Anne firmly declared.

"Take care, my dear," Lady Mary inserted. "We may need them after all."

"What is now to be discussed will not leave this room," Lord Rochford said with a look at all assembled. "If you do not wish to be a party to this, I will understand if you leave now."

Miss Metcalf rose, offering her hand to Lady Mary. "I am all sympathy my dears. If I do not hear anything of the plans and am questioned, I can in all honesty say I do not know a thing about the matter. I trust you will understand. I wish you only the best."

"I understand," Lady Mary replied, looking almost as grim as her nephew.

Mr. Parker rose and escorted Miss Metcalf from the house after claiming that as a Canadian he had no right to hear a word of what was to be said.

"I had thought better of him," Lady Mary mused softly. "Jane as well." She sank down upon the sofa on the other side of Anne.

"There is nothing like a scandal to show who your true friends are," Lord Rochford pointed out.

"Well, you know you can count on me to help in any way possible," Mr. Witherspoon vowed. His voice gruff with his feelings, he again turned to Anne. "We shall help you out of this ordeal, my girl. All will come about in the end, you'll see."

"I am not the only one affected. Lord Rochford is as well— to an even greater degree!" Anne turned an anguished look at him.

"I believe under the circumstances that we may use our Christian names. There was not the slightest hint of this action before today, was there?" Justin looked at Anne for confirmation of his belief.

"None. I cannot imagine who would encourage my uncle to do such a despicable thing." Anne searched the faces of the other three to see if they had any knowledge to offer.

"Alington," Mr. Witherspoon said quietly. "It is the sort of thing that would appeal to him. If he cannot have you, he wants you destroyed for anyone else. And under normal circumstances such a suit would destroy the reputation and standing of a girl."

"Never mind that probably half the English brides are in the family way on the day of their marriage," Lady Mary said bitterly.

Anne gave her ladyship a wide-eyed look, not having heard such things before in her life. "Oh, my!"

"Forget that I said that," Lady Mary said in disgust. "It is true, nonetheless. The court now sees itself as the guardian of public morality, and your uncle's barrister will claim his home and family have been dishonored. But who knows what he would permit? I read of a case where a mother abetted an affair by allowing a man into her daughter's bedroom for hours at a time, then sued him later when, well, you see what I mean," she concluded hastily with a dismayed look at Anne.

"I fear there is a great deal that Anne will learn in the coming weeks that she might rather have omitted from her education," Justin said wryly.

"While the suit is bad for me, I fear it is worse for you," Anne replied. "What can be done?"

"The first thing will be to attend the Eldon ball this evening. He was a previous High Court judge and as such will be fully conversant with the problems involved. I wonder how he will feel when it is one of his own friends unjustly accused?" Lady Mary mused.

"Do you think we will be welcome?" Anne wondered. "I would die of embarrassment were I denied entry at the door."

"You have a point there. What think you, Justin?"

"Perhaps our good friend here can do a bit of mousing about for us?" Justin turned to Giles Witherspoon.

"I shall stop by and have a brief chat with Lady Eldon," Mr. Witherspoon said with a wink at Anne. "I, er, know things about most everyone in Society, you see. There is not one soul in this Town who can cast stones at another without his or her own guilt behind him as it were. I'd not do this for just anyone."

So saying, he rose and charged off in the business at hand with the blessings of all ringing in his ears.

"Well, Justin, are you prepared for the coming evening? The Prince will attend, I imagine. Will he cut you?" Lady Mary inquired, hands tightly clasped in her lap revealing her tension.

"I do not believe he will. For one thing, I managed to alert him to the likelihood of a problem developing for Anne, although I admitted I did not know what form it would assume. *Now* he will know. I also strongly hinted that Alington would probably be behind any predicament that popped up in the near future. That future has arrived." Justin looked from Anne to his aunt.

"Trust Giles to work his magic with Lady Eldon," Lady Mary said, referring to Mr. Witherspoon with more informality than ever before. "We shan't be turned away this evening," she concluded with conviction, rising from the sofa to take a step toward the door.

"Come, Anne. We had better plan our wardrobe with greater care than usual. Justin," she said, pausing in the doorway, "I shall allow you a few minutes to discuss this with Anne. Then I expect her upstairs. We want to present the picture of perfect innocence combined with a dash of outrage at so dastardly a relative." With a grim smile, she left the room, admonishing Anne to follow her soon.

Rising to her feet, Anne held out her hands to Justin. "You cannot know how deeply I regret this. That you should be so ill-treated because you took pity on me! It is outrageous!"

"I could wish Hortense Finch to perdition if it would help any. It is her gossip that fueled your uncle's charges. Without her willingness to testify on his side, there would be nothing more than air to support his case."

"Shall I have to testify?"

"Only if you wish."

"And if I do not?"

"I have overcome worse."

"But in that event the jury might fine you a horrendous sum of money—money that my miserable uncle will use for his gambling. I doubt my aunt would see a penny of it." Anne stepped forward, fighting her tears. "It is so unfair, so wrong. I shall testify on your behalf, you may be sure."

Justin pulled her against him, stroking her back as though to calm a troubled child. "If we stay together, we can fight him."

"Surely the good God in heaven would not permit such a man to win over us?" Anne said, sniffing back a sob.

"Who can tell? Just say your prayers and follow Aunt Mary in this. She is a very wise woman."

"Shocking at times, as well," Anne said with a laugh that was half sob.

"Remember, I shall be there. Mr. Witherspoon will support us. Sidney will as well," Justin said with less assurance.

"Well, as to that, it depends on what Miss Price has said to her mother. Susan and Mr. Fairfax are, well, quite close at the moment. It is difficult to say if her mother will wish to annoy the man to whom Sidney is heir presumptive. She must know it is possible for you to alter that situation by changing your will?"

"Clever girl. I imagine he will be there and with Miss Price, I make no doubt. Are you prepared to face the firing squad? That is what it will be like. You will be stared at, gossiped about. Conjecture will swirl about you whatever you do, wher-ever you go, whomever you may speak with. Do not be surprised if there are people who give you the cut direct. Scandal is something that mothers with marriageable daughters seek to avoid at all costs."

"Goodness," Anne whispered.

"I fear goodness has little to do with it," Justin said, allowing himself to hold fast to Anne a few more seconds. Then he released her and walked with her to the landing, where he saw her on her way up the stairs to the bedroom floor.

When her skirts had disappeared around the corner at the top, Justin slowly made his way to the ground floor. After absently nodding to Potter, he stopped. Looking at the butler, who had so faithfully served Aunt Mary for many years, Justin said, "There is trouble brewing, Potter. I trust you to protect my aunt and Miss Anne from those who seek to harm them. Alert the rest of the household. No gossip, however trivial, is to be passed on by anyone employed here."

Obviously impressed by the dependence on his reliability, Potter assured Justin that he would do all that was necessary.

"We knew something was up, milord. Then I saw the papers today. May I offer my support, sir? May your innocence in the case be proven beyond a doubt."

Justin thanked the older man, then went on his way, wondering how he would fare this evening. Or Anne. His aunt he knew would sail through the scandal without a quiver.

It had been disquieting when Miss Metcalf and Edmund Parker had bowed out. Yet perhaps it was just as well, for Miss Metcalf spoke truly—what she didn't know she couldn't repeat, and she could claim ignorance of any plans with perfect honesty, as she said.

As for Parker, Justin was puzzled at his behavior. He had seemed almost too eager to escort Miss Metcalf for someone who was supposed to be nursing a *tendre* for Aunt Mary. Not wishing his aunt to suffer again, Justin wondered how best to handle the matter.

Yet it was with a faintly lighter heart that Justin returned to his town house. Aunt Mary would see to it that Anne did not stumble. And as for Anne, well, she had shown a fortitude that would do her well. He couldn't help but admire her for it.

*   *   *

When Anne faced Lady Mary before their departure for the Eldon ball, she nervously fingered the delicately embroidered pale blue glacé silk of the skirt. The fabric gleamed softly over a slip of cream satin. The neckline was higher than was being worn at the moment, but that was to the good. It was the most demure gown she had acquired from Madame Clotilde.

"Turn around. I see you wear your pearls. Good. A fan?" Lady Mary looked at the simple botanical fan with the delicate tracery of flowers and leaves and nodded her approval. "Very nice. Gloves spotless? Slippers comfortable? We do not want you to feel them pinch, then have you grimace as a result. Someone might think you make a face at something else entirely."

"I am as fine as I shall be, my lady. Besides, all eyes will turn to you, for you look beautiful."

Lady Mary smiled, murmuring her appreciation for the compliment, aware her plum sarcenet was the latest style. She nodded toward the door. "It is time to go."

Anne felt as though she were on her way to a hanging, not a ball.

Mr. Witherspoon met them outside the Eldon mansion, wearing a more genial look than usually sat on his kind face.

"You look pleased with yourself," Lady Mary said with obvious curiosity.

"Our way is paved. Seems Lord Eldon had quite his fill of those suits of seduction while he sat on the bench. I believe we may have a friend there."

"Oh, I hope so," her ladyship muttered in response.

There proved to be no impediment to their progress into the house and up the flight of stairs and corridor that led to the ballroom. At the entrance to the ballroom they all paused while Lady Mary handed over her card of invitation to the major domo. He glanced at it, then announced them to Lord and Lady Eldon as well as the assembled guests.

Soft music drifted across the room from the fine quintet hired for the occasion. Otherwise, the room was remarkably quiet considering how many people were already there. The scent of flowers hung in the air, as did a goodly number of suspended breaths.

"Dear Lady Mary, and Mr. Witherspoon," Lady Eldon gushed.

Then she turned to Anne, who had stood slightly behind the others, feeling shy and frightened. Anne curtsied.

"My dear girl, such a trial your relatives must be to you. Lord Eldon and I understand the situation far better than you can know. I hope that for one evening you may relax, secure in the knowledge that no one in this room will offend you." She glanced about the room as she spoke, exchanging looks with a number of her guests.

Anne suspected that if one person in the room failed to hear those words spoken in ringing accents, someone else would gladly repeat them. It was too delicious, for it presented an opportunity to discuss the latest scandal in the event that someone present had managed to miss the latest *on-dit* of the day.

"You are too kind, my lady," Anne said, then accepted the hand offered to her. Here was one person, and a powerful one, who seemed to be on her side for the moment.

"Well, my dear child, I knew Justin Fairfax before he became Lord Rochford, and there is not a more upright or moral man around," Lord Eldon declared. "He is often teased about being too proper. Your uncle selected the wrong man for his suit."

"Thank you," Anne said, although she suspected her face had turned pink with a blush.

"Ah, an innocent blush if I ever saw one," Lord Eldon said jovially.

Lady Mary and Mr. Witherspoon ushered Anne across the room toward Sidney and Susan.

"Head up, look victorious, my girl. You just won a great battle," Lady Mary murmured softly.

"How are you, Anne?" Susan whispered. "You look amazingly well. That gown is divine, and you look like a saint in it."

"I am so nervous I could scream," Anne whispered back, then turned to Sidney. "It is nice to see you."

"Justin said he would be here as early as he could make it. I believe he intends to join the Prince Regent's group."

Anne closed her eyes a moment, wondering if Justin had lost his senses. What if the Prince refused to listen to him, or ordered him to leave, never to return? The Prince was enormously sensitive to which way the people were inclined. He feared the public's rejection. He had known so much of it, most of that being his own fault, although he would never admit it.

"I trust Lord Rochford will be successful in his efforts," she replied.

Susan nudged Sidney, "Go on, do it."

"Miss Haycroft, would you do me the honor of standing up for the first dance? Seeing as how Justin ain't here, we—that is *I*—thought it would be a good idea."

Anne felt some of her fear recede. Sidney was so amusing with his earnest plea. "You are out to be as proper as your cousin?"

"Will you dance?" he persisted.

"Thank you, I would like that very much," Anne said graciously with a smile to Susan.

Rather than a minuet, the first dance was a cotillion. Lady Mary and Mr. Witherspoon joined Anne and Sidney to make a set.

Anne was conscious of many eyes upon her, watching, looking at her to find flaws, or merely with curiosity. She lifted her chin and moved through the dance with the fluid motion of one who has musical ability.

After that, George Harcourt asked her to dance, followed by Henry Metcalf.

"I am pleased to see my friends from the boating trip here this evening," Anne said during a pause in a country-dance.

"Well, as to that, we don't like your uncle much, and we know both you and Rochford. Just couldn't see either of you behaving in such a manner."

"In spite of what Hortense Finch claims she saw?" Anne asked, a twinkle restored to her eyes.

"It's been my observance that there are times when you think you see what you don't see at all," Henry said seriously as was his wont.

Anne smiled and continued on with the movement of the dance, thinking that although Henry sounded a trifle muddled, she understood him very well, indeed.

Mr. Parker had arrived with Miss Metcalf on his arm, looking fine as fivepence. Miss Metcalf looked like a cat that had walked off with an entire plateful of herring.

"How do you go on?" Miss Metcalf wanted to know of Anne.

"Very well, so far. Lord Rochford is supposed to arrive with His Highness shortly, and we shall see how matters stand then."

"Until then, do me the honor of a dance?" Mr. Parker led Anne onto the floor with a flourish after she nodded her acceptance.

It was evident to everyone present that the charming and quiet Miss Anne Haycroft had solid support from her friends, not to mention Lord and Lady Eldon. It was no small matter to have the sympathy of one who had previously been the Lord Chief Justice of the Kings Bench court. This courtroom was where the suit of seduction would be brought to trial. There was not one person in the room who did not wonder where the sympathies of the present holder of that title lay.

A stir at the door to the ballroom brought the dancers and music to a halt as the major domo announced His Royal Highness, the Prince of Wales. This was shortly followed by the names of those who accompanied the Prince. Justin was among the favored.

Anne had moved with Mr. Parker to the side of the ballroom, figuring that the dance might as well be over. No one could recall where he or she had been anyway before everything stopped for the Prince.

The Prince chatted for a brief time with his host and hostess, then began a slow progress through the room. Anne well knew how concerned he was becoming with propriety. Criticism of his way of life, his spending, his catastrophe of a marriage, not to mention the gossip of his mistresses, had repercussions. He was desirous to have respectability in those around him. She had high hopes that Justin had been able to plead his case successfully to him.

Finally the royal entourage reached the place where Anne and the others waited. She held her breath, seeking Justin's gaze before meeting the intense look from His Highness. She curtsied, then waited.

"Our esteemed friend Lord Rochford has explained what has been printed in the press. One cannot always be pleased with the press," he said with heartfelt tones. "We sympathize with your coming ordeal. It is not pleasant to be called before the court. Fortunately, you have excellent support, as does my friend Rochford. I trust you will prevail."

"Thank you, Your Highness," Anne replied, almost overcome with his words of kindness.

The Prince smiled at her, then moved on to the next group of people.

Anne dared a hesitant smile at Justin to be rewarded with a warm look.

"Justin is being very cautious," Sidney warned, speaking so that only Anne might hear him. "He thought that if you appear as polite friends, it would make your uncle's charges seem silly."

"How true," Anne replied with equal quiet, still watching Justin follow the Prince. Fortunately, everyone else in the room was watching the Prince, so there was nothing unusual in her regard.

At last the Prince indicated he would enjoy watching those assembled resume their dancing. Shortly after that, he set off for the room where the gaming was held. An inveterate gamester, he always enjoyed sampling whatever was available.

"Whew," Susan whispered to Anne. "I'd not have been in your shoes for all the tea in China."

"You did well, child. Now we must remain until His Highness leaves. It would not do to go before then. And do not look for Justin to join us. He will remain with the Prince for the remainder of the evening. We will hear more from him tomorrow," Lady Mary advised. "Shall we have more dancing?"

George Harcourt requested a second dance with Anne, then spent the entire time telling Anne what a beautiful woman Caroline Bonham was.

"I do not see her here this evening," Anne said, thankful she was at least spared that sight.

"Ah, no. She and Lady Eldon are not on best terms," he confessed.

"What a pity. This is a splendid ball," Anne declared, thinking that all of a sudden it was the truth. The ball she had feared had turned out for the best. Now if she could endure the coming days, not to mention deal with her uncle's treachery, all would be well. She hoped.

Chapter Twelve

Justin appeared the following morning about the time Lady Mary and Anne were sitting down to a late breakfast.

"Slugabeds," he derided with apparent good humor.

"How did the Prince behave to you last evening? What did he say when you told him your side of the legal action Mr. Haycroft has instituted against you?" Lady Mary demanded in rapid fire.

"Of course he had read the item in the *Chronicle*. What with having had such bad press himself, he was inclined to be sympathetic to another in the same circumstance," Justin said with a grimace. "Remember that I had already informed him after the levee that there might be trouble, which was to our good. Now he said he was not best pleased to see innocent people pilloried to enhance the pockets of a villain."

"You need not fear to offend me with that description," Anne said at the apologetic glance Justin had given her. "I deem my uncle the worst of villains. He is something that crawled forth from one of Mrs. Radcliffe's Gothic novels."

"Have you seen your solicitor?" Lady Mary inquired, acquainted with the early hours kept by those gentlemen.

"Actually I sent Quinlan a letter yesterday; he sent a reply that was awaiting me when I returned home from the ball. By the way"—the earl turned to Anne—"Mr. Kestell has taken ill. Quinlan will represent you now. When I met with him this morning, we went over the grounds of the suit. He advised we join with a barrister of high repute to take the case before the court."

"Which will be when?" his devoted aunt inquired.

"Quinlan went over similar cases yesterday as soon as the

papers were delivered to him," Justin said evasively. "We do have a problem in that Alington has made no secret of his intent to marry Anne. He bruited it about in the clubs and at social affairs, declaring Haycroft has as good as promised him Anne's hand in marriage."

"In that event I am surprised Lord Alington did not bring a breach of promise against me," Anne said thoughtfully.

"There is almost never a breach of promise suit brought by rich noblemen, my dear," Lady Mary said. "That sort of suit is left to the middling orders. Of course there are those other kind—the men who court the very wealthy widows and when they refuse marriage, sue for breach of promise. But I doubt that would be Alington's style," she concluded wryly.

"One thing in our favor is that both Anne and I have spotless reputations. A judge is apt to look more kindly upon proper souls such as we are," Justin said with a chuckle. "Never have I been so grateful for a reputation of being proper!"

"Proper sounds tedious," Anne said with a half smile. "I cannot think of you as being dull." Especially when she thought of his kisses. They were not boring in the least! He could make her heart race at the touch of his hand. Just to be with him was utterly beguiling.

"Well, that is something good at any rate." He studied Anne for several moments, then continued. "My solicitor, Mr. Quinlan, wants very much to have you testify. Do you think you could? It will be difficult. The other barrister will fire questions at you that may be distasteful, even nasty."

"Well, as long as I tell the truth, I shan't have anything to worry about, shall I?" Anne queried.

"As to that, a clever barrister can so confuse you that you may be willing to swear that black is white. However, my solicitor advised me that he consulted with a friend of his who is a barrister, Sir Oliver Knight, and he suggested we countersue."

"On what grounds?" Lady Mary said doubtfully.

"Defamation of our good names. I am known to be of very proper reputation, as is Anne. Neither of us has had a word of scandal ever attached to us until Hortense Finch had begun her tale. We can institute proceedings against Cosmo Haycroft, Lord Alington, who is a party to all this, and in particular, Hortense Finch. That woman has caused more trouble in this Town than any other one person I can call to mind."

"It is costly to sue—particularly if you lose the case," his aunt reminded him. "I have seen the reports in the newspapers of the settlements given by juries."

"On the other hand, with the current state of the judicial system, not to mention the disposition of the juries, I believe they would be most sympathetic. Particularly with an innocent young women whose uncle seeks to compel her to marry a man she finds abhorrent just for said uncle to line his own pockets at her expense."

"Perhaps if nothing else, it would force Hortense Finch to still her wagging tongue," Lady Mary said with a wry smile. "Besides, since jurists are drawn from those who can own land in London, I'd be surprised if she hasn't caused trouble for several of them one way or another."

"That would be a service to all of London, I fancy," Anne said with an equally calculating look. "I believe we ought to pursue that avenue. Could it not be to our benefit if we are summoned to appear in court for my uncle's case that we avow our innocence by this countersuit?"

"Clever girl," Justin said with admiration. "I instructed my solicitor to request Sir Oliver to proceed with the suit with all speed. I shall see him in a short while. If it becomes necessary for Anne to talk with him as well, I will send a message here. But I believe it best for Anne to avoid company."

"In the meanwhile, since *we* have not received a summons to go anywhere, I believe Anne and I will take a drive in the country," Lady Mary said, her eyes twinkling. "Perhaps we shall even take a picnic. If we are not *here,* we are certainly not at *home* anyway, are we?" she concluded, referring to the afternoon when she usually received callers.

Justin left the house first to see Sir Oliver and discuss the case with him, explore possible avenues, and see what could be done to prove their innocence.

By the time Lady Mary and Anne left the Lower Brook Street house in the careful watch of Potter, the landau had drawn up before the house and they had but to take a few steps into the carriage. The wicker basket with provisions for a picnic for two was already stored in the landau, ready for use. Two maids sat by the basket and a footman sat up with the coachman. They were not to be alone, by any means. But they saw no one they knew on their way through London.

"We shan't go into the parks," Lady Mary decreed. "We shall take a drive far into the country."

And so they did. In the shelter of a stand of trees they enjoyed a picnic, eating what they wished, then handing the rest of the ample contents to the servants for their enjoyment.

A stroll through bucolic lanes, along a picturesque stream, and the simple pleasure of birds and beauty of nature restored their good spirits.

"Perhaps," Lady Mary said with a look at her elegant watch suspended from a gold chain at her neck, "it is safe to return to the house. Potter will have dealt with the curious. We should be able to slip into the house and to our rooms with none the wiser."

Anne had her doubts, but readily agreed. The breeze had turned cool, and it looked to coming on rain. The landau was an agreeable carriage in good weather. It was when the top had to be closed over that the strong smell of the oil used to preserve the leather annoyed one. Indeed, Anne thought it a wonder that it did not render one unconscious with the strength of its smell.

They reached the house on Lower Brook Street without a wetting and without having to put up the top on the landau, most fortunately.

Anne changed out of her spencer and crumpled dress into a simple pink muslin gown with a demure frill at the neck. There were little frills at the wrists as well, and she thought she looked the epitome of a proper young lady. She even had the maid find a modest little cap of cream lace with knots of pink ribbon to cover her hair. If anyone dared to call so late in the afternoon, Anne intended to be ready.

They did have a caller very shortly, but it was one they deemed a friend. Potter ushered Miss Jane Metcalf into the drawing room with a nice show of civility befitting the spinster.

"How does it go?" Jane inquired nervously, glancing to where Anne sat with her hands primly clasped in her lap.

"Well enough, all things considered. Since you did not wish

to know details, I shan't tell you what is afoot at the moment," Lady Mary said with a slight pique.

"Oh, dear, I offended you," Jane said, fiddling with her gloves. "I merely worried about a slip of the tongue, you see. I would not be grouped with Hortense Finch." She gave her old friend a worried look.

"I doubt anyone is sufficiently horrible to be grouped with Hortense Finch," Lady Mary said grimly. "I should never have doubted your loyalty," she added as an apology.

"Well, I have been busy," Jane said simply. "I have called on everyone I could think of to drop my few words. I mentioned how odd I thought it was that the uncle sued someone as respectable as Lord Rochford, who is the epitome of propriety. And then our dear Anne is to be pitied, for imagine living in *that* household! Forgive me, my dear," she added to Anne, "but it seemed necessary to hint that you were fortunate to flee that house to a more agreeable one."

"Indeed, I am," Anne assured her with a smile. "You can say nothing about my aunt and uncle that I have not already thought to myself."

"Good. Mr. Parker also thought it a useful ploy. He accompanied me on the calls, and offered his opinion quite often that poor Lord Rochford was to be pitied having to put up with Mr. Haycroft, not to mention Lord Alington. I discovered that Lord Alington is not the least liked. Since the jury for the trial will have some of the better people on it, you may rest assured the case should go in your favor."

"I cannot help wonder about the gentlemen of the jury," Anne said with a worried frown.

"They should be respectable, being property owners of substance. I expect you will find out soon enough." If Lady Mary was perturbed to know that Mr. Parker had been squiring her friend Jane about town, she did not show her annoyance. But it seemed to Anne the two women had returned to a more amiable footing.

Anne was grateful that when Miss Metcalf left, no others dared to call. The house was in peace.

Justin returned in time for dinner, the later London hour of six-thirty.

"Sir Oliver agreed to go forth with the cases immediately," he reported at once. "I calculate the shorter time your uncle has to build his case the better for us. And we know we are innocent. I have made a rather formidable list of people who are willing to testify on our behalf. All of our servants will, of course. Nothing is private from the servants of the house. I believe I might even have the Prince, but there is the matter of his popularity. I do not think he would set well with the jury."

"I worry about the jury," Anne murmured.

"If you dress as demurely as you are now, I doubt there is a gentleman in all of London who would believe you guilty of what your uncle claims," Justin said with a smile.

"How does the precise wording of the Haycroft suit go, Justin?" Lady Mary wondered.

"Haycroft's solicitor has drawn up a suit containing the gist of his complaints. He claims I persuaded you to leave his house for my aunt's, that I seduced you *here,* and thereby prevented him from fulfilling the contract of marriage he had made with Lord Alington. He also claims that in abandoning his house you deprived him of the money he would have gained in marriage settlements. The suit alleges that I must pay him the vast sum of 5,000 pounds!"

"Good heavens!" Lady Mary cried. "Are fathers ever awarded such sums?"

"Sir Oliver said that usually it is a father demanding reimbursement for the loss of his daughter's earnings when she is in the family way that brings him money. That is usually around 200 pounds." He gave Anne an apologetic look for speaking so plainly.

Anne shrugged, thinking that she had learned far more of life since coming here than ever in the past.

"Dress very plainly, my dear," Lady Mary advised her nephew. "Anne will as well. Simple, demure, neat—that is the thing to wear. One must not appear wealthy!"

"Well, if my uncle has been dipping into my funds, I can scarcely look other than modest!" Anne declared.

"I mentioned that to the barrister, and he intends to bring that forth in the suit," Justin said after Potter had left the room. The conversation had been somewhat disjointed as they had not wished to utter anything of importance while a servant was in the dining room. Yet they all knew that a servant could easily listen at the door if curious about what was going on in the house.

"When is this ordeal to take place?" Anne asked hesitantly. She wished to know, yet she dreaded the answer.

"We have not received a court date at this point. But I stressed it should be soon. Neither of us wish to be living under this cloud." Justin played with his wineglass, looking from his aunt to Anne, both of whom wore worried frowns.

"Oh, I could do violence to that dreadful uncle of mine! Was ever a girl so treated?" Anne cried in vexation.

"Long ago you would have been locked in a tower and given nothing but bread and water until you agreed to your uncle's demands," Justin said with a grimace.

"Actually, I would not be surprised if my uncle and aunt would try the same thing now if it occurred to them."

The sweet course was abandoned; all claiming they had little appetite.

Following dinner, Mr. Witherspoon came to the house, requesting to see all of them.

"I wanted to know what has happened so far, my boy," the elderly gentleman said. "I am not just being curious, you know. I care."

Justin rapidly brought him up to the present on the situation, then awaited his verdict. There were few of any importance in London the older gentleman didn't know.

"I've met Sir Oliver. He seems a fine gentleman and has an excellent reputation as a barrister." Mr. Witherspoon accepted a glass of port, then reclined in a chair, studying Lady Mary, then the others.

"Anne and I will go in for our deposition tomorrow. I imagine any witnesses will be summoned as well. Do you mind being called?" Justin looked at Mr. Witherspoon, then his aunt.

"Not I," she said. "Nor, I fancy, does Giles. You know I would do anything to assist."

"This is all my fault," Anne stated in a flat voice. "Had I not accepted your kind invitation for help, none of you would be in this position." She took a handkerchief from her reticule and dabbed at her eyes and blew her nose.

"Now, now. That is all water under the bridge. We could never stand by and see you forced to marry such a one as Alington," Lady Mary said, her sentiments echoed by the others.

Mr. Witherspoon set down his empty glass. "'Tis drawing late. I had best go. Oh, before I do, I must tell you that my Canadian friend has come from Yorkshire. I sent him a letter inquiring about Mr. Parker. I trust my instituting a query will not upset you, but I have for some time been concerned about Parker. I'd not see you hurt, madam," he said to Lady Mary.

"Thank you, Giles. I would know all about Mr. Parker. Everything you may find out."

With a nod, Mr. Witherspoon bade them good night and left. Justin followed him shortly, after he informed Anne as to when he would come for her the following day.

The two women listened to the door close with a thud, then Potter locking up, closing the shutters on the windows below before coming to close the ones on the upper floor.

"Good night, my dear," Lady Mary said to Anne, offering a hand in comfort. "Try not to worry." She went on her way, leaving Anne to follow.

Anne paused before going to her room. Turning to Potter, she said, "You will be asked to give testimony in the law suit my uncle has instituted against Lord Rochford. My uncle claims that Lord Rochford seduced me while I have been living here."

The elderly, dignified butler bowed. "I am aware of the lawsuit and never heard such nonsense. And the two of you as proper as can be. Nothing would ever be learned peeping through your keyholes!" He nodded and continued about his nightly tasks.

Anne smiled grimly to herself. It was well known that servants tended to peep through the large keyholes that existed on most doors if they thought there might be something of interest afoot. No person could be assured of privacy in a London house, or anywhere, for that matter.

It was small comfort, yet it helped, to know that the servants would support the assertion that nothing untoward had happened in this house.

*   *   *

Anne dressed with great care for the deposition. She knew that no jury would be present, yet she felt it necessary at all times to offer the most modest of aspects.

"Will I do?" she asked Lord Rochford when he came to fetch her.

"Admirably. You look like a candidate for a nunnery!" His grin took any sting from his words.

"Will it be deemed improper if we drive there together? I'd not wish to have you compromised by my presence." Anne laced her fingers together, noting the fine weave of the glove fabric and the long time it took Justin to reply to her question.

"I believe we shall be all right. I doubt there will be any witnesses in the precincts of the Inn of the Court at this hour of the day. Is your uncle given to rising early?"

"Not usually." Anne sat in petrified silence the entire drive. She reluctantly left the carriage for the chambers of the barrister where the evidence was to be gathered. "I do not know if I can proceed with this. I am very frightened."

"It will not be as bad as you fear. I shall go first if you like."

But that was not to be. Within minutes of their arrival Anne found herself facing two strangers and a clerk whose job it was to take down what was said. Justin remained in the other room, and she was alone. Neither of the men allowed any feelings to show on their faces as they began to question Anne.

With a firm voice, Anne spoke. "I was not seduced by Lord Rochford at his aunt's house, nor at any other place. He was merely being kind to me. My uncle is a gambler. I did not wish to be part of any payment for his debts."

They questioned her, not harshly, but not gently, either. At last they permitted her to leave. Anne passed Justin on his way to take her place, and she grimaced.

"You survived. How did it go?"

"I told them nothing but the truth," she replied simply.

"Anne, when this is all over—" he began before he was cut off by the clerk, who summoned him to the other room.

Anne sank onto a wooden chair with a sense of relief and a devout wish she might be far, far away from London. What would happen were she to disappear? If she fled to some distant place? Likely poor Lord Rochford would be pronounced guilty and have to pay her uncle a horrendous sum of money.

She reflected on all that had happened, on what Hortense Finch thought she observed and how she had embroidered on it until there was scarcely a scrap of truth left to her observation. Then, there were her feelings for Lord Rochford. They had undergone a significant change. From her original admiration she had come to love him for the many fine qualities that had emerged, not merely because he was handsome and could turn her insides to jelly with a touch. This he did all too often.

Finally, Lord Rochford came from the room along with one of the men. "This is Sir Oliver, who will be our barrister for the cases. Relax, Miss Haycroft, he believes you and I are innocent of all charges." Justin ushered Anne from the chambers and down the steps with Sir Oliver right behind them.

"Would you have accepted the case if we were guilty?" Anne wondered when they left the building.

"Indeed, miss, but I would have charged a much higher fee," the gentleman said with a wicked grin.

"I see. Then I am very glad we are innocent," she declared with her own smile lighting her remarkable blue eyes.

"You are both dressed appropriately. See that you continue to do so. May I offer you a ride to Lady Mary's house, Miss Haycroft? It would be better if you were not seen with Lord Rochford."

"Of course," Anne replied instantly with a regretful look at Justin. "I worried about that on the way over here. Henceforth, perhaps it would be better if I have a hackney take me where I must go?"

"Perhaps—" the barrister began, to be interrupted by Justin.

"I shall arrange with Lady Mary's coachman that he will bring you wherever you must go. We cannot take any chances that Alington or your uncle might yet succeed in abducting you."

"Is it that grave, then?" Sir Oliver asked in astonishment.

"It is," Justin grimly replied. "She dare not be on her own for a moment."

Anne drove off with Sir Oliver, wishing she might look back at Justin, but not daring so bold an action. "I am grateful for your help, sir. Poor Lord Rochford, how ill paid he is for offering me nothing but pity and kindness."

"There was nothing else?"

Anne thought to the kiss and decided she must tell him. What if somewhere there was someone who had witnessed that innocent kiss and would now come forward to testify against him?

"When we first met in the church, he felt sorry for me and kissed me. There was nothing unpleasant about it, but should someone have seen him, it might be used against him."

"Hm," Sir Oliver murmured quietly, "an innocent kiss?"

"Well, I'd fallen asleep, and he gave me a kiss on my cheek, for I'd been crying and he pitied me. When I came to, I was about to scream out and he kissed me truly—to keep me quiet, I suppose."

"A most effective means, I am certain," Sir Oliver said with that wicked gleam in his eyes again.

"I believe you are right, sir," Anne said with a gleam in her own eyes. "I was quite silenced."

They had reached Lady Mary's house, and Sir Oliver assisted her from his carriage with a gentle hand. "I would see your hostess, if I may?"

"I should think she would agree to that, sir," Anne said, taking him with her into the house. She gave Potter a look, then inquired as to the whereabouts of his mistress.

"Awaiting you in the drawing room, miss. Shall I announce you and your guest?"

"No, do not bother. I shall introduce Sir Oliver to her myself."

Anne felt comfortable with the tall gentleman at her side and was surprised, given how stern he had been when he had questioned her at his chambers. They entered the drawing room together to find Lady Mary with a book in her hand.

"I have tried to read, but it was hopeless. How did it go, my dear?" She looked from Anne to the man at her side, a question in her eyes.

"This is our barrister, Sir Oliver Knight. You heard Lord Rochford mention him yesterday."

Lady Mary gestured to a chair, urging him to be seated. Anne poured a glass of canary for the barrister, then joined her hostess on the sofa.

They chatted a few minutes about the weather before Sir Oliver said, "I believe you must testify on behalf of your nephew. I was uncertain at first, but you have an air about you, madam, that is formidable. You will hold your own very nicely, I believe."

Gratified by this praise, yet appalled that she must go into the court to testify, Lady Mary asked some questions before the gentleman begged to be excused and departed.

They were quietly seated, with Anne explaining all that had occurred, when Mr. Witherspoon huffed his way into the drawing room.

"Good heavens, Giles, what is the matter? You look most alarmed!" Lady Mary cried in dismay.

"My friend from Canada. Recall I wrote him about Mr. Edmund Parker?" he asked Lady Mary.

"Indeed, I do. Did you learn anything we didn't know before?" she queried in return.

"The man is already married! If a woman were to wed him, he would be a bigamist!"

"But how can this be?" Lady Mary demanded, her face pale, yet determined.

"Parker insists the marriage in Canada is not legal. He says the woman used fraudulent means to trick him into marrying her. But my friend says that is not the truth of the matter. He claims that Parker needs money and is here to bilk a rich woman. Once he is out of the country with her and her money, there's nothing she will be able to do!"

Anne shifted until she was sitting close to her ladyship and took an icy hand in hers to offer comfort.

"How do we learn the truth of the matter?" Lady Mary wondered aloud. "He is very smooth, glib almost. Can we trust the man we knew as a boy, simply because we knew him as a boy?"

"That is for you to say, dear lady. I thought you would wish to know at once."

"Indeed. He was out with Miss Metcalf paying calls, you know." Lady Mary raised her brows, giving her old friend an arch look.

"I am aware of that, yes," Mr. Witherspoon answered quietly.

"How is it you seem to know everything?" Lady Mary cried in frustration.

"Oh, yes, there are one or two things I do not know that I would like to know. Perhaps they will be revealed in time, however. I have high hopes of it," he said simply with a curious expression that Anne observed but she doubted if Lady Mary did, occupied as she was in staring at the book on her lap.

He left soon after that. His departure made the room seem terribly empty.

"I miss Giles when he goes, you know," Lady Mary murmured. "He has been a good friend for many years. I would hate to lose that friendship."

"Indeed, ma'am," Anne said in reply, wondering why Lady Mary thought the friendship was in danger.

Chapter Thirteen

There was little time to consider the matter of Mr. Parker and his supposed Canadian wife in the following days. Lady Mary may have fretted over the matter of Mr. Parker, but as nothing was forthcoming from Mr. Witherspoon, and nothing was seen of Mr. Parker, there was not a great deal she might do. And at any rate, the two lawsuits that had been filed were far more absorbing.

Common law, contrary to canon law, was satisfied with only one witness. Hortense Finch gloried in being the sole person who supposedly had observed the crime in action, so to speak. Naturally she did not claim to have actually witnessed the so-called seduction, but she had seen quite enough to make it plausible! Or so she insisted.

However, Sir Oliver Knight, the barrister employed by Lord Rochford, took depositions from all the servants in Lady Mary's household, collecting the statements one by one into a veritable onslaught of testimony to the propriety of both Miss Haycroft and Lord Rochford. As Anne had behaved most correctly at all times, and as there was rarely a moment when at least one servant was not around, their accumulated testimony was impressive.

Lady Mary's sworn statement held not only the strength of a member of a very old family known for its respectability, but her personal reputation for veracity was unassailable. She had never been known to be a gossip, and so all could swear.

Mr. Witherspoon, as a confidant of the family and frequent caller to the house, was also called upon to give his attention to the character of the couple. Since Giles Witherspoon was everywhere known and much liked—in spite of his somewhat testy disposition—his word was greatly respected.

It was some days later Anne came down to breakfast to find Lord Rochford seated at the breakfast table with his aunt deep in a discussion.

"My dear, Justin has good news for us. Rather than dragging on for weeks or months, the barrister has managed to have the defamation suit brought before the court this week. I should not be surprised if Lord Eldon had something to do with our advanced hearing date. He was most sympathetic and still dabbles in the law, I understand. I suppose that fills you with apprehension, but Sir Oliver thought the sooner, the better. It would be intolerable for all of us to live under this cloud for long."

"I think it to our benefit that we have *our* case heard first," Lord Rochford added with a concerned look at Anne's pale face.

In the looking glass that hung above the sideboard she could see that she strongly resembled a ghost. Well, she thought, shock sometimes did that. She slid onto a chair, deciding it best to be seated when discussing things of this nature.

"I agree. And when does the other suit, the one for the supposed seduction go to court?" she inquired, her small appetite utterly gone at hearing the news.

"We have not heard anything as yet," Lord Rochford said. "But as to the first trial, Sir Oliver is bringing it forth as an action against your uncle. We claim he holds us up to ridicule, and in particular impugns my integrity and reputation by his suit of seduction. Your uncle or his counsel will be required to set out the facts—not hearsay. What that does to Miss Finch's testimony you can imagine. She can only testify to that which she actually saw. And Sir Oliver will quiz her most carefully regarding that kiss on the hand that she thought so reprehensible."

"That you should be put to this expense for so little a thing!" his aunt exclaimed.

Anne looked down at the table. How crude that the charming kiss bestowed so lightly on her hand should be vilified. Actually, it was not the kiss that had set her heart racing—it was the look from his dark eyes!

"Well, Miss Finch has slandered nearly everyone in the *ton* at one time or another. I doubt she will find much genuine sympathy on her side," his lordship said. He took a swallow of his cooling coffee, then looked to his aunt.

"I cannot find it in my heart to feel the slightest pity for her," Lady Mary said over her teacup. "Not after all the trouble she has caused us!"

It was agreed that they would attempt to go on as usual in spite of the coming trial. Anne thought it impossible, but Lady Mary was indomitable and not about to be reduced to hiding in her bedroom. They took the air in the park, and it seemed that no one of importance snubbed them. Indeed, Anne thought Lady Mary handled everyone superbly, even the most intrusive of questioners.

Miss Metcalf came for tea, but was most subdued. Perhaps she felt pity for them regarding the coming trial, but she avoided talking about it. And perhaps that was for the best.

Anne was pleased that Lady Mary appeared to have forgiven her old friend for her association with Mr. Parker. Of course Lady Mary's emotions might be based upon the assertion that he was married. He had not mentioned a wife, only that he had a list of things to buy for someone in Canada. Should he not have divulged his married status at that time?

It seemed to Anne that Lady Mary had entertained more than a slight fondness for Mr. Parker. She had revealed a touch of jealousy when he escorted Jane Metcalf about, in spite of Jane's naiveté regarding the matter.

Anne wondered at Mr. Witherspoon's delay in placing charges against Mr. Parker—not legal ones, but private accusations. When she asked him about it, Mr. Witherspoon declared he wanted corroboration from at least one or two more sources. After seeing what a false charge could do to a person, he wished to be supremely cautious.

Anne and Lord Rochford met several times with the barrister in his chambers to go over what might be asked, what ought to be said, what might be expected. After each meeting, Anne went back to Lower Brook Street in Lady Mary's carriage, while Lord Rochford went his own way. With each meeting Anne grew more nervous, her apprehensions assuming the guise of living a nightmare. It might have calmed her fears had she been able to speak with Lord Rochford and be reassured by him.

But they had no time together, as they had before. Anne missed conversation with him, and above all, missed looking at him. She found comfort and reassurance in him.

Justin was seldom seen in Lower Brook Street, for he was quite preoccupied with the trial. Friends sought him out to advise him and to tell him of Alington's latest wild talk. And there was no staying at home. Rochford went everywhere, noting his popularity had not declined. A few mothers, high sticklers of the snobbish sort, kept their precious girls away from his presence. But on the whole, he was not disheartened. He missed seeing Anne, but had deemed it politic to avoid being in her company. He felt, as did Sir Oliver, that being seen with Anne added fuel to the fires of gossip. If he went with others, like the beautiful Miss Bonham, he would be free of that censure.

What he did not reckon with is that the word came back to Anne that he was squiring Caroline Bonham about Town again, and that it appeared he was quite in her pocket.

Anne felt as though she were the one who was being shunned because of all the slanderous talk. He clearly avoided her as a result of the gossip. And hadn't Sir Oliver told her that the main reason one could institute a suit of defamation was because the victim had been shunned by others, ridiculed, and so forth? She might not have been ridiculed, but it seemed Lord Rochford wanted nothing to do with her. Perhaps he felt a stigma from this dreadful scandal? And so her muddled thoughts went round and round.

At last the day came when Anne was to appear in court. She had gone to Westminster Hall the day before so she would be somewhat acquainted with the conduct and proceedings of the court. It appeared much the same today, with a slight rearrangement of people here and there.

Beneath the lofty ceiling of the Court of King's Bench, Judge Ellenborough sat behind a relatively narrow wooden stand, his elaborate wig looking hot and uncomfortable. Behind him hung a tapestry with a lion and unicorn rampant in the design. Immediately below him sat a number of clerks, wearing black robes and white wigs, although not quite as elaborate as the one worn by the judge. Opposite the judge, beyond the floor of the chamber, a vast number of gentlemen also garbed in black robes and wearing those pompous white wigs ranged behind a wooden barrier. They could be seen talking to one another, some reading papers, or in one case, snoozing. A few were actually paying attention to the testimony.

To the left side of the room was the panel of twelve jurors. They appeared to be moderately prosperous gentlemen, and their faces gave no clue as to their opinion of the case's merits.

Out in the center of the floor stood Sir Oliver, holding a paper and encouraging his witness to testify.

To her right was the witness stand, where Potter now stood giving testimony regarding his employer's nephew and her guest. Behind him stood or leaned against a wooden barrier other witnesses. Anne was the only woman present other than Lady Mary. Miss Finch was no doubt kept with Uncle Haycroft's witnesses.

Now Anne was to present herself to repeat the information she had given at the deposition. She trembled with apprehension. Going before all those strangers was difficult for a shy young woman. To speak, to answer questions seemed beyond her powers. Yet go, she must.

In the dim recesses of the back of the court she saw her uncle, looking rather serious, standing beside Lord Alington. He as usual appeared somewhat absorbed with the scene before him, intent in his gaze.

Anne was thankful for the distance between them. They could not reach her here.

A man, presumably a clerk of the court, ushered her to the witness stand. There was no sign of Lord Rochford.

Miss Anne Louise Haycroft was duly sworn in to testify. Sir Oliver led her through the embarrassment that had occurred as a result of Miss Hortense Finch's gossip and defamation of her character. All of the witnesses he had called to this point had testified to her propriety. Her behavior had never before been questioned; indeed she had been set as an example for younger girls to emulate. Yet she'd had to endure public humiliation as a result of Miss Finch's slander. Sir Oliver touched lightly upon the resultant lawsuit brought about by Miss Finch's oft repeated remarks.

Then he inquired about the scene Hortense Finch claimed to have seen.

"Lord Rochford had taken me to his aunt's house since she had offered me shelter. Because we arrived so early, he stayed for breakfast and conversation with his aunt. Upon his departure, I went with him to the front door to again express my thanks for his help. He accepted my thanks and kissed my hand when I offered it in farewell."

"And what time of day was this?" Sir Oliver gently asked.

"It was ten of the clock by the time he departed," Anne replied, conscious that Sir Oliver had instructed her to keep her answers brief and offer no more information than necessary.

"Why did you leave so early in the morning?"

"My uncle informed me that he intended to marry me against my will to Lord Alington as soon as possible. I was afraid of my uncle as well as his lordship. In effect, I ran away and found refuge with Lady Mary."

"And Lord Rochford took you there in his carriage?"

"Indeed, he did."

"He behaved with correctness?"

"Yes," Anne replied with a nod. "He was at all times proper in his behavior to me."

Additional questioning revealed that her uncle had berated Anne for denying him the financial gain that was to be his as a result of the contract of marriage that he had arranged with Lord Alington.

There had been a stir, followed by muted discussion, in the gallery of black-robed gentlemen when Anne had stated under oath that her uncle had intended to compel her to wed Alington against her will. It wasn't all that unusual for a father or guardian to arrange a marriage or for a girl to be unwilling. Nor was the revelation that he wanted the marriage for financial gain deemed reprehensible. It was that the man involved was Lord Alington. Few men would come to his defense. Indeed, although a few gentlemen took note of Mr. Haycroft and Lord Alington at the rear of the courtroom, no one spoke to them.

The questions from the opposing barrister were more easily dealt with than Anne would have expected. He queried her behavior in Lady Mary's house, but as it had already been established that her reputation was spotless and she had acted with modesty, there was little he could imply regarding her behavior.

At last Anne was invited to step down, which she did with weak knees. She went to the back of the area behind the witness stand to watch while Justin was interrogated.

Normally the person directly involved was not permitted to give evidence, but the judge allowed Justin to make an unsworn statement.

Justin Fairfax, Earl of Rochford, presented his statement on his own behalf with a calm, deep voice. He was unshaken in his charge that his character had been vilified, that he had been held up to ridicule, and that there were persons who now avoided him as a result of the slander that had been spoken against him. All that he said confirmed what Anne and the others before her had presented as testimony to his unblemished reputation and the damage to it as a result of the slander of Miss Finch as well as the suit filed by Cosmo Haycroft.

It was then that Hortense Finch was brought to the stand to answer the accusation of slander. Defamation was not an uncommon charge, and cases were often brought to the King's Bench courtroom. That this case involved the worst gossip in all of London who obviously had accused a most proper young lady and a gentleman of the highest repute held special interest for those who watched.

It was doubtful if there was one person in the courtroom who at one time or another had not been the victim of this woman's slanderous tongue. Only Lord Rochford had the temerity to challenge the tattler in court, daring to bring suit against her. Perhaps in other cases there had been an element of truth, so the victim had not dared sue. Miss Finch had attacked the one man and one woman in all of London who were quite innocent of her charges.

Stillness filled the room when Sir Oliver began his questioning. Miss Finch's barrister had merely asked what she had seen and left it at that.

Even the best of barristers would have had a difficult time of it to paint Miss Finch in a charitable light. Few witnesses would testify to her solid character. She fired her servants so often that there was no old retainer to vouch for her. She had no true friends.

Sir Oliver demanded to know precisely what Miss Finch had seen. When she tried to deviate to speculation, he stopped her. "What you say is that you saw Lord Rochford kiss the young lady on the hand. Have you ever been kissed on the hand, Miss Finch?"

Someone chuckled when the spinster admitted she had not.

"Do you consider it a reprehensible act of a depraved man?" He toyed with the quizzing glass he dangled in his hand, tilting his head while he awaited her reply.

Another chuckle was heard when she said "No, it is not."

"Nothing more occurred?" She affirmed this as true.

"So the remainder of your tale was fabrication? You were not witness to a seduction?"

"Well, no, but the early hour!" she said with a flutter of lashes and a shrug of her thin shoulders.

"It has been shown Miss Haycroft feared her uncle for what she considered a good reason. Is it so reprehensible and unreasonable that the gentleman who helped her escape from the unwanted marriage to Lord Alington would collect her quite early in the morning? And that he brought her directly to his aunt's house?"

Miss Finch admitted it was not.

"And is it bad that Miss Haycroft wished to thank the gentleman for his assistance? What would you do, Miss Finch, in like circumstances were a gentleman to help you?"

The spinister admitted she would indeed thank the man.

When she was finally excused from the witness stand, Judge Ellenborough turned to the jurors to give them instructions. "I wish you to consider the conduct of these people, their reputations and character as established by those who know them. Do you believe they are the sort to behave in such a manner as mentioned by a woman who is established as a gossip?" He went on to remind the jurors what else was required to render their verdict, then sent them to the room where they were to deliberate. Since a jury would normally hear several cases in a day, the verdict would be given soon.

Anne left the area where she had listened to Justin and Miss Finch testify for the cool spaciousness of the hall outside the courtroom. Justin followed her, and within minutes Lady Mary and Mr. Witherspoon joined them. Sidney Fairfax appeared, having, unknown to Anne, been present at the rear of the chambers throughout the trial.

"I could not bear to remain in there, knowing that on the other side of that door twelve men were deciding on our reputations," Anne explained. She did not mention her fears regarding the proximity of her uncle and Lord Alington. Surely they would not dare to abduct her within the confines of Westminster Hall? Yet her uncle was brazen, and he wanted this marriage of hers very much.

"After Miss Finch's testimony I have little doubt but that you and Justin will be completely vindicated," Lady Mary declared.

"I wonder what the judgment will be?" Mr. Witherspoon said quietly. "Miss Finch has little money. A monetary award would be of little use if it puts her in bankruptcy."

"Ellenborough indicated he wanted a verdict promptly. He has little patience with juries that take much time in deliberation," Justin said.

Anne edged away from him, standing close to his aunt and Mr. Witherspoon. "I should like to leave London, but I shan't give that woman the satisfaction of thinking she has driven me away," Anne said, looking anywhere but at Lord Rochford.

They could see Miss Finch with her barrister at the other end of the hall, deep in conversation. Where her uncle and Lord Alington were, Anne didn't know. But they had not joined the key witness in the suit of seduction. Perhaps they had remained at the rear of the courtroom to learn the verdict.

Anne was surprised when Sir Oliver came to get them, explaining that the verdict was to be read.

"So soon? It did not take those men very long to decide," she whispered, thinking it could not be good, if it had come so quickly.

Judge Ellenborough appeared very stern, looking first at

Anne and Justin, then at Miss Finch. Therewith he began his reading of the verdict.

"Cosmo Haycroft is hereby ordered to cease and desist any imputations against Lord Rochford." The judge continued by declaring the sum of £2000 be paid to the earl. Judge Ellenborough then impaled Miss Finch with his chilling stare. "The jury finds Miss Hortense Finch, spinster, guilty of defamation. She is ordered to dress in a white gown and pick up small feathers which will be tossed from a pillow casing in the middle of Hyde Park at five in the afternoon at a date to be selected."

At first there was silence. Then a chuckle was heard, followed by another, and within moments laughter rocked the courtroom, with a solemn-faced Judge Ellenborough hammering his gavel to regain silence. When at last the room had returned to its more normal stillness and order restored, he spoke once more.

"I believe the accused Miss Finch will find it as difficult to gather small feathers as to recapture the words she has spoken. Once spoken, words cannot be retrieved. I would charge you, Miss Finch, to be very careful what you have to say from this day forward!"

Thus admonished, they were dismissed, and the next case to be heard was summoned before the court.

Anne hurried ahead of the others with Mr. Witherspoon at her side. "Would you please take me back to the house, sir? I have no wish to talk about the case, or that woman. Never mind that she will reap her just deserts. I just want to go away from here."

"Of course. I believe I understand how you feel. Come, I ordered my carriage to stand ready." They waved to the others in farewell.

The others were deep in discussion, with Lord Rochford and Sir Oliver being congratulated by one and all. Of Miss Finch there was no sign.

Mr. Witherspoon took Anne by the elbow and ushered her from Westminster Hall with all dispatch.

Anne doubted very much if Justin had even observed her departure.

Within a brief time they had left Market Street behind and

were heading toward St. James's Park. Anne was conscious that Sidney had come running after them, but kind Mr. Witherspoon paid not the least attention to his call.

"It is good to have that nastiness behind you. I would not be surprised if your uncle would decide to call off his suit of seduction after this trial. After all, he was ordered to cease and desist. And Miss Finch is totally discredited as a witness."

"Ah, yes, Miss Finch," Anne mused. "One could almost have it in the heart to pity her in Hyde Park, garbed in unsuitable, girlish white trying to capture elusive feathers at the height of the fashionable hour. All those carriages of people driving past, the riders observing her from their horses, the strollers who pause to stare at the spinster so foolishly occupied would vex her exceedingly."

"If the case is dropped or settled out of court, you will be free. What will you do then?"

"I am not sure. It would be best if I leave Lady Mary's household. She has been more than generous and gracious to one who has brought terrible expense and near disaster to her dearest nephew."

"Where would you go?" he inquired gently.

"I have some cousins here and there. Perhaps I can go to one of them for a time." Anne wondered if she even had the direction of any of them. The only one she had been in contact with was the cousin in South Yorkshire.

"I do appreciate your friendship, Mr. Witherspoon. I trust that all will be resolved for you and Lady Mary in due time."

"So . . . you believe there is something to resolve?"

"Indeed so," Anne shot back, somewhat recovered now from her ordeal in the courtroom. "She remarked that she was very lonely when you were not there."

"Is that so?" the good gentleman asked. "Perhaps there is hope for me yet?"

"I would suggest that if there is someone you want that you do not dawdle. If you are truly partial to Lady Mary, go about making her yours without delay." Anne gave him a shy smile, aware she had stepped out of line a trifle, but wishing with all her heart that the two people she had come to love would find happiness together.

"I see," Mr. Witherspoon said slowly. He left St. James's Park to drive through Green Park at a moderate pace before continuing to Lower Brook Street.

When he brought the carriage to a halt before Lady Mary's house, he turned to Anne and said, "You have given me much to think about. I shall leave you now, but I will return later. I expect there will be some sort of celebratory dinner party or something of that sort."

"And I shall be there to encourage if you wish."

"I suspect I shall need all I may receive," he replied with a chuckle.

It was a broadly smiling Potter who opened the door to Anne. "We did it, did we not, Miss Anne? They are all up there awaiting you. It is champagne today!"

"Thank you, Potter." Anne trod the steps with lagging feet, then entered the drawing room with a pleasant smile pasted to her face. Never would she allow her inner feelings to show.

"Anne, where is Giles? He must join us as well," Lady Mary cried, looking behind Anne to see if her friend was there.

"He will return later, perhaps this evening." Anne gave no other explanation for, indeed, she didn't know of one.

That Lady Mary was disappointed was evident. Miss Metcalf had joined the group as had Mr. Parker. Justin—Lord Rochford—stood with Sidney, probably discussing the case in detail.

Potter carried in champagne brought from Justin's cellars. Anne sipped from her glass, looking across to the man she had come to love. How hopeless was her passion. She had been nothing but grief to the man. Doubtless he'd hope she would go away soon and he could be rid of her and her problems. She owed him a great debt of gratitude, beyond anything she could ever repay. That was scarcely a basis for anything romantic!

"Anne, come here, my dear. May I tell you how well you did on the stand?" Lady Mary said.

"You are all graciousness, ma'am," Anne said with a smile. She truly loved this woman and would be sorry to bid her good-bye. "When one has nothing but the truth to reveal, it is not so difficult. I fancy that I feared coming face-to-face with my uncle more than I did that other barrister!"

They all laughed as she had intended.

"So it is over now," Justin said to Anne. He had crossed the room when she looked elsewhere, and she was startled at his proximity.

"Indeed," she said cautiously. "I pray the other suit will be dropped. Mr. Witherspoon seemed to think it might. With Miss Finch so utterly discredited, they have a greatly diminished case."

"Let us hope this is the end of it all, then."

"I imagine you will think twice before offering help to anyone again?" Anne suggested with a wistful smile.

Justin opened his mouth to reply, but Anne was never to know what his answer would have been.

Mr. Parker commanded attention with a loud "Ahem!" All turned to look. "While we are in a celebratory mood, I have good news to announce. Miss Metcalf has done me the honor of agreeing to be my wife."

Mr. Witherspoon had quietly slipped into the room, standing near the door, unnoticed until now by the others. "That is interesting, considering you have a wife in Canada. Do you intend to be a bigamist, Parker?"

Chapter Fourteen

The room fell silent. The very air seemed to sizzle.

Anne exchanged horrified looks with Lady Mary, who in turn took a step toward her old friend.

Miss Metcalf drew away from her betrothed, turning to face him with a wary gaze. "Can this be true?"

"It is a lie," Mr. Parker said calmly, looking defiantly at the others.

"Would that it were," Mr. Witherspoon said into the deadly quiet of the room. Two men followed him as he entered the drawing room. Mr. Parker appeared to lose some of his confidence as he caught sight of the newcomers.

"Your ladyship, Rochford, Miss Metcalf, Anne, and Sidney, may I present my Canadian friend, Ian Wilmot, and another Canadian, George Farmer. They are both acquainted with Edmund Parker *and* his wife, and are willing to give testimony or proof against Mr. Parker." He gave the bewildered fiancée an apologetic look. "I am sorry to distress you, Miss Metcalf, but is it not better to know now, rather than later? 'Tis a shock, true, but later it could be a disaster."

Jane nodded, seeming confused about the matter.

Anne wondered if the spinster would rather have known a brief time of marriage than to face the rest of her life alone, knowing she had been wooed for her money by one who was no more than an opportunist and a fraud.

"You are right, as usual, Mr. Witherspoon." She drew off the dainty ring Edmund Parker had given her and handed it back to a speechless Mr. Parker. "Please leave now. I do not think I can bear to see your face any longer." Miss Metcalf turned toward Lady Mary, holding out her hand in a gesture of supplication.

Instantly, her old friend was at her side, giving Mr. Parker the most haughty of frowns. "Good-bye, sir. I trust we shall not meet again."

Mr. Witherspoon pointedly stood aside from the doorway, gesturing toward it somewhat theatrically. "Be gone, knave. To prey on ladies of quality who have no one to protect their interests is lower than a slug."

There was little Mr. Parker could do in the face of such total opposition. He lifted his chin and strode out of the room with the appearance of great indignation.

"What a debt I owe you, Mr. Witherspoon," Miss Metcalf said hesitantly once Mr. Parker had left. "I might have married that man and traveled with him to Canada only to find a nightmare once I landed."

"*If* you landed, dear lady," Ian Wilmot said with a knowing look. "I have heard stories of English women who depart this country never to reach their destination."

"Once you married him, your newly found fortune would be his," Mr. Witherspoon reminded.

The two Canadians remained at Lady Mary's insistence, chatting with Miss Metcalf, who was of an age with them. They explained something of the irregular marriage that Mr. Parker had entered into with the deaf but very rich Elspeth Jeacock. Apparently she was satisfied to live in the country while Mr. Parker lived in Halifax, continuing on with her father's shipping business. They lived apart, each content, so it seemed.

"Well, it was very cruel of him to so deceive our Jane," Lady Mary stated firmly.

Jane still seemed a trifle dazed by his defection, whereas Lady Mary was roundly indignant.

"Well," Mr. Witherspoon softly said to Anne, "did I do right in bringing those men here? Should I have waited to bring them later?"

"No, it is best that an attachment be cut off as quickly as possible if it is not to be." She darted a look at Lord Rochford, thinking that perhaps it would be good were she to leave this house as soon as possible. Where she might go was a distinct problem. Young women of quality simply did not set up a household of their own, even if they possessed a fortune, albeit a modest one. She could not return to her aunt and uncle. That would be impossible even were she so stupid as to consider such a thing.

"What will you do if and when the suit of seduction against Lord Rochford is dropped?" Mr. Witherspoon inquired. "With Miss Finch so utterly discredited, they will have a difficult time to establish their case. The court requires only one witness for such a lawsuit. Any personal correspondence might also be used as evidence against you." Mr. Witherspoon gave Anne a sharp look. "He never sent you a written message, did he?"

"No, but if someone is as determined as my uncle, it would be possible he could hire a forger." Anne studied the Persian rug at her feet, hating to admit what a scoundrel her relative was, yet knowing nothing was beneath him.

"I said she was clever and she is," Lord Rochford said from behind her, causing Anne to spin about. "You think your uncle may try to forge our writing?" The earl stood looking at her, a quizzical expression on his handsome face.

Anne stared at him a moment, forgetting the problem and her uncle. Justin was so compelling. How was she to live without seeing him, loving him? Her heart ached at the mere thought of living without him. Then she recalled that he awaited her answer. "Indeed, sir. He is a prince of rogues. With him, anything is possible."

"We can only hope his barrister gives him some sound advice in that event. No barrister may bring forth evidence he knows to be false, nor can he assert that which he knows to be a lie. Of course there is the possibility your uncle may make a case by some other means or trickery. On the other hand, perhaps he will drop the suit."

"Mr. Witherspoon thought he might. But . . . what if he does not?"

"Quinlan has been checking into the matter of your funds to see if any illegality has occurred in the transfers and accounts. We could always sue your uncle for fraud." Justin raised his brows at her frown.

"Lawsuits and more lawsuits. I hope I never see the inside of a courtroom again," Anne declared with some vehemence.

"You did well, however. No one would have known you were quaking in your shoes." He grinned at her start of surprise.

"Then how did *you* know?" Anne said, her ire fading.

"Because I quaked in my shoes as well," Justin said simply.

Anne laughed then, a silvery sound of pure delight that brought an answering smile to Justin's lips.

"More champagne?" Justin said, handing her another glass before she could refuse. "It is good for you, and will give you an appetite for dinner. I have noticed that you have eaten very little these past days. That will not do, you know. I personally believe that there will be no need to return to King's Bench Courtroom. Have hope. Rest easy."

Anne smiled at that nonsense. *Rest easy?* How like a man, to suggest she had no more worries now. But it surprised her to learn that he had been watching her. *When?* It seemed to her that whenever she had stolen a look at him, his gaze was elsewhere.

"Of course you cannot return to your aunt and uncle," Mr. Witherspoon inserted, giving voice to Anne's earlier thoughts. "To do so would make all our efforts in vain. He would have you married to Alington in a minute."

"You are right. But there are other options," Anne said quietly, gazing into the depths of her glass as though she might find the solution lurking at the bottom.

"I seem to remember your mentioning a cousin?" Justin asked politely. "He or she does not sound very promising if you have corresponded but infrequently."

"My cousin's name is Penelope Tyler. We are related on my mother's side," Anne added by way of clarification if any were needed. "I feel certain she would give me shelter." Anne knew little of the more distant branch of her family that included Mrs. Drummond-Burrell. She'd not turn to them.

"Well, that is to the good, at any rate," Justin said heartily, tucking that name away in his memory. "But I do not want you to worry on that score. You have friends, and we shall see you safe."

Anne gave him a doubtful look. She had known little help over the years—until she had met Lady Mary and Lord Rochford.

"I believe I shall go home now, dearest Mary," Jane Metcalf said with a rueful look. "I am slightly overset."

"That is small wonder, given the shock you have had. But I do not like it that you go alone. Stay on with us, please. It is no problem to add another person for dinner."

Ian Wilmot quietly spoke then. "My wife would be vexed with me if I and my good friend Mr. Farmer did not serve as escort to the lady whose happiness we served to blight. By the bye, Mr. Farmer is a bachelor gentleman with nary a wife in view, unlike Parker. But I shall see that all is proper, you may be sure," he concluded with a twinkle in his fine gray eyes.

Miss Metcalf looked rather overwhelmed at the idea of two escorts on the short walk to her house on the next street. "Very well," she said when she recaptured her breath. "I should like that exceedingly."

Once she had departed with Mr. Wilmot and Mr. Farmer, Lady Mary sank down on the nearest chair to declare, "Well, I'll be!"

"Indeed, you shall," Mr. Witherspoon. He gave his old friend a fond look.

"And what do you mean by that, sirrah?" she asked in a somewhat arch manner for Lady Mary.

"Well, if you come for a drive in the park with me, you might find out," Mr. Witherspoon said in an amazingly crafty way for one his age.

Lady Mary looked up at him with an arrested expression. "I shall collect my bonnet now," she said as she crossed the room, prepared to fetch her outdoor things at once.

"I will be waiting," Mr. Witherspoon said. He gave a satisfied sigh, then strolled from the drawing room and down the stairs without another word to anyone.

"How extraordinary!" Anne whispered, not wishing Mr. Witherspoon to hear what she said.

"Indeed," Sidney murmured, edging toward the door as though he wanted to confirm with his eyes what his ears had just heard. "I believe I shall walk to Justin's. Walking is supposed to be beneficial, you know."

He quickly disappeared from view, heading down the stairs,

ostensibly to go to Justin's, though it was more likely he wished to see Mr. Witherspoon take up Aunt Mary in his carriage.

Anne knew that although Lady Mary and Mr. Witherspoon had been friends for an age, they had never gone beyond that stage. Lady Mary had once mentioned Giles to be a confirmed bachelor who never intended to marry. Had he perhaps changed his mind—or heart?

"I think the world has turned topsy-turvy," Anne declared as Lady Mary whisked herself down the stairs and from the house.

Potter collected the glasses, then silently departed.

"Everyone has gone," Justin said.

"Yes," Anne replied, retreating a step. She continued to look at him, cherishing the face she would soon have to forget. How difficult it would be to leave here forever.

"I do not want you to go away," he chided. He touched Anne lightly under her chin. "And I believe you are about to flee London the first opportunity you have. Am I right?"

"I cannot remain here forever," she protested.

"I doubt it will be necessary for much longer. Allow your uncle's suit to be concluded one way or another. Then we can talk about what your future is to be." He moved closer to her, intimidating in his nearness.

"I think I know yours," Anne charged with a laugh that sounded forced even to her ears. She toyed with her glass, then set it down on a small table. Bravely, she turned to face him, lifting her chin in a challenging manner.

He took a step closer, then another. "What might that be?"

"I have heard that you are often in Miss Bonham's company. Am I to wish you happy?" Anne said, her mouth dry, wondering if she was to hear news of his engagement to that young lady. Such was her confusion, she forgot all he had said about Miss Bonham before.

"You cannot believe that of me! Surely you can't?" Justin gave her a look of unfeigned amazement. "You must have known I could *not* come to see you, or take you about. It would have given credence to Miss Finch's lies. Even now there is danger for us."

"Danger?" she whispered, finding her throat oddly constricted. One hand flew to her neck in dismay.

"Oh, yes," he murmured. "Because I might do this." He enfolded Anne in his arms. And then he kissed her with far more than the light touch she had known before. When he at last lifted his head to gaze into her eyes, he whispered. "And this." And once again he found her lips. This proved to be longer, sweeter, and more enervating than the previous. "And we might never stop."

Anne was certain her knees had melted and she would never be able to stand alone again. It took every ounce of strength, both of character and of physical, to wrest herself from his arms. "And if a servant saw us or a member of the *ton* walked in, we would both be compromised beyond all hope."

"That would be so terrible?" Justin asked, not allowing her to stray too far from his side.

"You must know it would not do. We have just endured a dreadful ordeal in court. You cannot toss that all away for the sake of some . . ." She could not complete the sentence, for the words would not come.

"Utterly delicious, wonderful kisses?" he concluded for her with a smile.

"Were they?" she said skeptically. Any man who could squire Caroline Bonham around Town just to fool people, Anne thought, might well try to fool herself as well.

"You know they were."

At that moment Potter entered the drawing room, first giving a slight cough. "Sir, there is a man below. A Mr. Quinlan urgently requests to see you."

"How curious. Of course, I shall come down to speak with him at once."

Justin turned to Anne, taking her hand in his to place a lingering kiss on it while gazing deeply into her eyes.

She wore no gloves. The effect of his warm mouth on her tender skin was almost as astonishing as the other kisses he had given her. She failed to snatch her hand away from him as she ought. Like a fool she stood, unable to move.

"I shall see you later. I suspect that Quinlan has news of some import that will require some attention on my part. Tell Aunt Mary I was called away." He glanced at the door to note Potter had gone, and added, "But nothing else."

"You may be certain of that, sirrah!" Anne said with a spark of fire lighting her eyes.

"Ah, blue ice now, I perceive." He flashed a grin at her. "Take care, lest we have a repetition. A man can endure only so much, my heart."

And then he was gone, and could be heard on the stairs. Anne wondered what the admirable Mr. Quinlan knew that required Justin's immediate attention.

She reflected on what had just happened and shook her head. Potter appeared at the door, and Anne turned at the faint sound. "Yes?"

"Is there anything you wish, miss?"

Anne looked up and said, "No, there isn't a thing I want, thank you." Unless, she added mentally, it might be a new brain box, or common sense. Why, with all the people in London, did it have to be Lord Rochford who had paused to help her that day in the church?

Retreating to the peaceful quiet of her room, she sat staring out of the window until sometime later when she heard the sound of Lady Mary's return from her carriage ride. Anne jumped up and dashed down the stairs to the first-floor landing. She said nothing, but watched her hostess most carefully.

"Come into the drawing room with me, Anne. I would talk. Oh, Potter," she said, raising her voice slightly, "tea if you please. On second thought, perhaps a glass of wine would be better."

Curious, Anne followed Lady Mary into the drawing room, crossing to stand by the fireplace. "Well? You have an air of suppressed excitement about you, ma'am. Am I to guess? Or will I hear the news in due time?"

"Naughty girl. I shall tell you all when Potter comes with our wine." She sat on the plum damask sofa with a regal air that became her well. When Potter entered, she ordered him to remain.

"I wish you both to know that Mr. Witherspoon has asked me to be his wife."

"I think that is fine, ma'am," Anne said with a clap of her hands.

"Very good, my lady," was Potter's response.

"I shall need you with me in my new household, Potter. Mr.

Witherspoon said he'd not have it any other way. You have been with me for many years now. I'd not like to accustom myself to another butler."

"I am pleased to go where you go, my lady," the distinguished butler said with a broad smile.

When he had left the room, Lady Mary turned to Anne. "He does not want to wait. Giles wishes to be married as soon as possible. Can you believe that all these years he has been wishing for me, but thought I pined for Edmund Parker? If I had but known. What foolishness we women believe at times," she said absently, looking down into her glass much as Anne had done not so long before.

"That is very true, ma'am. Why, I believed that Lord Rochford was escorting Caroline Bonham around Town because he had an interest in her . . . a particular interest."

"And you discovered that he did not have a . . . particular interest?" Lady Mary said with a shrewd look at her guest.

"Yes," Anne replied, thinking that with all the wine she had drunk this afternoon she was feeling just a tiny bit tipsy.

"Giles will be joining us for dinner," Lady Mary said as though she were still in a dream.

"Oh, dear, I fear I cannot be with you. I am promised to Miss Price for dinner. It was a last-minute invitation to fill in for someone who is ill," Anne said, fabricating as she went. "How fortunate the weather is still so fine. She said something about a picnic."

"I do not like the idea of your going out alone. Either Justin or I ought to be with you." Lady Mary gave Anne a suspicious look, but then turned her thoughts to a menu and within a few minutes Anne escaped to her room.

"A fine kettle of fish you are in now," Anne scolded the image in her looking glass. "Susan is not having a dinner party, nor are you invited on a picnic." Thinking a few moments, she crossed to the little desk by her window to dash off a note to Lord Rochford, explaining her dilemma. If Lady Mary wished her to depend on her nephew, the least Anne could do was to obey!

Potter was only too happy to be of service in dispatching the note to Lady Mary's nephew. "Shall I have the footman wait for a reply?"

Anne paused at the bottom of the stairs, then nodded. "Indeed, I expect that would be best."

It was about thirty minutes later that the footman sought out Anne at the pianoforte, where she practiced with a distinct lack of enthusiasm.

Thanking the young man, Anne broke the seal to unfold the crisp white paper and read. "Ah," she sighed, "he is truly a gallant gentleman to come to my rescue."

Thus it was that Justin came to collect Anne for the impromptu picnic later, intending to inform his aunt of his escort.

"Justin," Lady Mary said with a somewhat rueful expression, as though she expected his amusement, "I am to marry Giles Witherspoon, and soon if he has his way. You do not think me foolish?"

"Never," he replied fondly. "I think it high time you enjoy your life." With an indulgent look, he left the room as Anne reached the landing.

They both wished Lady Mary a pleasant evening with her affianced gentleman.

And so it was that Anne, properly garbed for a late afternoon or early evening picnic, left the house on Lower Brook Street to ride off in Justin's curricle.

"We shall meet Sidney and Miss Price near the park. How far are we supposed to go on this lark of a picnic?" the earl queried with an amused glance at his companion.

"Not far at all. I merely felt that after waiting so long to find each other, Mr. Witherspoon and your aunt ought to have time alone."

"Aha! A romantic, I see." He teased her; she could tell that, yet she didn't mind, for she was too pleased with her little scheme to take anything amiss.

Sidney and Susan awaited them in his curricle, with a similar picnic basket along.

"What a clever idea. I trust you will not be vexed that I suggested Henry Metcalf and Miss Green join us as well?" Sidney asked with a smile.

"Why not?" Justin said dryly. "The object is to surround ourselves with people, is it not?" He looked at Anne while he spoke, his voice amused.

"It is likely the most sensible thing to do, would you not agree?" Anne replied, pleating her blue muslin skirt with suddenly nervous fingers.

"By all means. I'd not be surprised to see the estimable James in attendance." At Anne's rueful look, he laughed. "He is behind us in another carriage."

"I knew your aunt would fuss otherwise. She insists my uncle may still attempt to snatch me away."

"It would assuredly cancel the suit of seduction—if Alington had you, there would be no need to sue. But on the other hand, that may not come about. Mr. Quinlan found some interesting and most curious figures while looking into your funds as well as their dispersal. He will investigate further on your behalf."

Anne sat still for a moment while the others selected a place that would be suitable for their impromptu party. It would be interesting to know precisely what was involved in a seduction. How was a girl supposed to avoid such when she didn't know what it was? Her aunt had said little on the subject, other than for Anne to behave herself.

"Well, I am not certain what all is involved with the suit, but I expect it is one of those things I ought not know."

Justin glanced at her and chuckled. "Remind me to give you a demonstration of it someday."

"It most likely is improper," Anne mused.

"Highly," Justin replied, an inflection in his voice Anne found intriguing.

For an impromptu meal, the various cooks had done splendidly. Cold gammon, salads and rolls, and various other delights to tempt the palate were placed on the checked rug by Sidney and the earl with the airs of conjurors.

"I think having a picnic was a lovely idea," Jemima Green said. She forked a pickled cucumber onto her plate with enthusiasm Anne found delightful.

"Miss Haycroft needed to get away from the house for a time, and this seemed an ideal choice. She has been under a great deal of strain the past days."

"It must have been very difficult for you to testify before Lord Ellenborough and the jury," Susan said with sympathy.

"Actually Uncle Cosmo's barrister was the most troublesome." Anne set her plate down, her meal forgotten for the moment. The memory of the court with the high windows shedding but faint light on the room below returned. The serious, almost hostile, looks from all those severe gentlemen had been most unnerving. Then she picked up her plate again, unwilling to share her woes. "But it is over, and God willing, I shan't have to testify again."

"I think you ought to leave London, go as far away as you can, just to thwart your uncle. If he cannot reach you, he can scarcely force you to marry that man," Susan declared. "Where could you go?"

Anne avoided a direct reply. "It may be necessary for me to leave soon anyway." Anne shared a look with Lord Rochford, wondering just how much she ought to reveal to the rest of the party.

"I believe you refer to my aunt's intentions?" the earl inquired, his gaze friendly.

"I shan't spoil her surprise, but yes, it does involve your aunt."

The place they had chosen was not terribly far from the road. There was little traffic, only a lone carriage dashing along the lane. It looked familiar, but then, there were so many carriages of that type in London. Anne sat up when the vehicle drew to an abrupt halt, the horses rebelling at the sudden stop. "What . . . ?" she wondered with a frown.

"I believe we have a guest." Lord Rochford reached into his basket to withdraw a rather nasty-looking pistol, large and ungainly, but formidable all the same. He partially concealed it with a linen napkin.

Lord Alington approached the group, his pistol in hand, a menacing fellow walking behind him. "Ah, an alfresco supper. How charming! The man I've had watching you was correct— you are indeed in the park. There is little you can do, Rochford, to prevent me from escorting my dear fiancée home to her aunt and uncle. Very soon she shall be mine."

Alington strode across the grass to grasp Anne's arm. He pulled her roughly to her feet.

Not about to go to her doom meekly, Anne struck out at him. "You toad! I'll not go anywhere with you, much less marry you."

"Let her go, Alington," Lord Rochford said in a firm, quiet voice. The gun he had so providently thought to bring along—fearing something of this sort—was now aimed directly at Alington's heart.

"You'd not dare to shoot me," Lord Alington sneered.

"No? You are willing to put me to the test?" The earl eased the trigger a trifle.

Alington pulled Anne against him, using her as a shield. "I do not think you will shoot now. You would hit Miss Haycroft, and that would never do."

He began to back toward his carriage when such a flurry of activity occurred that Anne scarcely knew which way to look.

James, that most excellent and burly footman, attacked Alington's servant, dispatching him with ease, while Sidney and Henry tackled Alington from behind. As he struggled, Justin plucked Anne from Alington's side with dispatch, safely away from the wicked gun. Then he assisted in completing the job of escorting the two men to their carriage. What threats were issued could not be heard by the girls, but the menace in Lord Rochford's voice was unmistakable.

Anne had willingly hid behind the solid and comforting figure of the earl to watch her enemy thwarted. Once she saw Lord Alington being led away, she breathed a sigh of relief and retreated.

Susan and Jemima had prudently hidden behind the shelter of a large oak. Now they ventured to Anne's side, silently watching with huge eyes while the carriage disappeared down the road.

"My," said the prosaic Susan, "this is far better than seeing Mrs. Radcliffe's drama on the stage."

"Mr. Fairfax and Mr. Metcalf were exceedingly brave," Jemima said breathlessly.

"Do not forget how the earl dared to aim that gun straight at the villain," Susan added. "He is like the hero in the play."

Anne was beyond speech at this point. Justin might have behaved like a hero, but they had all been in great danger, one way or another. It seemed to her that as soon as the lawsuit was over, she *must* disappear. No one was safe until then.

All thought of eating had fled. The remains of the supper was quickly gathered, the three carriages loaded with hampers, and all the participants hurriedly set forth to the house on Lower Brook Street.

Chapter Fifteen

The babble of voices in the drawing room stilled only when Lady Mary stamped her foot. "May I request silence?" she demanded in her most dignified manner. "What has happened to put you all in such a pother?" She gave Mr. Witherspoon a warm look, then motioned for him to sit at her side. "Justin, perhaps you could explain?"

"The six of us went on a picnic—with your estimable James also in attendance. We had about finished with our meal when a familiar black carriage approached. It proved to be Alington. I knew he has had a man watching Anne, so I decided it would be prudent to bring a gun with me—in the event he just happened along."

"He has had a man watching where I go, what I do?" Anne cried, her anger clear against the man who so tormented her life.

"From morn until late evening, yes," the earl replied smoothly.

"How dare he!" she cried, utterly outraged.

"He dares quite a few things that a person would normally not do," the earl replied.

"Mr. Fairfax and Mr. Metcalf were exceedingly brave," Jemima declared with an admiring look at Henry Metcalf.

"Indeed, after James, your footman, subdued that dreadful servant who came with Lord Alington, they jumped his lordship. I do believe Lord Alington now has a rather horrid nose, for it bled all over his cravat," Susan said with surprising relish. "Mr. Fairfax was splendid!"

Sidney Fairfax appeared a bit embarrassed by this praise. He cleared his throat and rubbed his hand over his chin before adding. "Well, as to that, Justin was the one who polished the bounder off. Never saw such a handy bunch of fives."

"That will be quite enough, Sidney," Lady Mary insisted firmly. "I gather that your supper was not quite the ordinary picnic. Susan and Jemima, I shall refrain from repeating this to your parents. They might not understand," she concluded in a masterful understatement.

"But poor Anne, to be so plagued," Susan said with a concerned look at her friend. "I do not think I could survive for long, nor be as brave as she."

"We shall have to do something about that," the earl said, seeming equally concerned. What his solution might be, he didn't say.

"She is welcome to remain here for a time. But I must tell you that Mr. Witherspoon and I are to be married as soon as this trial business is over. We thought to take a trip to Sweden. If Anne can find a chaperon to reside here with her, she is welcome to stay."

"What about my aunt?" Henry Metcalf said. "I feel certain she would be happy to offer a place for Miss Haycroft to live until the trial is over."

"That may never come about," Justin said thoughtfully. "It is possible . . ." He stopped and said no more.

"Possible what?" his aunt demanded.

"If we find that Cosmo Haycroft has cheated Anne, we may be able to call a halt to the suit for seduction. At least persuade Haycroft he would be better off to either drop the suit completely or perhaps settle out of court," Justin said.

"Threaten a countersuit for mishandling an estate?" Mr. Witherspoon asked.

"Fraud!" Lady Mary declared emphatically.

"Well," Justin said, "Mr. Haycroft is a trustee for Anne's remainder from her father's estate. She is an only child, and her father left the entire estate to her, in the keeping of two trustees. Am I correct so far, Anne?" Justin looked to her for corroboration.

"I believe so. The other trustee is my solicitor." Anne perched on the edge of a chair, absorbed in what Justin had to say.

"Mr. Quinlan has recently taken over as Anne's solicitor—Mr. Kestell became quite ill not long ago. It is difficult to step in and assume such a burden, but he and her solicitor were partners, and as such it is perfectly proper. He has had nothing to do with her estate until now. I trust him to find any irregularity."

"Interesting," Mr. Witherspoon inserted. "What, if anything, has been uncovered to make Quinlan suspicious?"

"Considering the sum of money that existed when Anne's father died and that the sum had been invested in government consols, it would appear that no interest has ever accumulated."

"Haycroft has been skimming the interest from the estate? What about the land?" Witherspoon asked, leaning forward with concern.

"There appears to be a question there as well. Upon looking over the books. Quinlan believes payments have been incorrectly accounted. It will take a little more time, but I would not be surprised if there was sufficient evidence to put Cosmo Haycroft in prison. Certainly he has no means of paying back what he has stolen."

"He could if he sold the London house," Anne said quietly. "I know it is his and not leased."

"If there is no lien against it, that might do. He would be forced to return to the country. He'd not have the money to rent a dwelling in London."

"My Aunt Haycroft would detest living in the country," Anne said with a wry look.

"I feel the man cannot be trusted," Mr. Witherspoon said. "Until Anne reaches the age of twenty-one, he can legally have control of her life. Even if you can prove he skimmed money from her estate, I doubt a court would do much to him. He can simply claim it was for her expenses. Never mind that she saw precious little of those monies," he asserted. "Haycroft has assumed the place of her father and feels that she is now his property. He also feels that he is entitled to damages since you, Justin, in effect seduced—or convinced—her to refuse the marriage he lawfully arranged for her. Remember that he sought to sell her to Alington. If he cannot sell her, he wants money from someone. And that someone appears to be Justin."

"And if he sells the London house to pay back what he owes, he would be free from prosecution," Justin said thoughtfully.

"*If* we can persuade him by one means or another. In the meanwhile, Anne must take refuge where he—or Alington—cannot find her," Mr. Witherspoon pointed out. "At least until she is of age or is married, whichever might come first." He eyed Justin, who sat quite unperturbed at the scrutiny.

"Where might such a place be?" Jemima wondered. "Her country home would be the first place her uncle would look."

"True," Anne agreed. "Besides, he rented the Kent house, although the home farm is still being managed by the tenant who has been there for ages."

"I shall think of something," Justin said with a glance at his aunt. "Since his home is to the south, we shall send Anne north."

Beyond that, he said nothing more—to Anne's frustration.

The conversation turned to more interesting matters, such as the coming wedding and the wedding trip to Sweden.

"It is a pity that that Corsican monster is still loose to create havoc on the Continent," Lady Mary said wistfully. "I should have liked to go to Switzerland."

"Some day we shall, my dear," Mr. Witherspoon said with optimism.

"What about you, Anne? Where would you like to travel?" Justin inquired thoughtfully.

"I was reading Mary Wollstonecraft's *Letters*. Did you know she went to southern Norway? From her accounts it is a delightful place, and I think I might like to visit where she went."

"Dreadful woman, that Wollstonecraft," Lady Mary said with a sniff. "No morals, a most radical thinker."

Justin immediately changed the direction of the conversation to a safer topic. He suggested that perhaps they ought to all depart, since the evening had been so exhausting.

"And perhaps we might consider refraining from mentioning to others what happened while on our picnic. You know how people can misconstrue things," he added with a glance at Anne.

The others agreed with alacrity, quite pleased to be trusted with a secret. They straggled from the room, clattering down the stairs by twos, talking over the evening's events with great animation.

"No matter what," Mr. Witherspoon said quietly, "I am quite sure that Anne will cope with whatever comes in a most admirable way."

Anne thanked him, offering a demure smile.

Nevertheless, once all the guests had departed, Anne walked up to her room, knowing her days in this house were numbered. However, she was so delighted for Lady Mary she could not feel sad.

The following morning found Anne at the pianoforte when Justin came to call. Lady Mary had sallied forth to Madame Clotilde, intent upon an entire new wardrobe. She declared she could not be married in her old rags!

"I gather my aunt has gone out?" Justin said from the doorway, careful to leave the door wide open as he entered.

"Shopping for new clothes. Weddings and honeymoons are times when a woman is supposed to outfit herself in new styles." She gave him a worried look. "Do you have any news of Alington or my uncle?"

"I believe we have your uncle right where we want him. Quinlan—with the help of a skilled accountant—has determined where the losses have occurred. I must admit, your uncle is extremely clever. Mr. Kestell never noted anything amiss. It was only when the account was handed over to someone younger and inclined to be inquisitive that it came to light."

Anne rose from the chair by the pianoforte, crossing to the earl's side. "What can be done?" she pleaded. "I want nothing more than to end this horrible nightmare."

"Poor girl. It has not been easy for you, has it?"

Anne gazed into those dark brown eyes so full of compassion and sighed. "Indeed not." How she yearned to cast herself on his broad shoulders and seek comfort from him.

"It shall all be over soon. Quinlan is going to see your uncle today, inform him of what has been learned and threaten to sue for recovery of property." Justin took Anne's hand, leading her over to the elegant damask sofa.

"I can scarce believe he can actually compel Uncle Cosmo to

sell the house, much less return the money he stole from me," Anne declared, sitting down on the sofa, while watching the earl. "I do not care as much about the money as I do about my freedom from fear and the threat of marriage to Lord Alington—or any other man my uncle might find who would offer more advantages to him."

"The man has no conscience," Justin said, walking from where he stood by the sofa to a spot by the fireplace. He paced back and forth, glancing at Anne from moment to moment.

"When is your birthday?" he asked abruptly.

"June seventh," Anne replied.

"Of course, you told me before. There are too many things going on; it is difficult to keep track of it all," Justin said, looking as though he felt foolish.

"I am surprised you can recall what day of the week it is. You have had very little time in which to enjoy the Season." Anne's guilt hung over her, seeming a monumental barrier to vanquish. How could the earl ever care for the woman who had brought such scandal to his name?

"I have no complaints—at least not about missing the usual entertainments of the Season. It has been a challenge to help you, even if it did involve taking Miss Finch to court. Have you heard anything about what has happened to her?"

"Nothing, at all."

"Well," said Lady Mary from the doorway, giving her nephew an approving look for his discreet behavior, "I heard she is to do her feather-chasing two days from now. I, for one, intend to watch her mortification. Anne, do you join me?"

"If Lord Rochford says I may. I'll not jeopardize my safety nor our suit by opening myself to trouble."

"What a wise woman!" Justin said with a look of respect. "I should think that between me and the estimable James, Anne ought to be safe. I'll admit I should like to see the feather-chasing myself. In fact, I should think it would be expected of us."

"In that case, Sidney Fairfax and Henry Metcalf ought to come along as well. They served admirably as assistants before." Anne compressed her lips lest she smile. It was not a smiling matter, yet she knew it best to tease, else she might end up weeping.

It was agreed that the group would assemble in the park at the site and time fixed for Miss Finch to perform her feather-chasing punishment.

"I cannot imagine Hortense Finch wearing a white gown. It is the worst color in the world for her!" Lady Mary exclaimed, her eyes twinkling with mirth.

A door slammed, and shortly Sidney dashed into the room. "Have you heard the news? Alington is dead! His house caught fire, and he perished trying to save some of his precious collectibles!"

"Good grief," Lady Mary whispered, sinking onto a chair.

Anne also sought a chair, stunned into silence.

"That is the end of his persecution of Anne. I cannot think any of us will grieve. Now if only her uncle will cease to plague her," Justin said quietly.

"Indeed," Anne agreed, relief washing over her.

Two days later, Anne drove to the park with Lady Mary, Mr. Witherspoon, and Lord Rochford in the landau. Each lady had a hat decorated with white feathers—Anne's a blue velvet, Lady Mary's hat a stylish rust silk. Behind them Miss Metcalf and Mr. Farmer, who had never heard of such a spectacle, Henry Metcalf, and Jemima Green traveled in a landau. Both women also had white feathers secured to their bonnets. Susan and Sidney drove in his curricle. Susan had been clever in arranging tightly curled white feathers and pink ribands on a straw bonnet.

"I hear," she confided to the other ladies when they reached the park and joined as a group, "that Nickolay's is entirely sold out of white feathers!" She referred to the elegant fur and feather manufactory on Oxford Street, the scene of frantic shopping the past few days. "Nearly all the women who were victims of Miss Finch's gossip sought white feathers to wear on their bonnets. I believe every one of them intends to stand somewhere in the park to view Miss Finch's comeuppance."

"I say, does this happen very often?" Mr. Farmer wanted to know.

"Never before to my knowledge," Mr. Witherspoon replied. "I daresay half of London is in the park today. It is quite an event." He gestured to the vast circle of people, both men and women, who had come to see their detested foe receive her due. Many of the women stood, arms crossed and eyes narrowed in anticipation. Justice was indeed sweet.

Justin offered his arm to Anne, then assisted her over the coarsely scythed grass to a place where they could watch the scene. She trembled at the feel of his muscular strength. His closeness was bittersweet; too soon he would be but a tender memory.

They did not have long to wait. Miss Finch, garbed in a white gown, arrived in a plain carriage accompanied by a member of the court staff. There were no white feathers on her small chip bonnet.

Another man, carrying an enormous sack of goose feathers, strode to the center of the open parkland that had been selected for Miss Finch's ordeal. He climbed upon a high, small platform and began to shake his sack. Small white feathers drifted with the gentle breeze, flying this way and that, catching on branches, tangling in tall grass. Only when the sack was empty was Miss Finch given the selfsame sack and permitted to gather feathers.

Her task proved more than difficult. She caught a few, stuffed them in the bag, then chased some more, only to have them elude her. Frustrated, laughed at, mocked, she looked close to tears. She continued on by order of the court staff member. There was little chance that she could recover even half the feathers that had been released.

"Do you suppose she will learn anything from her ordeal?" Anne wondered to her escort.

"Only time and Miss Finch can tell. Perhaps she may think twice before spreading her malicious rumors again."

"I have seen enough, thank you. I do not enjoy the humiliation of an older spinster, no matter how well deserved it might be," Anne said, turning away from the pathetic sight.

Justin bestowed a look of approval on the young lady at his side. "Your sensibilities do you justice. Come, we will drive away from here. I rarely have you to myself these days. Sidney will lend me his curricle. He and Susan can go back with my aunt" He drew her more closely to his side, wanting to protect her. At least they no longer had to worry about Alington.

It was as he said, with Sidney happy to be of service.

"It seems like a lifetime since I first saw you in that church," Anne said when they had achieved some distance from the feather-chasing Miss Finch.

"I hope that we may go there again before too long," Justin said.

Anne gave him a confused look. What did he mean by such a remark? He did not elaborate on the intriguing statement.

"Shall we go to Quinlan's office?" he suddenly suggested. "It is possible he may have returned from the meeting with your uncle. I feel certain you would like to know the outcome as soon as possible."

"Indeed, I would. Yes, yes, by all means, go to Threadneedle Street and the solicitor," Anne urged.

Traffic was heavy, in spite of the huge gathering at the park. Drays and hackneys vied with landaus and curricles, gigs and whiskeys for a space in the streets. Overall was noise and the smell that comes with horses.

Threadneedle Street was little better, being narrow and dusty. Justin handed the reins to a young fellow who dashed out from the solicitor's office as they drew to a halt. "Good lad," he said with approval for so quick and thoughtful an action.

Mr. Quinlan wore a look of immense satisfaction when Anne and Justin were ushered into his office. Tea was brought for Anne, and Justin was offered a glass of superior claret.

"We have something to celebrate. When I called upon Mr. Haycroft and revealed the results of our findings as well as the only means he had of redeeming his losses, he was eager to drop the suit of seduction."

"Oh, wonderful!" Anne exclaimed with heartfelt joy.

The solicitor looked down at his desk, then at Justin. "I fear I was not very lenient with him. I presented him with the documentation of his thievery regarding the inheritance belonging to his niece. Then I persuaded him to sign the papers that would drop his suit."

"What is to happen now?" Justin wondered.

"First of all, he is to be removed as her guardian and trustee. The court takes a dim view of this sort of swindle."

"Can this be true?" Anne whispered, turning to Justin for his confirmation of what she heard. At his nod, and a reassuring pat on her hand, Anne settled back to sip her excellent tea.

"I advised him the only recourse he has to survive financially is to sell the London house to repay his debt to you, Miss Haycroft, as well as to pay his settlement to Lord Rochford. He seemed to think his wife would take it greatly amiss."

"Indeed she will," Anne said with knowledge of her aunt's hatred of the country.

"As well, I advised him to seek counsel with his own solicitor. I felt it fair and honest that he be aware of the ramifications of his actions. His own solicitor will tell him the truth of the matter."

"So . . . when am I freed of his guardianship?" Anne quietly demanded.

"As soon as a new one can be appointed."

"Could you assume the duty of guardian as well as trustee?" Anne questioned.

"It is possible. I can place a petition before the court to have the guardianship transferred from your uncle to me. It may not be difficult, as I am also a trustee. I am honored that you would consider me in that light." Mr. Quinlan studied Anne, a serious expression on his face.

"You appear an honorable man, sir. That is far more than my uncle ever was."

"Perhaps as a younger man he had scruples he later abandoned?"

"Perhaps, but somehow I doubt it." Anne rose, placed her empty cup and saucer on a small table, then looked to Justin. "Could we go?"

"Before we leave, I should like to know if Miss Haycroft is now free to go where she pleases? I believe she would like to leave London, her uncle, not to mention the memory of the court appearance far behind her." Justin took Anne's hand and placed it on his arm, his stance protective.

"That is certainly understandable. If I am to assume the role of guardian, I would like to know what she intends to do." His gaze shifted from Anne to Justin.

"She is going north to Derbyshire to visit my mother."

One of Miss Finch's feathers could have knocked Anne clear off her feet.

"That sounds like an excellent idea. I imagine Miss Haycroft has not known a pleasant Season." The solicitor rose to stand by his desk, looking at Anne with a kindly expression.

"God willing, she will have a better one next year," the earl said firmly before ushering Anne from the office.

Once again seated in Sidney's curricle, Anne gave the earl an exasperated look. "I was unaware your mother had invited me to visit her," she said with commendable restraint.

"She has not done so as yet. But she will. You will like Derbyshire. It is one of the loveliest places in all of England. I think it will be good for you." Given his love for his country estate, he could be forgiven the trace of pride in his voice.

"I didn't even know you had a mother," Anne said, rather disgruntled at having her life arranged for her yet another time. Did all men have a tendency to manage?

"We all have had one at one time or another," he said, sounding quite amused.

"That is not what I meant. You have not mentioned her to me before. I suppose I assumed she was no longer living," Anne said virtuously, her pretty face set in prim lines.

"In a way she is a little like you," he said, his words tantalizing.

"Like me? How?" Anne wondered. She couldn't imagine anyone like her.

"She is very feminine, is gentle and kind, enjoys music, and is also very stubborn," Justin concluded with a wry glance at the young woman at his side.

"I am not stubborn," she insisted. "I never demand my own way, nor do I *usually* involve others in my affairs," she said with a wistful air not totally lost on her companion.

Even in the midst of London traffic he could detect that plaintive note. "No, I don't suppose you do," he said.

It was late in the afternoon when they returned to the house on Lower Brook Street. The sun cast long shadows on the buildings across the street.

"We had best go up. Aunt will be wanting dinner before long."

"Are you to stay?" Anne inquired with a very revealing look, one that certainly gave hope to her escort.

"I believe my aunt would not deny me a meal," Justin said.

However, when they reached the drawing room, they found a rather hostile group. Mr. and Mrs. Haycroft were seated on two chairs—the hard ones, Anne noted—while Lady Mary and Mr. Witherspoon sat on the plum damask sofa.

"There she is!" Mrs. Haycroft exclaimed.

"Tell me this is a daymare, that I am dreaming," Anne murmured to Justin.

"I fear you are wide awake," he muttered back. Of his aunt he asked, "What is this all about, pray tell?"

"Oddly enough, the Haycrofts have come to fetch Anne. They have a paper that claims to order her to go with them."

Anne felt a reassuring touch on her arm, but when she looked at Justin, she found a warning in the earl's eyes.

"Strange," Justin said, not leaving Anne's side. "We have just now come from Threadneedle Street and Mr. Quinlan. He informed us you have signed a paper dropping the suit of seduction as well as promising to sell your London house in order to pay back what you have stolen from Anne as well as the settlement due to me."

Mr. Haycroft jumped to his feet. "Here now, you cannot slander me in such fashion!"

"The truth is not slander, sirrah. However you choose to phrase it, I call it stealing when you take money that does not belong to you," Justin declared.

Anne felt the earl's hand tighten on her arm.

"It was for her education, clothes, and food," Mr. Haycroft said as a defense.

"I saw the sum. Hundreds and hundreds of pounds to feed and clothe a slip of a girl each year? Her education was not costly, not such as Oxford would have been. No, Mr. Haycroft, I'll not yield Anne to you!"

"But I have an order remanding her to my care," Mr. Haycroft blustered.

"You will have to come again tomorrow with your solicitor to convince us of the authenticity of that paper." Justin stood firm, refusing to let Anne free, as though he feared her uncle would snatch her away from him.

"Very well, we shall return tomorrow with my solicitor. But you had best be prepared to leave with us, missy. Even though I dropped the suit of seduction, and Alington is no longer with us, I can still marry you off to another." With that threat, Cosmo Haycroft stomped from the room, leaving his acidulated wife to trail behind him.

Once the Haycrofts were out of the house, Justin spun Anne about to face him. "You must leave here as soon as possible. If he really does have a valid writ, there is little we can do. Until Quinlan is able to change the guardianship, your uncle retains hold over you."

"I am his property," Anne said bitterly in a soft voice, "as Mr. Witherspoon said. And where am I to go?"

"As I said before, Derbyshire." Justin whispered. "Pack what you need, and I will have a carriage ready for you. Take a maid along for company and propriety. I cannot come with you. I shall remain in London to throw off any suspicion of where you have gone."

"Derbyshire!" Anne repeated.

"Go, girl. I'll send one of the maids to you. When Justin returns, you must be ready to depart," Lady Mary said.

"And I will make certain there is no one watching the house. Aunt Mary, I trust you will not object if I send the estimable James along? In the event there is a need to crack a few heads, he is most handy," Justin said in a low voice. "Hurry, Anne. There is no time to lose."

"Take care," Anne cried from the doorway.

Justin stared after her, wondering when he had fallen in love with this girl who had brought him nothing but trouble.

Chapter Sixteen

It was decided that Anne should flee in Lady Mary's traveling coach since she would travel with Mr. Witherspoon in his.

Thus it was but a few hours later Anne was ready to enter that well-upholstered vehicle, hastily packed and prepared to leave all of London behind her. That she would also leave Justin Fairfax behind forever, she knew all too well.

Justin had gone immediately to his town house to send a servant northward with a message to his mother warning her that a guest was on her way and relating something of the circumstances. He did not reveal his love, however.

Returning to his aunt's home in time to bid Anne good-bye, he stood in the chill mist of the night, staring down at the women he loved. A flickering flambeau before the house lit her face. Why had he not known it before? He hungrily searched her face, those amazing blue eyes. Small wonder that no other woman had captured his interest. Anne totally eclipsed all others.

How he longed to kiss her. Yet if he did, he knew he could not send her away from him, far north to Derbyshire. Firmly setting aside his desires, he placed his hands on her arms, ready to swing her up to the coach, where the maid awaited her. James sat with the coachman, ready to depart.

Anne shivered with the night chill as well as the knowledge she was leaving the man she loved, most likely forever. All she had given him was trouble and expense, not to mention scandal. She had yearned for a love match. There would be no love match for her now. How could she think of another man when she loved Justin?

Before she could reconsider the matter—or recall the few

servants about—she stretched up to place a kiss on his lips; she'd have to remember it forever.

"Anne . . ." His murmur was lost as he crushed her against him. He kissed her back, fervently, lovingly. Only the impatient movement of the horses brought him back to his senses.

Within minutes Justin assisted Anne into the coach, shut the door, and the vehicle began its journey to the north. It rattled to the corner and turned, lost from view at once. Justin felt as though a part of him had been torn away, and he felt the loss keenly. He shivered.

"Come inside," his aunt beckoned from the door. "Hot coffee and perhaps something to eat will restore you."

Anne was out of his care now, and he could only pray that the estimable James would keep her safe. There was nothing more to be done at this hour. He followed his aunt inside and along to the breakfast room. He accepted the coffee, then absently ate what was set before him, his mind miles away. After a cup of coffee and a roll he was ready to sleep a bit before morning arrived.

"Well, that is that," his aunt said with a sharp look at her nephew when they paused in the entry, "once the Haycrofts are persuaded she has gone to the south, you will be free to do as you please. What *do* you intend to do?"

"I will see you wed, then leave London." Justin said, wondering where the coach was at this moment. Did they traverse the highway to the north yet? Islington, perhaps?

"You wish to visit your mother?" she guessed, shrewd as always.

"Indeed," Justin said. And Anne as well. He knew hope, for a young woman like Anne would not have bestowed that kiss unless she cared very much for him. It had been a kiss of barely leashed passion, promising much.

Hours later, they were again sitting in the breakfast room, discussing the Haycroft suit, when Potter ushered in an agitated Henry Metcalf.

"This is an early hour of the day to come calling, Henry," Lady Mary said, a question in her voice.

"It is Aunt Jane! She has run off, gone to Canada with Mr. Farmer!"

"Well I never!" Lady Mary declared, setting her cup down with a loud clink.

"She left a deed to her house—deeded to me—and a letter of explanation. She also arranged for me to have a sizable sum of money from her inheritance! I cannot believe it!" Henry sank down upon the nearest chair, the stunned look on his face almost comical.

"Well, it would be good were you to think about marriage. You would have a very nice house and a goodly income, if well invested," Lady Mary said. That she was amazed at the impulsive action of her old friend could be seen on her face, yet she neither condemned nor praised.

"Where is Miss Haycroft?" Henry finally wondered, looking about him in surprise.

"Anne went to her home in the south, somewhere in Kent, I believe," Lady Mary said with deliberate care. Only the staff who went with Anne knew the truth. The maid, James, and the coachman weren't around to talk, and the trusted Potter never would reveal what transpired.

"Rather sudden," Henry replied with a puzzled frown.

"Indeed. I believe she sought to get away from her aunt and uncle," Justin said with perfect truth.

"Oh, Miss Green wants to know when your wedding is to take place. There has been nothing in the paper, and she would very much like to attend if that is agreeable. We are both fond of you, you know," Henry said.

"The ceremony is set for Tuesday at St. George's. Mr. Witherspoon has a special license, so we need not wait. At our age it seems rather foolish."

"I should say it is foolish to wait at any age, dear aunt," Justin added, thinking of Anne.

"By Jove, you are right there. I'm rather fond of Jemima as well, Lady Mary. Now that I have a house and a modest fortune, her parents might agree to our marriage."

"I should think that likely." Lady Mary gave him a kindly smile before leaving for her room. "There is much to be done.

Giles thinks we shall sell this house upon our return. I want to order certain belongings packed."

"Sorry, Rochford," Henry muttered. "Somehow I thought you and Miss Haycroft would make a match of it."

"Well, as to that, who knows? My aunt and yours as well are living proof that it is never too late for happiness." But Justin was surprised that Henry had reached such a conclusion. Perhaps Henry mistook Justin's sympathy for something more? Justin hoped that Anne might as well.

The two men left the house soon thereafter. Henry went on his way to inspect his new dwelling more carefully. Justin returned to his town house to prepare for the meeting with the Haycrofts. He was not certain how they would react to the news that Anne had gone. Nor did he know what their solicitor would do.

It was some hours later after he had returned to his aunt's house that he faced the angry pair with their solicitor. They were not pleased with his news. He wondered what they would do when they learned of the change in guardianship. But their threat to Anne had been real—Cosmo Haycroft did not give up easily when it came to money. Who knew what manner of man he'd pick next?

"Gone? Impossible! I demand to search the house," Mrs. Haycroft said, her voice strident as usual.

"It would be useless, but you are welcome if you wish," Lady Mary announced from the doorway. "I fear there is considerable confusion here as I am to be married Tuesday and many of my things are being packed away."

"If Lady Mary is leaving here, Miss Haycroft has had to seek another abode," the solicitor pointed out.

Concealing his delight at besting this pair. Justin said, "I fear there was nowhere for Miss Haycroft to go but her own home. I believe she mentioned it is in Kent?"

"We shall find her, wherever she might be," Cosmo Haycroft warned, his plump face red with anger.

"I expect you will," Justin murmured as he ushered the unwelcome callers to the door.

"Are they gone?" his aunt demanded some minutes later. "I did not hear any screaming."

"The solicitor kept a lid on any displays, I fancy," Justin replied. "I will not rest easy until I know that Anne is safe with Mother."

"Well, it ought to be interesting, the meeting between your mother and Anne." Lady Mary paused at the bottom of the stairs, her hand resting on the railing.

"How so?" Justin asked, perplexed.

"They have much in common. They both love you," Lady Mary said before she hurried up the stairs to her room.

Justin stood rooted in place for a moment absorbing his aunt's words. *Could she be right?* Did Anne truly love him as Aunt said? The idea bolstered his spirits through the following days.

Anne found the trip north fascinating. Betsy, the maid given her for company and propriety, was young and shy, but competent. They both enjoyed the scenes viewed from the carriage. If Anne's thoughts frequently strayed to the man she had left behind, she gave no clue to her companion.

It was but 153 miles to Bakewell, the town nearest Lord Rochford's home. They glimpsed Woburn and admired various large country homes to either side of the road, and spent two nights at excellent inns. Once past Derby, they crossed a canal, then headed north, pausing at the Kedleston Inn for a light repast.

Anne also changed into her most becoming day dress. She thought it most important that she present a good impression to Lady Rochford upon arrival.

One thing Anne had decided while bowling along the highway was that she would spend but a few days, a week at the most, at Rochford Court. She had no desire to be more beholden to the earl or his family. She had imposed quite enough.

The house impressed one even from a distance, rising importantly on a hillside. Rows of windows sparkled and the pale stone gleamed in the late afternoon sun. Tired as she was from three days of travel, Anne felt revitalized when she considered that this was Justin's home, a place he obviously loved a great deal from all he had said about it.

The traveling coach drew up before an imposing pair of

stairs that winged upward to a terrace. Above that rose a covered entry boasting four Ionic pillars crowned by a majestic pediment, all in exquisite Palladian taste.

A footman helped Anne from the coach. She was anxious to meet Lady Rochford, hoping they might get along tolerably well. As the mother of the man Anne loved, she was sure to be a delightful lady.

Betsy and James were to return with the coach in two days' time. Anne was pleased the coachman and maid could have a rest before turning back to London. Her thoughts would go with them.

The climb up the stairs gave her a chance to survey the house some more. It was truly magnificent. Inside the house, she found the entry impressive. It was vast, for one thing. Why, she thought, the carpet alone must have cost a fortune.

"Follow me, miss." The footman led her through a bewildering succession of halls and rooms until she entered a rather pretty room done in pale gray with accents of a delicate violet that instantly charmed. On one of the deep violet sofas of the very latest design sat a slim, very pretty woman with gray-streaked hair and the same dark eyes her son possessed. Anne thought it would be impossible not to like her, for she was so like her son.

"And you are Anne Haycroft. I trust you had a tolerable trip? Justin sent word that you were to come. 'Hastily fleeing London,' was the way he phrased it," Lady Rochford said in an attractive low voice. "Come, join me if you are not totally exhausted, and we shall have tea."

"I stopped at Kedleston for a cup of tea, but I would welcome some now. The road was dusty," Anne said simply.

"We are due for rain. While we wait for our tea, we can become acquainted. Justin said he found you in a church."

Anne could hear the question in those polite words. "Indeed. He came to my rescue much like someone would a stray cat or puppy. I desperately needed help. Lady Mary has been wondrously good to me, taking me into her home and caring for me as though I were her own. Did you hear about the lawsuit?" Anne asked with caution.

"No! A lawsuit! How exciting! You must tell me everything!" her ladyship exclaimed in a cozy manner, so much so that Anne found herself telling the very charming mother of the man she loved the entire tale of the lawsuit and countersuit and the highly successful outcome.

Tea came and was drunk, and the two sat deep in conversation until dinner was announced.

"Good heavens, I have not given you a chance to change or settle in your room. Forgive me, but it is all so fascinating! Do you wish to change, or could we dine while you continue the amazing tale from London?" the countess beseeched.

"I changed at the Kedleston Inn, ma'am, so it is quite all right to dine now as far as I am concerned." Anne was starved, though too polite to say so.

They adjourned to the yellow dining room, to sit at one end of a vast table. While she consumed a substantial meal, Anne continued to reveal the hair-raising events leading up to her departure.

"I must say, your aunt and uncle sound most unpleasant," her ladyship commented at the conclusion of Anne's story.

"I have but a little over a week until I turn twenty-one. After that, I may deal directly with the trustee. I feel confident that Mr. Quinlan, my solicitor, will find a way to eliminate my uncle from my life."

"You have Quinlan as well? Justin says he's a fine man, extremely clever. Now, what is this about Mary? Never say she is to be wed! I thought she pined for Edmund Parker." Her ladyship ordered tea at the end of the meal, and they settled at the table to talk some more while Anne disclosed the duplicity of Mr. Parker and revealed Mr. Witherspoon's undying love.

"Fancy that," Lady Rochford said at last. "Mary wed to Mr. Witherspoon. They have been friends for ages."

"I should think friendship a solid basis for a good marriage," Anne suggested.

That launched another discussion, and it was late indeed before Anne saw her room. But never before in her life had she talked with another woman who felt so much as she did, or saw things as Anne would see them. Why, it was as though Anne had known her all her life.

As to Justin, Anne eagerly drank in every word his mother

had to say about him. And what mother does not enjoy an appreciative audience when talking about her son?

The days slipped by one after another. It rained and they played cards and Anne entertained at the pianoforte, an elegant instrument made by Broadwood. The chair before it was the latest in Greek revival and covered with the countess's favorite violet.

Anne felt herself slipping into the fabric of the house, becoming almost a part of it. It was a shock when she realized she had been at the Court for a week. That day she revealed her plan to the countess.

"Leave! But you cannot leave. I will be bored, desolate without your charming company," the countess cried. "No, I cannot bear to see you go. One more day at least?"

Anne smiled and gave in, but insisted, "I must go the day after that. I would see my cousin. We have been apart for so many years." Anne did not add that her cousin had never been close to her, nor that she had no idea Anne intended to visit her. A post chaise was arranged for the journey, an expense the countess insisted upon bearing.

It rained the morning Anne was to leave. She sat at the lovely rosewood table in the breakfast room, staring out at the water dripping from the trees. It was not a good day to travel.

"You must not go," the countess declared as she breezed into the room. "That rain will make the roads utterly dreadful. You will have to crawl through ruts a foot deep at the very least."

"You have been most kind, but I cannot impose any longer," Anne said with firmness. The countess was too charming to easily resist.

Thus, two hours later, Anne set off in a post chaise brought from the Kedleston Inn for her travel. It nearly broke her heart to leave. Sheltered under an umbrella, the countess stood at the top of the stairs, waving until Anne could no longer see the house. The young maid who was to go as far as Hull, sat quietly opposite.

The countess's prophecy about the conditions of the road was wrong. They were worse. Anne jounced and bumped along the wretched roads, wishing she had remained at Rochford Court. Every stop for a change of horses enabled Anne and the maid to huddle by a fire for a brief time, perhaps with a cup of tea, then on again. The inns were dreadful, the food indifferent. Sheffield and Doncaster passed in a film of rain. At Thorne the skies lightened, and the day she woke in Howden the sky was gray, but no rain in unceasing monotony.

Penelope Tyler lived just west of Hull on the edge of Kingston, a main shipping port on the east coast. Although the River Humber ran not far from her modest property, one could smell the sea. In Hull were the docks from whence one could sail to Holland or Norway, even France when there wasn't a war.

Anne got out of the post chaise with more than a little trepidation. She didn't even know if her cousin was at home! After instructing the postilion and maid to wait, she approached the house. Several firm knocks on a stout oak door finally brought an elderly maid, her mobcap askew, and her apron damp where she must have hastily wiped her hands.

"I am Miss Anne Haycroft, cousin to Miss Tyler, come to visit." Anne gave the woman an expectant look. This brought a wider opening of the door and a grudging reply.

"She be home. Come in." Two cats, one ginger, one black, stared at Anne with unblinking eyes.

Behind her, the postilion removed her little trunk and dropped it before the house. The maid remained in the chaise, ready for his return.

Feeling as unwelcome as she had felt welcome at Rochford Court, Anne followed the unkempt maid down a long hall of flagstone. It was as cold and as forbidding as the woman who announced Anne to the lady of the house.

The woman who greeted Anne had aged considerably from when last seen. Wisps of gray hair peeked out from beneath a tidy white cap, spectacles perched on a determined nose below the family blue eyes, now somewhat faded.

"Well? And what brings you here? Come to importune your old cousin, have you? What has happened, pray tell, to bring you so far from London?" Sharp eyes took note of the little case and the anxious expression on her visitor's face.

"I have fled my Aunt and Uncle Haycroft," Anne promptly revealed. "They wished to marry me to a cruel man who frightened me horribly. I'd have no part of such a life, so I ran away. I shall be twenty-one in a few days. Then Uncle can no longer demand I marry where he wants." Anne dropped her small traveling case on the floor, then added, "May I stay a week?" She guessed that a week was about all her cousin might tolerate.

"A week, no more," was the reluctant answer. "Supper will be on the table in an hour."

So dismissed, Anne picked up her case and returned to the cold hall to find the maid waiting for her. The door opened for her revealed a simple room, but the bed looked clean. There was a wooden chair and table by the lone window and pegs for her clothing in one corner of the room. It was a far cry from the luxury of Rochford Court, where her pink and white room contained every comfort one could desire.

Resolute and determined to make the best of things, Anne thanked the maid, asked that her trunk be brought up, then set about unpacking a few things from her traveling case. It was a good thing she hadn't brought a maid. There was obviously no place for one in this house!

Over dinner, Penelope inquired about the Haycrofts. They were only distantly related—since Penelope was on Anne's mother's side, while the Haycroft family was on the other.

"Can't say as I am surprised at Cosmo Haycroft treating you like that. I met him when your mama married your pa. Thought he had a loose screw back then, and I can see he didn't improve with age."

That ended her curiosity. In fact, that ended the conversation. Instead of the delightful chats Anne knew with the countess, there was silence. Obviously since Miss Tyler lived alone, she was accustomed to a lack of speech.

The next morning being a fine day, Anne set out to explore the area. She walked down to the riverside and sat on a rock, wondering where Justin was, what he was doing, and what in the world was to become of her.

A week after Anne had left, Justin entered the same church where he had met her. Looking about, he saw the chair where she had sat. It was still pushed to one side as it had been left weeks ago. He went to set it neatly against the wall, finding comfort in touching the humble object before he took his place beside his aunt. It was his pleasure to give her away.

A great number of people had assembled for his aunt's marriage to Giles Witherspoon. His aunt had said it was a pack of nonsense to have a big fuss. She claimed to be too old for that, but Justin thought she looked pleased to see so many of her old friends in attendance.

He suffered through the wedding breakfast, then saw the pair on their way.

It took a day to consult with Quinlan and Sir Oliver regarding the conclusion of both the suits. Justin was satisfied that Hortense Finch intended to mend her ways. However, the matter of Cosmo Haycroft was something else.

It had taken Sir Oliver some clever manipulation and a good many meetings with Haycroft's solicitor to reach a satisfactory solution.

Quinlan was now the sole trustee, Cosmo deciding that it was futile to locate Anne when she was not found at her family home. He admitted he had searched for her. He charged Justin with concealing her whereabouts. Justin had merely laughed in his face—politely, of course.

The "remainder" of Anne's inheritance, was placed in Quinlan's capable hands to administer for her. Cosmo had been required to sell his town house to pay back what he had stolen. Justin was ruthless regarding that matter. That this crumb of a man should steal from his niece to finance his gambling was beyond the pale.

At last Justin was free of it all, the suits, his aunt's affairs, all. He had avoided *ton* parties, fearing to encounter Caroline Bonham. Now he was unfettered. His own affairs could now be pursued.

He headed north at first light, pushing his horses to the limit with each change, covering about seventy-five miles the first day, the remainder in the second. He was tired and worn when he drew up before his home. But it was worth it. Anne would be here.

His mother fluttered down the steps, running into his arms in greeting. "She isn't here, Justin. She left a few days ago, insisting she had overstayed and that she must see some cousin east of here. I suppose you wish to follow her?"

"Mother, I pushed to make it here in two days. I need food and sleep before I can think."

"Yes, dear." She dismissed the coachman with a nod.

Bitterly disappointed but not as surprised as his mother expected, Justin had a meal and then headed for bed.

The next morning he felt more alive and relaxed over his morning meal while listening to his mother talk. And what talk it was—stories about Anne, what she had done, said, how she had played the pianoforte so beautifully, did quite well at cards, and in general he received a detailed accounting of the time Anne was at the Court.

"It's a pity you were not able to get here sooner," she concluded when she ran out of words.

"And I think it even more a pity that you did not keep her here. I had hoped . . ." He paused, then asked, "You liked her? You found her company pleasing?"

"Indeed, I did. She is a charming girl. I could wish for no one better."

"What do you mean by that?" he queried sharply.

"Unless I miss my guess, you are going to follow her to ask for her hand. If you want my blessing, you have it."

"I would marry her anyway, you know," he said with a grin. "But I appreciate your approval."

"Justin, it was as though I had known her forever. Instant understanding like that is very rare. I shall look forward to the wedding."

"I suspect she will wish you to remain here since you got on so famously. As well, she is too tenderhearted to think of your leaving what has been your home." Justin said.

"How thoughtful, dear. As to that, I shall visit from time to time, but I believe I will visit your sisters, my sister, friends, and probably settle down in the dower house with great contentment."

Thus assured, Justin took care of some pressing business on his estate, then ordered the traveling coach to be brought around once again the following morning. He left at break of day for the north and east.

"Kingston is on the Humber River, sir. That's where Hull is as well," the coachman said, having made use of his time to study *Patterson's Roads* for the best route.

"I must make up for lost time, so I will spell you from time to time," Justin said before entering the coach for the first lap of his journey after Anne.

The roads hadn't improved very much in the days since Anne had traveled over them. Someone had tossed a few rocks into the worst of the holes, and the puddles had gradually dried. He figured it would be some time before the new and improved road building methods used on the Brighton and Holyhead roads came north to this area.

They drove late, taking few hours to sleep, then on again, covering the miles much faster than Anne had.

When they came within sight of Kingston, Justin first knew fear. What if he couldn't find Anne's cousin, or Anne, for that matter? He recalled the cousin's name. Tayler . . . or Tyler it was. Penelope Tyler, he concluded with a sigh.

The coachman entered the town at close to a walk, for which the horses were undoubtedly thankful. Justin had joined him outside on the bench of the vehicle, searching the paths, hoping against hope that he would quickly find his Anne.

She was not to be seen.

At last he sought an inn, the best in town. Here he quizzed the landlord about one Penelope Tyler. She was unknown.

"Surely you must know the woman? She has lived in this area for years, so I'm told," Justin said, utterly frustrated with the blank wall that faced him.

It seemed that if Penelope Tyler had been a resident, she had been a reclusive one, sending a maid on errands and paying cash for everything. She wasn't one to come to the inn, at any rate.

Justin slept poorly that night, knowing Anne must be near, but not knowing where. Then he recalled what she had said about going to Norway and that was the end of sleep for him. She had funds, thanks to Quinlan, and she could sail from here. He finally dressed and went for a long walk.

The docks of Hull loomed in the distance. On the off chance that Anne might have inquired about passage, Justin sought out the booking agent. Here he had luck. One Anne Haycroft had booked passage to Oslo this coming Friday, providing the winds held and the ship arrived on time.

Justin made note of the time and the ship, then meandered back toward Kingston. It was clearly a smallish place, but growing. A chap had established a ferry service, and Justin wandered down to look at the boat.

He turned then and looked along the beach. There was a girl walking on the broad, sandy riverbank. She was slim, had a halo of ash blond curls, and he would bet everything he owned that she also possessed the clearest, truest blue eyes that could be seen. He ran.

Anne looked up to see the stranger running toward her and wished she had taken a stick for protection. She was about to flee when she heard her name. Looking again, she suddenly knew who was running toward her. She froze, unable to move another foot.

"Anne!" Justin cried, sweeping her into his arms and swinging her in a circle of joy. "My love, I found you."

"Indeed you have, sir! Oh, Justin, why did you come? I cannot forget you if I see you," she wailed.

"Ah, my love, I cannot forget you whether I see you or not. You are with me every moment of the day and night." At that he could wait no longer and held her tightly in his arms while he made a splendid job of kissing her senseless.

"Anne, will you marry me? I had the forethought of bringing a special license. My dearest love, I cannot wait long to make you my own. Tell me you do not desire a fancy wedding such as we saw the day we met?" He swung her about again, lifting her high in his arms, kissing her when he caught her close.

"Justin, oh, yes indeed, I accept! And I believe I should rather have you in a simple wedding and tomorrow, if you please. I shall be twenty-one and not accountable to anyone." She grinned at him, love in her heart and in her eyes. "But I do love you, Justin. I shall have my love match after all."

"Indeed you shall, my little love. It's a forever sort of love, the lasting kind. Mother insists I bring you back, and it will be as my wife. I believe she loves you almost as much as I do, and that is a very great deal."

And so the pair of lovers strolled along the sandy bank toward their future together. They were lost in their love and dreams, seeing nothing but each other.

Author's Note

The idea of arranged marriages is somewhat foreign to us today, but in the Regency period, as had existed for many years prior, the practice continued. Marriages were usually arranged for financial gain, either money or land or both. There had been little opposition to these arranged marriages in the eighteenth century, but toward the end of the century and into the Regency period the idea of romantic love and marrying for that love grew considerably. Young women began to demand a say in their futures. More and more parents listened to their daughters' requests. Because a young lady of the upper class rarely met a gentleman other than of her own status, there was often no opposition. She knew that there were limits and was content to select a husband within those limits.

The suit of seduction mentioned in the book was something that began around 1653, expanded in the eighteenth century, blossoming into the Regency period until it ended in 1844. Mostly, the father of a girl who had been promised marriage and yielded to the urgings of her lover brought about the suits when his daughter became pregnant. When the lover refused to marry the pregnant girl, the suit brought either a marriage, or enough money so the girl could in effect buy a husband.

At first the suit was limited to damages for loss of services, considering she was of little use to the father during her pregnancy. No mention of the pregnancy or seduction was made in the suit, rather only the loss of her services.

The action took on new life in the Regency period when the lawsuit seemed more an action for the protection of public morality. The suit became a punishment, with the court a guardian of public morals. In 1844 Chief Justice Tindal reviewed the long history of the suit and dismissed the case before him, citing it was restricted to actual loss of services, which apparently did not apply in that case.

Justin is called an old wigsby—and that was a narrow-minded, crotchety old man, hardly complimentary.

Gossipers were called prattle boxes or tattle-baskets, dishing out bits and scraps, scandal-broth, and usually got by with their tales. A suit of defamation would have undoubtedly silenced more than a few tongues. Libel was also brought to court, as people increasingly wrote their opinions of public figures. Between 1808 and 1810 there were eighteen trials of journalists. One, Cobbett, spent two years editing his radical newspaper from jail.

The London Belle by Shirley Kennedy

When her father gambles away the family fortune, a beautiful young lady must decide whether to marry a wealthy man whom she does not love or accept a position tutoring the son of a notorious rake. But even as she helps a lonely boy emerge from his shell, she also melts the heart of her employer....

0-451-19836-0/$4.99

The Misfit Marquess by Teresa DesJardien

While fleeing the embrace of a false lover, a beautiful young woman is rendered unconscious in an accident. Discovered by a handsome lord, the marquess frets over her reputation and pretends to be a little daft. The lord's suspicions of her arise with his desire to help her...and to have her. But the villain who pursued her will not surrender her without a fight....

0-451-19835-2/$4.99

To order call: 1-800-788-6262

SIGNET

REGENCY ROMANCE

On Sale September 13th 1999

Fair Game by Diane Farr

A young woman of unearthly beauty. Her unscrupulous mother. A powerful womanizer demanding repayment of a large debt. All amount to a most peculiar sojourn in the country, a tangle with a hat pin, and a shocking barter that leaves everyone fair game....

0-451-19856-5/$4.99

The Magic Jack-O'-Lantern by Sandra Heath

A heartbroken—and invisible—brownie hitches a ride with an angelic heiress...and brings his mischievous brand of Halloween chaos to high society. The problem is, the pompous Sir Dominic Fortune doesn't believe in such superstitions...until the magic of love makes his heart glow brighter than a jack-o'-lantern.

0-451-19840-9/$4.99

The Wily Wastrel by April Kihlstrom

Juliet Galsworth was surely unmarriageable—imagine a lady interested in fixing mechanical things! But then James Langford came to visit, revealing the fine mind of an inventor behind his rakish exterior. Shared interests turned to shared passion. But would dangerous secrets close to James's heart jeopardize their newfound love?

0-451-19820-4/$4.99

To order call: 1-800-788-6262